OH, WHY DID HE HAVE TO BE SO BLASTED HANDSOME?

Honesty peered at Jesse through lowered lashes in what she hoped was an inviting manner. "I don't think your li'l ole tub is big enough for the both of us."

She pulled free of his hold, and his hot, hungry stare bored into her back as she crossed the room. Honesty put a saucy swing into her step, hoping he couldn't see how badly her knees knocked together.

At the dresser, she quickly pulled her chemise back up, releasing a pent-up breath. How had the tables turned so quickly? She was supposed to have been seducing him, not the other way around! It was definitely time to put an end to this little charade.

As Jesse closed his eyes to rinse his hair, Honesty slipped a trembling hand into her skirt pocket and pulled put a packet of powders. "I'll bring you another whiskey," she said, stirring the powders into his glass.

As she approached him, a devilish smile appeared on his fallen-angel face and a wicked promise glittered in his eyes. Men like him were dangerous as sin.

She handed Jesse his glass, lifted her own in the air, and, hoping he never knew how dearly she regretted what she was about to do, proposed a toast. "To an unforgettable night."

RACHELLE MORGAN

An Unlikely Lady

AVON BOOKS
An Imprint of HarperCollinsPublishers

This is a work of fiction. Names, characters, places, and incidents are products of the author's imagination or are used fictitiously and are not to be construed as real. Any resemblance to actual events, locales, organizations, or persons, living or dead, is entirely coincidental.

AVON BOOKS
An Imprint of HarperCollins*Publishers*
10 East 53rd Street
New York, New York 10022-5299

First Avon Books paperback printing: August 2001

Avon Trademark Reg. U.S. Pat. Off. and in Other Countries, Marca Registrada, Hecho en U.S.A.
HarperCollins ® is a trademark of HarperCollins Publishers Inc.

Printed in the U.S.A.

10 9 8 7 6 5 4 3 2 1

The Pinkerton Code

Accept no bribes.
Never compromise with criminals.
Partner with local law enforcement agencies,
when necessary.
Refuse divorce cases or cases that initiated
scandals of clients.
Turn down reward money.
Never raise fees without the client's pre-knowledge.
Apprise clients on an ongoing basis.
Never fall in love with a suspect.

Chapter 1

Last Hope, Colorado
1886

She didn't know who looked worse: the man, or the horse he rode in on. Both carried the mark of miles of weather and wear in their slouched postures and dust-caked hides, both looked as if they hadn't seen a meal in ages, and both seemed incapable of taking another step without toppling over.

From her room above the saloon, Honesty McGuire squinted through the window for a better look at the lone rider as he drew closer, stirring up dust on a street that hadn't seen traffic in weeks. To her dismay, the worn brim of the Stetson pulled low over his brow cast most of his

face in shadow, and the heavy whiskers around
his mouth and jaw hid the rest. A filthy duster
covered him from neck to spur, and dirty, matted
hair fell past his collar. He was a bit too scrawny
for her tastes, too, but often what a man lacked in
brawn he made up for in speed.

All right, so he wasn't the knight in shining
armor she'd been hoping for; considering her
choices to date, he was by far the most promising of the lot. At least he was young. And sober.
And breathing.

And who knew? His disreputable appearance might even play to her advantage, giving
her the opportunity to search places she
wouldn't dare explore alone. If Honesty had
learned anything in her twenty years, it was
never to overlook an opportunity.

No matter how pitiful it appeared.

So that left only one question: since the mines
had played out, only two kinds of people ever
showed up in Last Hope anymore—those looking for someone, and those running from someone. Which was he? The hunter? Or the hunted?

A drink, a meal, and a bed. Jesse Justiss
craved all three so badly he'd have given up his
four-dollar boots for just the sight of them.

Navigating around yet another pot hole in
the road, he directed his horse toward a warped
hitching rail and forced his weary body out of

the saddle. A sharp hiss tore through his lungs the instant his boots hit the ground and a spear of agony shot through him from heel to heart. His knees came close to buckling.

Jesse dropped his sweat-drenched forehead against the saddle skirt and cursed ten ways to Sunday through gritted teeth. Twice before, he'd found himself at the receiving end of a bullet, and he couldn't remember taking this long to recover.

Maybe he should have heeded the doc's advice and given his shoulder a couple more weeks to mend before tearing up one side of the Rockies and down the other. Maybe then it wouldn't now feel as if hot railroad spikes were being driven through his chest. But Jess never had been very good at taking advice.

Once the pain finally subsided to a dull, tolerable ache, he pushed away from Gemini's side and circled the horse. Fresh blood on the animal's foreleg caught his eye. "Hell and damnation," he swore under his breath. "What have you done to yourself this time, old pal?"

Gem nickered and bobbed his head.

Crouching low, Jess ran practiced hands along the black stocking, careful to avoid the ragged gash just below the knee—a fresh cut, more than likely from the trip down the mountain where sharp limbs and scrub littered the aspen-populated slopes.

Well, he couldn't detect any swelling. That was a good sign. But it didn't mean the animal hadn't pulled a tendon or suffered an even more ruinous injury. It just meant Jess had caught it in the early stages.

He wiped his hand down his sunburned face and cursed again. So much for making it to Canon City by nightfall. The last thing they could afford was another delay, but neither would he risk riding Gemini now and crippling him for life. The mustang had been a gift from the prettiest horse thief he'd ever had the pleasure of knowing. Jesse had laughed when Annie Corrigan had told him he'd never find a finer mount or more faithful friend, but over the last eight years he'd lost count of how many times Gem had proved her right.

Jess brushed his hands together and straightened, then squinted into the sunlight to give the town—if it could be called that—a full sweep. It looked like any of a dozen there-then-gone mining communities he'd passed through, with false-fronted structures lining either side of the road. What windows weren't busted through or covered with boards wore a layer of grime so thick he couldn't see through them. Paint peeled from signs that creaked on rusty chains. Patches of weeds had sprung up between cracks in the boardwalk and were taking over sections of the packed dirt road, and a general odor of defeat had settled over the area.

"We picked a helluva place to land in, didn't we, Gem?" Jesse grumbled.

With a sigh as dismal as his surroundings, he turned toward one of the only establishments still open, a two-story lumber structure with THE SCARLET ROSE GAMING PARLOR AND SALOON painted in bold, sweeping strokes of red across a whitewashed backdrop. It couldn't have been more appropriately named, for the building stood out from the others like a perfect blossom in a row of tumbleweed.

As if to remind him that even the most perfect blossoms had their thorns, the hair along Jesse's arms suddenly stood on end. The cords in his neck went rigid. Prickles of unease danced up his spine.

He shifted his left hand to the holster at his hip and scrutinized the street behind him. It remained as empty as it had been a few minutes ago—not a soul in sight. But just because he couldn't see someone watching him didn't make it any less true. That sixth sense had saved his hide too many times for him to start mistrusting it now.

An ambush? One deft flick of his finger popped the safety strap. It wouldn't be the first one, that was for sure. No matter how many times he changed his appearance, there always seemed to be one dog in the pack who recognized him.

When nothing untoward stirred in the street, Jess turned his attention to the saloon. He glanced up, searching the second floor balcony. A flutter of curtains had his sights honing in on the last of four windows set into the false front. Jesse pulled his Colt from its holster and gripped the nickel-plated handle with swift familiarity.

Several seconds passed with no further movement. Jesse pressed the barrel of his revolver tight against his thigh and sidestepped onto the boardwalk. He pushed the door open and stood half in, half out of the double wide doorway, his nerves stretched tight as sunbaked rawhide, his senses kicked into full alert.

As he scanned the interior of the Scarlet Rose, the old adage "seeing red" took on a literal meaning. The brazen color dominated everything: the skirting around a stage at the south end of the room; the printed drapes flanking tall windows set high on either side; the balustrade rimming a staircase and the upper balcony. Even the dozen vacant tables scattered about wore red mats.

A flicker of movement near the bar had Jesse arcing his arm and taking aim. The woman who appeared in the doorway gasped and slapped her hand to her breast. Mid-twenties. Upswept hair frizzing around an oval face lightly powdered with rouge. Curvy in all the right places.

"Land's sakes, you scared the fooley out of me!" she cried.

Obviously not his spy, he decided from the genuine surprise in her tone. Jesse slowly reholstered his Colt and touched his fingers to the brim of his hat. "My apologies, ma'am." He kept his hands in sight and a good distance between them, letting her know he posed no threat. "Are you Scarlet Rose?"

"The one and only. Who's askin'?"

Still wary. Smart woman. "Nobody who means you any harm." With a final sweep of the room satisfying him that no danger lurked in the corners, Jesse strode with feigned casualness to the polished mahogany bar that ran the length of the north wall. Bottles in all shapes, sizes, and colors sat upon ceiling-high shelves built around a scroll-framed mirror that many a poker player had no doubt used to his advantage.

Scarlet Rose, recovering her surprise, brushed her hands down the trademark red fabric stretched tight across her midriff and took up a position behind the bar. "Now that I've got my heart back in my chest . . . what's your pleasure?"

Still edgy with his surroundings, Jesse

hooked one spurred heel over the brass rail below. "Whiskey—if you've got it."

"That's about all I've got—for five cents a shot." She plucked a bottle from beneath the bar and filled a squat glass with two fingers of whiskey.

Jesse plopped down a few nickels dug out of his vest pocket, then tossed back a swallow. The first taste stung his cracked lips and scored its way down his throat; the second washed through weeks of accumulated dust and sent a blissful fire spreading through his belly.

"We don't get many visitors around here since the mines ran out."

He didn't miss the inquisitive gleam in her green eyes or the subtle question in her statement. *Fishing for answers without outright asking.* He liked her style. He also knew the game well. Hell, he'd been playing it for years. "My horse pulled up lame." He pushed the glass forward. "Any idea where I might find a good hostler?"

"In Last Hope? You'd have better luck finding gold." She tipped the bottle and poured him a refill. "Folks expected this to be another Leadville. Miners hit color twice, but the shafts played out within a year. Then everyone pulled up stakes and moved on to richer pickin's."

"You're still here," Jesse pointed out.

One shoulder lifted in a shrug. "Stubborn, I guess. There's still a couple of prospectors up in the hills who swear they won't leave till Last Hope becomes Lost Hope." A crooked smile played on her rouged lips. "Can't seem to bring myself to give up till they do."

"Persistent as well as beautiful." He saluted her with his glass. "Now that's a combination a man finds hard to resist."

The blush staining her powdered cheeks only reinforced his opinion that there wasn't a woman alive who couldn't be plied with a little bit of flattery—even a woman as worldly as Scarlet Rose.

With a rag retrieved from beneath the counter, she began polishing the already spotless bar.

"So have you ever been to Leadville?" he asked conversationally.

The rag stopped in mid-circle and Scarlet tensed. "Once. It was an experience I don't care to repeat. Then again, I expect there ain't a body alive who hasn't had one of those."

Jesse could certainly relate to that sentiment. He'd had several.

"What about you? You look like a well-traveled man."

He swallowed a mouthful of spirits and nodded. "Just came from there, as a matter of fact. I was supposed to meet up with a pal of mine, but he never showed. He might even have passed through here in the last few weeks," he ventured, as if the thought had just occurred to him. "Big fellow, red hair, thick Scots brogue . . . ?"

"Sorry, sugar. The closest thing to Scotch I've run across in this area is the bottle I've got collecting dust in my storeroom."

Jesse bit back the urge to ask her if she was sure. Not that he doubted her, exactly. He'd just learned that folks tended to overlook the insignificant, and a little prodding often helped them with their recollections.

But Scarlet Rose, for all her good humor, had the shrewd feline eyes of a woman who had seen it all and forgotten nothing, and the fastest way to raise her hackles was to pelt her with a bunch of questions. Jess hadn't survived the last twelve years in his profession by making stupid mistakes. "Ah, well." He forced a smile. "It was a long shot anyway."

He doused his disappointment with another swig of the rotgut Scarlet passed off as whiskey. Duncan McGuire was known to frequent larger towns that provided a variety of opportunities either to load or lighten his purse—depending on which way the wind was blowing. One look around told Jesse that his quarry would have avoided this place like smallpox.

His hostess crossed her arms on the counter and leaned forward with a smile. "Tell you what, sugar, I've got a stable out back where I keep my mule. If your horse don't mind putting up with Bag-o'-Bones caterwaulin', he's welcome to rest up there for twenty-five cents a night."

The price was a bit steeper than he expected, but Jesse didn't dicker. He could hardly blame the woman for trying to make extra coin. "Much obliged. I'll be needing a room myself for the night, too, if you've got one to spare."

"Got half a dozen sittin' empty upstairs. Fifty cents a day, including meals."

Jesse almost choked on a swig of whiskey.

"You pay whether you eat or not, so you might as well eat." Pointedly taking in his appearance, she quirked one brow. "And no one gets a room without a bath."

"I suppose you know just where a man can find a bath hereabouts, too," Jesse countered with a crooked grin, fully aware that it, too, would come with an outrageous price tag.

"Now that you mention it, I've got an old tin tub in the pantry I'd be willin' rent. A dollar a filling—a dollar fifty if you want hot water."

"That's robbery!"

The mischievous smile she gave him made her look more like an adolescent girl than a calico queen. "There's always the creek."

That ribbon of mud and muck just outside of town? Jesse heaved a sigh of part despair, part amusement. At this rate, he'd be flat broke by nightfall. "You drive a hard bargain, Scarlet."

"So I've been told. But I make it worth every penny."

The smoky lilt of her voice left no mistake that they weren't just talking a room, a meal, and a tub of water. "How much more for personal treatment?" he couldn't resist asking.

"Depends on how personal."

"A back scrub and hair washing—for starters."

"Well, normally that would cost an extra ten cents, but for you . . . it'd be on the house." Her voice dropped a notch. So did the direction of her gaze. "Anything more will be up for negotiation."

The first genuine smile Jesse had felt in months tugged at his mouth. He was hardly a stranger to a woman's advances; hell, they'd been throwing themselves at him since he'd picked up his first straight razor. He never quite understood what it was they found so appealing about him, but neither did he question his good fortune. Passable looks were as much an advantage in his line of work as his sharp wits and nose for the truth—three gifts that Jesse never failed to use when necessary.

But, if he looked half as bad as he felt, it was a wonder any woman would look at him twice, much less flirt with him so brazenly. Then again, women of Scarlet's profession would flirt with a fencepost if it meant adding to the till.

Just as he started to ask where he might find the old tin tub, warning prickles once again danced up the back of his neck. Jesse reflexively shifted his hand to his hip.

"There you are, Honesty," his hostess called out, looking past him. "We've got us a visitor."

The guarded glance Jesse cast over his shoulder became an eye-popping double-take as his sights filled with the most stunning vision he'd seen in years. She stood halfway down the staircase, five feet six inches of temptation wrapped in red satin, with one hand on the banister, the other propped lightly on her hip. A mass of thick, amber ringlets tumbled from her crown down her back, with stray wisps framing a fine-boned face that belonged on a cameo pin. Slender brows arched over wide eyes with impossibly long, sweeping lashes, her nose was small and narrow bridged, and her mouth . . . Jess swallowed hard. Oh, mercy. Lips that ripe and full were known to lead a man down the long road to trouble and make him thank God for the trip.

Even the dress she wore should have been outlawed. Jess swore the shimmering red silk hugging her figure from bodice to knee had been designed solely to drive a man crazed with lust. And if all that red wasn't enough torture, black lace edged the slopes of her breasts and wrapped around her waist to form a ruffled bow at the low of her back.

"Honesty, why don't you show Mister—"

"Jesse," he supplied, finding his voice. "Jesse Jones." The false name fell from his lips with surprising ease, considering his tongue seemed to have affixed itself to the roof of his mouth.

"Show Mr. Jones to his room while I scare up something for supper?"

"Sure thing, Rose," she replied in a spun velvet voice that wrapped around Jesse's vitals. "Follow me, cowboy."

Anywhere, he thought, watching black lace brush across her red satin clad bottom as she started up the stairs. A forgotten fever surged through his bloodstream and settled below his buckle. With her being just a few inches shorter than his own five feet eleven, it didn't take a scientist to figure that their bodies would fit together like heat on fire, and the picture that formed in his mind sent desire slamming through him with the force of a cannon ball. Jesse saw himself walking up behind her, pulling her back against his front, her bottom to his groin, sliding his hands down either side of her rib cage, her hips, her thighs, then slipping up again beneath her hem to the dark stockings beneath . . .

She paused on a middle step and twisted around. The up and down gander she gave Jesse, as if judging his worth, left him with the impression that she found him sorely lacking. "Are you coming?"

Not yet, but he would if he stared at her much longer—right here in the middle of the Scarlet Rose.

Jess thanked the week's growth of whiskers for hiding the color heating his cheeks. Never in all his thirty years had he felt such a swift and immediate response toward a woman; the fact that one sultry-eyed saloon girl could affect him so strongly, and at a time when he needed all his wits about him, left an acrid taste in his mouth. "I'll be along after I've seen to my horse," Jesse announced, pushing away from the bar. Best put some distance between himself and this lush-lipped distraction till he got himself under control.

With a tip of his hat, he strode out the door.

Long after he disappeared from sight, Honesty stared after him, her mouth agape, her heart tapping faster than musician's spoons. Never in all her born days had a man looked at her like that—as if he'd waited his whole life to see her and finally got the chance. It was humbling and astonishing and . . . thrilling. Every inch of her skin tingled, and a strange, faintly wicked sensation danced deep in her belly.

"You gonna give me a hand, or are you gonna stand around gawking all day?"

Wrenched from her musings, Honesty snapped around to find Rose watching her with amusement. Good cow feathers, what was wrong with her? If she didn't know better, she'd think the feelings their guest had stirred inside her were desire. Honesty shook off the disturbing thought. Impossible. The only feeling men roused in her anymore was disgust.

"I wasn't gawking," she denied, following Rose into the kitchen.

"You were gawking. Not that I blame you— that one's got the makin's of a true Lothario."

Warmth flooded Honesty's cheeks. "If your tastes run toward the scrawny desperado type."

"You just ain't looking at all the possibilities." Rose opened the door to the cast iron stove and started shoving chunks of pine into its mouth.

Possibilities? Honesty caught sight of him through the window, leading a muscled brown horse across the back yard. Good gravy, he looked as if he'd been dragged through a riverbed and hung out to dry. It wouldn't surprise her if his face was plastered on wanted posters from here to Mexico. All those whiskers, that long, matted hair . . . hadn't she heard somewhere that long hair often hid the cropped upper ear marking a horse thief?

Yet despite his scruffy appearance, Honesty couldn't deny that there was something about the man that sent her heart racing. Maybe it was the way he walked, with the straight-shouldered confidence of one at ease with himself and the rest of the world. Or maybe it was the aura of unleashed power and mystery he exuded.

Who in God's green pastures was he? And what was he doing in Last Hope?

"Fetch me a kettle out of the pantry, will ya, hon?"

Once again snapped to the present, Honesty did as Rose bade and brought a large copper cooking kettle from the pantry, as well as a pair of banded wooden buckets to haul bath water. Thanks to Rose's Uncle Joe, they weren't forced to heat water over the stove the way they used to. He'd rigged up a cistern out back that sat upon a constant flame, so when visitors like Mr. Jones showed up, they wouldn't have long to wait.

After filling the buckets she returned to the kitchen, where Rose was chopping a slab of beef into pieces. "So what does he want?" Honesty asked, hoping the woman read nothing more into the question than idle curiosity. She wished she could have heard the conversation between the two of them, but the stranger's voice had been too low pitched to make eavesdropping possible.

"Same thing as every other man." Rose shrugged. "Good whiskey, a hot bath, a soft bed, and a willing woman to share it with."

She should have guessed, Honesty thought with a grimace. Why should he be different from nearly every other man she'd encountered? "He didn't have to make a trip all the way out here for that."

"He didn't. Apparently his horse went lame."

"Do you believe him?"

"Don't see why I shouldn't. No one comes to Last Hope willingly anymore."

That was an understatement. Even she wouldn't be here if fate hadn't struck such a cruel blow. But when a girl found herself dodging predators left and right, the best place to hide was the last place anyone would look. A nearly deserted town in the Rocky Mountain foothills worked quite nicely.

"That water should be plenty hot, hon," Rose remarked, steering Honesty's thoughts back to the subject at hand. "So go on and take him his bath while I throw a stew on for supper."

A sudden flurry of panic erupted in Honesty's middle at the idea of being in the same room with the stranger. "How about if I cook the stew and you take him his bath?"

Rose's brows dipped into a V; her face softened in concern. "Honesty, are you afraid of him?"

"Of course not!" She wasn't afraid of any man. Cautious, yes. And why not? Her father had been a master swindler, and in the three months since his death, she'd found herself pursued relentlessly by every mark he'd ever swindled. Who wouldn't be wary after that? "I just can't shake the feeling that his showing up here isn't as innocent as he wants us to believe."

"That may be true, but his reasons aren't any of our concern. He's the first customer to walk through that door in weeks, and as long as he's got the coin, we'll oblige his every whim."

The thought of obliging the stranger anything made the disturbing sensation in Honesty's middle return full force. She couldn't forget the hungry look he'd given her—as if given the chance, he'd gobble her whole . . .

"Look, hon," Rose broke into her thoughts, "you and I both know I didn't hire you to decorate the mantel. But I also know you've had a rough time of it lately. So go on and take him his bath. If he wants more than a good scrubbin', just turn him over to me."

The wink told her that Rose wouldn't consider the task much of a sacrifice, and she drew comfort in the fact that the option was there if she needed it. Unfortunately, if she ever hoped to leave this place she had to make money, which meant doing the job she'd been hired for—tending to the customers.

Besides, maybe she was overreacting. If it turned out that Mr. Jones was her best chance of solving the mystery Deuce had left behind, could she really let a few silly worries get in the way of finding out whatever secret he'd kept from her all these years?

Managing a smile braver than she felt, Honesty patted Rose's hand. "Don't worry about me. I can take care of myself." She'd had plenty of practice in the last three months.

She turned from Rose and headed for the stairs. He was just a man, after all, she told herself, with a man's strengths as well as his weaknesses. And if he wanted more than a good scrubbing . . . well, she hadn't spent a lifetime with the greatest con man in the West without tucking a few tricks in her pockets.

Chapter 2

Calling the ramshackle structure a stable was being generous, Jesse thought, leading Gemini across the yard behind the saloon. The gaps between the boards were big enough to fit a fist through, the tin roof bore rust holes the size of pie tins, and termites had chewed their way through several rafters. But if it kept the elements off the animals, Jess supposed he had no call to complain.

He guided Gemini into an empty stall next to one holding the sorriest excuse for a mule he'd ever had the misfortune to view. His nose curled as a stiff wind stirred up an unpleasant odor. "I hope that's you stinking to high heaven," Jesse told the mule. But he knew good and well where the odor came from—endless

21

days of sweating under the hot sun and interminable nights of sleeping wherever his body
landed.

No wonder his hostess had been so insistent
on that bath. It was a wonder she'd even allowed him through her doors.

He took his time tending to Gemini—bathing
the wound, bandaging his leg, then brushing
him down; doing his best to apologize for pushing him so hard lately and causing the injury.
But even if the horse hadn't needed the extra attention, Jess would have used it as an excuse to
get himself under control.

What had come over him back there? So Scarlet's girl was a looker. She wasn't the first pretty
woman he'd met in his travels, and he doubted
she'd be the last. And the last thing he had time
for was a blonde-haired, brown-eyed temptress
distracting him.

Then, with a grimace, he realized that until
Gem's leg healed, all he *had* was time. Too much
of it.

"What kind of trouble have you landed me
into this time, huh, Gem?"

The horse looked at him with soulful eyes,
then turned back to the bucket of oats Jess had
filled for him. With a sigh, Jess gathered the
strips of cloth and tin of ointment he'd used to
doctor the wound, and stuffed them back in his
packs.

Once he had Gem groomed and settled, he grabbed his saddlebags, returned to the saloon, and mounted the steps to the room he'd been assigned. The accommodations weren't much to boast about. Plain walls, an iron bedstead and side table, two chairs tucked under a small round supper table, and a claw-footed wardrobe that smelled faintly of cedar. The red calico screen in the corner probably hid a commode and wash stand, if past lodgings were anything to go by. He'd slept in worse places, though. It came with the territory.

Jesse set the saddlebags on a chair near the door, then sat on the bed; the ropes strained and screeched in protest to his one-hundred-seventy-pound frame. The spread was a bit frayed, but at least he didn't have fleas jumping at him from out of the mattress or questionable stains on the sheets.

After discarding his duster, he pulled off his Justins, draped his gun belt around the foot-post, and topped it with his hat. The few shots of whiskey he'd consumed had his head pleasantly buzzing. As promised, a tin tub sat in the center of the room, waiting for water. Once it showed up, he planned on indulging in the first good soaking he'd had in weeks and a full night's sleep. Then, once Gem's leg healed, he'd resume his search for "Deuce" McGuire.

A floorboard squeaked under his stockinged

feet as he wandered to the window overlooking
the deserted street below. It still amazed him
that the case had been open for sixteen years!
Just as amazing was that it had taken so long to
call in professionals and expect them to close it.

Hell.

Jesse leaned against the window frame and
wondered for the hundredth time what had
possessed him to accept this assignment? A kidnaping didn't run to his usual tastes. Cattle
rustling, train robberies, stagecoach heists, and
horse thieving . . . now, those were the cases he
fed on.

Had fed on, he corrected himself. After
twelve years, he was just fed up. He wouldn't
even have accepted this assignment if he could
have avoided it. But with a majority of the
agents tied up with the McCormick strike and
the Denver Branch just getting on its feet, Bill
McParland had thought Jess the most experienced man to take over such an important and
highly confidential job. The West was his do-
main, after all, and discretion his middle name.
What was a fellow supposed to do when the
man who saved his life asked for a favor?

Jess rubbed his shoulder and continued staring out the window at the shades of black and
red being thrown across town by the setting
sun. Damn, he wished he had more than the
scanty information he'd been given. Duncan

McGuire, commonly known as "Deuce," was wanted for the abduction of the daughters of San Francisco shipping magnate Anton Jervais.

"But as often happens in cases like this," Bill McParland had informed him two months earlier, "he fled with the ransom money without ever returning the girls."

With the pitifully thin file lying open on the desk before him, Jesse scanned the items his superintendent had collected—the profile sheet William Pinkerton had developed several years back for each subject the agency pursued, a couple of newspaper articles, a sketch of McGuire and another of two flaxen-haired, cherub-faced little girls. "What happened to them?" he'd asked, though he wasn't sure he really wanted to know.

Bill's silence and averted face bespoke the worst. "Both of them drowned in San Francisco Bay."

In spite of the emotional detachment Jesse tried to maintain as a Pinkerton Operative, his heart gave a tug.

"Whether McGuire committed the actual murders is still in question. He was a notorious con artist with a penchant for get-rich-quick schemes, but he wasn't a killer." Bill tapped the file. "The uncle, on the other hand, was a desperate man. According to reports, Phillipe Jervais had been in financial trouble for years. I suspect he never intended on them being returned. Not only would the ransom take care of his financial woes, but their permanent disposal would ensure that his son inherited the Jervais fortune."

"And all this is coming to light sixteen years after the fact?"

"Local authorities worked on the case for a couple of years without a single lead. Phillipe Jervais covered his tracks well. He died last year, though, and some incriminating evidence was found among his personal belongings: directions to the ransom drop-off point, written in Phillipe's hand to his hireling, Deuce McGuire, so a solid link between him and the abductions could be established. Anton Jervais found it and contacted us."

"So what are my orders?"

"Find McGuire. Obtain a confession. Bring him back to San Francisco to stand trial."

Simple enough, Jesse had thought at the time. Now he wasn't so sure. After two months, he was no closer to finding McGuire than the day he'd started his search. The man moved around more than a Cheyenne hunter. A few days here, a few days there. Hell, Jess had had more luck tracking a raindrop through a downpour.

He'd thought he'd finally gotten a break down in Durango when McGuire had hightailed it north after shooting a man. According to witnesses, the unfortunate victim had shown an interest in a pretty dance hall girl McGuire fancied. McGuire ambushed the man in a back alley, then fled the scene with the woman. Jesse managed to track them as far as Silverton, where, the trail went colder than a Montana winter. He'd covered every nook and cranny between Durango and Leadville without a single trace of the fellow or his companion.

Well, he'd root McGuire out of whatever hole he'd crawled into—eventually. Jesse hadn't earned his reputation without cause. And once he wrangled a confession out of the worm, he'd take him back to San Francisco as ordered. Then he was done with the Pinkerton Detective Agency. Sure, Bill had promised him his pick of future assignments. But the prospect of jumping into another ruse just didn't fill him with the same sense of anticipation it used to. A man could spend only so many years being shot at and beat up and left to rot in places unfit for the human race . . .

Jess pushed back the incident chewing at his memory. Yeah, the sooner he located McGuire and turned him over to the authorities, the sooner he could turn in his resignation and decide what he'd do with the rest of his life.

Unfortunately, "sooner" was taking its own sweet time getting here.

"If I were a Scotsman, where would I be?"

A rap on the door broke into his musings. Jesse crossed the room, cracked open the door, and found Scarlet's girl standing in the hallway balancing a stack of towels and soap in one hand and a yoke of water buckets across her neck.

As before, the sight of her commanded his full and immediate notice. Even with a yoke weighing down upon her shoulders, she carried herself with a regalness that made him want to touch her and keep his distance at the same time.

"Are you going to make me stand out here all day or are you going to let me in?"

Jess jerked himself to awareness and stepped away from the doorway with a grimace of self-disgust. What was it about this girl that just the sight of her had the ability to chase all conscious thought from his head? He hadn't felt so tongue-tied and muddle-minded around a female since Christina Flowers had proudly displayed her blossoming wares to him in her daddy's barn the spring of his thirteenth year.

When Scarlet's girl—Honesty—set the buckets down beside the tub, Jesse belatedly realized that the least he could have done was to relieve her of her burden, but he seemed incapable of doing more than staring at her like a simpleton.

As she laid the towels on the bed, then poured the buckets into the tub, he leaned against the window frame with his arms folded across his chest. "Honesty. An unusual name."

"My father was an unusual man." She swiped a stray curl from her cheek. Steam billowed around her face and put a sheen on her flushed skin. "Do you plan on bathing with your clothes on?"

Ah, a forbidden subject, he thought, recognizing the diversionary tactic. He could respect that. He didn't much care to discuss his father, either.

He pushed away from the wall and unfastened first one cuff, then the other. "So how'd a pretty girl like you wind up in a godforsaken place like this?"

"They don't call it Last Hope for nothing."

Jesse peered quizzically at her from under half-masted lashes. He would have pursued that remark, but again she steered the subject from herself.

"You might want to test the water before you get in," she said, gesturing toward the tub.

After scooping his hand through the water and finding the temperature to his satisfaction, he finished unfastening his shirt and tossed it carelessly on one of the chairs.

"Good cow feathers, what happened to you?"

Jesse didn't have to look at the weblike pattern above his heart to know what she referred to. "I had a fight with a Winchester and lost."

He unbuttoned his trousers and she whipped away to face the wall. Jess quirked his brow at her peculiar reaction. Hell, she acted as if she'd never seen a man undress before.

"Does it hurt?" she asked, busying herself with the items on the bed.

"Only when I breathe."

"You're lucky you're able to do that. An inch lower and you'd be dead."

"That was the plan." He shucked his pants, then lowered himself into the steaming water with a sigh. The tub was almost too small to hold him; Jess had to fold his knees to his chest just to fit. "You can turn around now."

She peered over her shoulder, as if checking to see if it was safe, before lifting her chin and approaching to kneel behind him. He heard her lathering her hands, and a spicy scent mingled with the vapor rising up from the water. He nearly melted when her soap-slick palms glided across his upper back.

"You're a long way from Texas, cowboy."

"Is it that obvious?" Jesse asked, knowing full well that it was. Though he hadn't been in the Lone Star state for several years, he'd discovered that the affected dialect seemed to open more doors for him than any other. Few seemed willing to question a Texan, especially one in the Stetson and spurs of a cowboy's trade.

"I recognize the accent." She slid the rag

across his shoulders, back and forth, her touch light and heavenly. "So what brings you to Last Hope?"

"Just passing through."

"Unless I miss my guess, you do that often."

She must take fishing lessons from Rose. "Often enough."

"Are you a miner?"

"Not hardly."

"An outlaw?"

"No."

"A gambler?"

That made him smile. "Only when it suits my purposes." He wondered where she was heading with the conversation. Most sporting girls cared only how loud the jingle was in a man's pocket. "Are you always this nosy?"

"Only when it suits my purposes."

The sideways grin she gave him struck Jesse as so pure and innocent that a moment passed before he remembered that purity and innocence were hardly words that belonged in the same context as her profession.

"Close your eyes so I can wet your hair."

He did as she bade, and as warm water tumbled over his head, a groan of pleasure rumbled up his throat. Damn, but that felt good. The scouring of her fingers against his scalp felt even better.

Jess leaned back as far as his spine would

bend and allowed himself to enjoy the full extent of her ministrations. Lilac perfume and a woodsy scent he recognized as patchouli thickened around him as fingernails gently scored his scalp from brow to nape. Her hands circled his neck, then ran across his shoulders and down his chest, taking extra care around the puckered scar.

Oh, to hell with the meal—this bath was heaven itself.

When he opened his eyes, he was treated to the delicious sight of Honesty's breasts trying to push their way out of their tight confines. She had beautiful breasts, what he could see of them. Full. Firm. Flawless. *Yep, definitely heaven,* he thought with a smile.

Just then a glitter of gold caught his eye. Languidly, he slid his forefinger beneath the chain and lifted an object from the valley it called home. A gold ring set with a small, oval-shaped ruby raised his eyebrows. "What's this?"

Soapy hands gently extracted the jewelry from his grip and dropped it between the pale swells. "A gift."

"You must be quite talented."

"From my *father*."

Even if the correction had called for a reply, the appearance of a straight blade in her hand warned Jesse against voicing it.

"I hope you aren't too fond of that scruff on

your face, because you and it are parting company." She gripped his chin between her thumb and forefinger. "I can't abide whiskers." Only then did Jess realize how rich a brown her eyes were, the color of hot chocolate—though right now they glittered with a determination that set his nerves on edge.

She drew her bottom lip between her teeth and tilted her head first one way, then the other. The sight of those pearly whites nibbling on pink flesh had the temperature in the room rising several degrees. "Have you ever shaved a man before?"

Perfectly arced eyebrows shot upward. "Do I *look* like a woman who has never shaved a man?"

Put that way, shaving was no doubt a drop in the bucket of services she offered.

The images that popped into Jesse's mind would have made even the most seasoned harlot blush. Suddenly his skin became overly sensitive to the water, his senses acute to the woman beside him. The rasp of steel scraping away beard and her gentle breaths were the only sounds in the room.

Normally he avoided bedding saloon girls; he well knew the kind of men who paraded in and out of their beds each night, and had no desire to take with him any souvenirs gained from a few minutes of pleasure.

So the swift and gripping interest in bedding this one was odd—and a little unsettling.

It had to be the whiskey dulling his wits, not her flowery-fresh fragrance, so out of place among the smells of steam and spice and whiskey and sweat. Not the glossy brown-gold curls piled atop her head. Not the beads of bath water dotting her skin.

Closing his eyes, Jess reined in the desire climbing through his veins and forced himself to think of something—anything—other than the woman kneeling over him.

His mother. Thinking of his mother should overcome this damnedable weakness he had for soft skin and sweet scents. Hoping the old trick would serve its purpose, he called forth an image of Rowena Randolph as he'd last seen her, standing on a depot platform in Cheyenne, Wyoming, recruiting other suffragettes to close down a bordello. He'd just about succeeded when a soft gasp echoed through the room.

He opened his eyes and found Honesty staring at him in wonder. "Oh, my lands . . . you're beautiful!"

His brows shot up. *"Beautiful?"*

Her cheeks turned a becoming pink, and she self-consciously dabbed at his freshly shaven face with a damp cloth. "You needn't act so surprised. I'm sure people tell you that all the time."

"Not if they want to live," he said with a sardonic twist to his mouth. *Beautiful* sounded far too feminine, and much too much like the derogatory names thrown at him all his life by his own gender. Angel-face, pretty boy, buttercup . . . and those were the polite ones.

Of course, as Jess had gotten older, he'd learned to close his ears to the slurs and use his looks to his own advantage: women seemed to appreciate them, and men were so busy underestimating him because of them that they never realized how much danger they were in until it was too late.

Strangely enough, coming from her, the comment sent a surge of warmth through his chest instead of the usual resentment, a rush of power—as if she could pay him no higher compliment. It didn't make a lick of sense. Hell, for all he knew, it could be part of her routine. All harlots had one; some were just better than others.

And Honesty was infinitely better than most, he decided, when her hand delved beneath the water. Her fingertips grazed his hips, and Jesse couldn't decide if it was a designed move to arouse or an innocent mis-aim. Either way, it had hot blood centering in his groin. He seized her hand under the water in a tempered grip. "Do you tend to all your customers so thoroughly?"

She blinked. "Rose said to oblige your every whim."

His every whim, huh?

Well, why the hell not? When a man found himself stranded with a beautiful, willing woman, he shouldn't complain. He should fall on his knees and thank the gods.

How long had it been since he'd lost himself in a soft, warm body? Too damn long, now that he thought about it. After two months of diligent tracking, didn't he deserve a night off? And if that night included being pleasured by the prettiest sporting girl this side of the Rocky Mountain Range, he'd consider himself richly rewarded. "Honesty?"

"Hmm?"

"I've got a whim that needs obligin'."

He dragged her hand to his hard shaft. Dark eyes widened in alarm, she sucked in a breath, and her entire body went tighter than a lodge-pole pine . . .

For a moment Jess wondered how experienced she could be at pleasuring a man, when she acted as if she'd never touched one before.

Then her fingers closed snugly around him, and he couldn't think at all.

"Ah, God!" he gasped, sinking back against the rim of the tub, pushing himself further into her palm.

As if emboldened by his body's reaction, her

hand moved up, then down. "My, my, that's quite a loaded weapon you're packin'," she drawled in that red-velvet voice.

Stars burst behind Jesse's eyelids and every last drop of blood in his body seemed to rush to his groin. The air around them grew hot enough to peel the hide off an armadillo.

He gritted his teeth and fought for control. "You keep touchin' me like that and it won't stay loaded for long."

She licked her lips again, and seeing that pink tongue sliding across the seam of ripe flesh proved his undoing. With a half-groan, half growl, he cupped the back of her neck and dragged her face down to his.

The instant their lips met, light exploded into tiny shards behind Honesty's eyes. She couldn't deny that she'd been kissed before; over the last few months, there'd been more than she wished to count, and most of them had been like this— demanding and possessive and self-satisfying.

None of them had ever rocked her down to her corset strings.

As his mouth devoured hers Honesty tried to call upon the methods Deuce had taught her over the years to fend off overly bold advances but not a one came to mind. Even if any had, she didn't think she could muster the strength to use them. Her heart pounded so loud she swore he could hear it; her hands felt sweaty

and clammy at the same time. A wild craving
unfurled low in her belly, a restless urgency she
could neither define nor fight.

Honesty moaned and leaned closer into him.
She'd never dreamed a kiss could be so. . . . en-
joyable. His tongue felt like velvet sliding
across hers and the pressure of his lips as entic-
ing as paradise.

He shifted, and Honesty realized that she
hadn't yet moved her hand. She'd never
touched a man's. . . . privates before—she'd always managed to keep the game from going
that far. But as Honesty once again stroked his
stiff organ, she marveled at the texture of him.
He bucked his hips, fueling a sense of power
and control she'd never felt before. His fingers
tightened in her hair; his tongue followed the
rhythm set by her hand, driving into her
mouth, then retreating. And she thrust back,
tasting whiskey and soap and man . . . oh, so
much man.

Driven by an insane need to touch him, she
dragged her palm past the soft, wet hair that
nestled at the core of him up to a stomach rigid
with muscle, then glided up the tight, slick wall
of his chest. How could she have ever thought
him scrawny? Lean, yes, but hardly scrawny.
There was no mistaking the solid ridges of muscle beneath her fingers.

His kiss gentled then, his mouth no longer

bruising, his tongue no longer aggressive. It slid across hers with maddening leisure, coaxing, teasing, tasting; magnifying her awareness of his power and her weakness. Then he drew her tongue into his mouth and. . . .

Oh, God.

Sensations swept through her in kaleidoscopic colors—the blue of desire, red of fire, purple of need . . . she plunged her fingers into his soapy hair, gripping the back of his head, if only to ground herself from the dizzying assault.

"Damnation, but you taste sweet," he murmured against her lips.

He tasted like . . . a summer storm.

Reeling, Honesty's head felt too heavy to support, and fell back. He took that as an invitation to blaze a hot path down her neck with his mouth. Her limbs turned to liquid, her blood to lava. Her breathing grew so ragged she feared she would faint.

"And your skin is so soft . . ."

And his was so . . . hot. She'd go up in flames if he kept this up.

But she'd die if he stopped. Everywhere his lips touched, her skin burned. Down the cords of her neck, along the ridge of her collarbone, across the slopes of her breasts . . . They strained against her dress, growing so heavy and painful she could hardly bear it. In a daze, she watched as he gave the scooped neckline of her chemise a fierce tug; one breast spilled out over the top of her corset and eagerly filled his hand.

His mouth latched onto her nipple and Honesty nearly came out of her skin. Her fingers gripped his slick shoulders, her leg lifted over the rim of the tub. She hardly noticed that the toes of her slippers dipped into the water, or that splotches of water stained her skirts. She knew only an intense need to be rid of the restless, aching feeling Jesse had created inside her.

"Enough—I want inside you now."

The words, raw and determined, reached past the fog and slapped her like a sheet of cold rain. Honesty stilled instantly; she glanced down at the top of Jesse's head.

Oh, God . . . what was she *doing*?

Her mind spun back to the moment it all began. If any other man had taken such liberties, she'd probably have clubbed him over the head with the closest chair. But Jesse had the strangest ability to make her forget the role she played and remind her that beneath the sporting-girl guise beat the heart of a woman.

Breathless, she pulled back, knowing that if she didn't put some distance between herself and this tub full of temptation, she'd never regain control of the situation. "How about we take this to drier ground?" she suggested in a ragged whisper.

His grip tightened. Eyes impossibly thick-lashed and such a rich shade of green they put mountain aspens to shame studied her with a twinkle of mischief. His hand swept under her skirt and slid up her stockings, past her garter, and curled around the back of her thigh, his fingertips mere inches from the damp heat of her. "What's the matter, darlin'—afraid of gettin' a little wet?"

Honesty's breath caught at the bawdy remark. She didn't know whether to laugh or spit in his face. Alarmingly, she couldn't find the will to do either. Oh, why did he have to be so blasted handsome? Earlier, with his hair in soapy tangles, shaving cream and bits of whiskers smeared all over his face, he'd hardly been an appealing partner. But with the grime washed away, his hair had turned the light blond of a sunbeam and fell across his shoulders in tumbling disarray. Brows a shade darker arced above those smoldering eyes, and lines extending from the corners suggested that he spent a lot of time either laughing or squinting into the sun. His nose was straight bridged and narrow, and below was the most perfect set of lips, the lower slightly fuller than the upper, that she'd ever seen in her life.

She licked her own lips, swollen from his kisses, and peered at him through lowered lashes in what she hoped was an inviting manner. "I just don't think this li'l ole tub is big enough for the both of us."

She pulled free of his hold once again. This time he made no move to stop her, but his hot, hungry stare bored into her back as she crossed the room. Honesty forced herself to remember her role and put a saucy swing into her step, hoping he couldn't see how badly her knees knocked together.

Once at the dresser, she pressed her hand against her breast, closed her eyes as she quickly pulled up her chemise, and released a slow, pent-up breath. How had the tables turned so quickly? She was supposed to have been seducing him senseless, not the other way around! Good gravy, the whole purpose of working in places like the Scarlet Rose was to get money! How could she hope to hire an escort without funds to pay him?

It was definitely time to put an end to this little charade.

She threw a quick glance over her shoulder. Much to her relief, he was bowed over in the tub, pouring a bucket over his head to rinse away any remaining suds. Honesty quickly slipped a trembling hand into her skirt pocket and withdrew her "secret to a man's greatest pleasure." The packet of powders had come in handy more times than Honesty cared to remember. "Would you care for another whiskey?" she asked, amazed that she could even talk for the tumult inside her.

"I've had enough, thanks."

"Surely you won't make a lady drink alone."

With determined movements, she poured them both a glass of whiskey from the bottle Rose always kept in the night stand, then watered down the contents in her glass. She'd never had much tolerance for spirits, and getting soused would quite defeat her purpose.

But as she opened the packet and lifted it to the rim of his glass, she found herself fighting a sudden impulse to toss the powders aside. Take the passion Jesse offered, and hang the consequences. For the first time in her life, a man's attention was less like a bullet to dodge and more like an adventure to savor. Did it really matter that this gorgeous cowboy would be gone tomorrow? In fact, wouldn't it be better if she didn't have to see him again?

Then Deuce's face appeared before her—laughing Scottish eyes, stern father's mouth, and a truth left undiscovered—and she knew she could not let herself be diverted from her goal, even for one night.

Honestly pressed her lips tightly together, dumped the powder into his whiskey before she changed her mind, then turned around—

And nearly dropped their drinks. "Oh, m-m-my . . ."

Jesse stood in a ray of setting sunlight in all his naked glory, every lean, tapering inch of him, beautifully bronzed and exquisitely proportioned. The air around her went tight and humid. She teetered on the verge of swooning.

Speechlessly, she let her gaze roam over the body bared to her view. Bad enough he had a face so beautiful it almost hurt to look at him, but did he have to have a body to match? Wide shoulders, chiseled chest, abdomen flat and rippled with muscle.

Her gaze dipped, drawn against her will to that fine line of hair extending from his navel to the impressive and unmistakable evidence of his desire.

Oh, lands, she was in trouble. All that power, all that sensuality tucked into one masculine body . . .

Even as she watched transfixed, the corners of his mouth turned upward in a smile of awareness, whether at his own power or its effect on her, she couldn't say. But despite her embarrassment, she couldn't tear her eyes away as he crossed the room with a loose-limbed stride that made her heart stutter. He then flipped the sheets over on the bed and climbed in. With his back propped against the headboard, arms winged behind his head, a devilish smile appeared on his fallen-angel face and a wicked promise glittered in eyes. Men of his caliber weren't harmless—they were dangerous as sin.

And resisting him was going to be harder than she'd ever dreamed.

Aware that he was waiting, she forced her wobbly legs to carry her to the bed. She handed Jesse his glass of whiskey, lifted her own in the air, and, hoping he never knew how dearly she regretted what she was about to do, proposed a toast. "To an unforgettable night."

Chapter 3

H e couldn't remember a damn thing.

With his elbows propped on splayed knees, his head cupped in his hands, Jesse sat at the edge of the bed, naked as the day he was born. Around him, the scents of sweat and lilacs swirled together in a dizzying aftermath.

His gaze turned to the woman in his bed. Her pale hair fanned across the pillow slip, silky tangles against pristine white. A vague image of burying his fingers in that hair stirred at the back of his memory, yet he couldn't quite grasp it.

She rolled onto her side. Her eyes were closed, her lashes casting shadowed crescents on flawless cheekbones. Her nose nuzzled the sheet as if inhaling its scent, and her lips curved into a smile of wistful bliss that had his gut knotting.

Abruptly she stilled. A frown creased her brow. Then she shot up off the bed, giving him only a glimpse of bare back and pale, curvy bottom before snatching a blanket over her nudity. Eyes as wide and frantic as a stormy sea searched the room, then anchored on him.

"Jesse?"

"Expecting someone else?"

"Oh my gosh," she whispered. "Oh my *gosh*!"

Through bleary eyes, he watched her throw a wrinkled chemise over her head, then wriggle into a pair of ruffled black drawers. Seeing her in the dark undergarments had as much an impact on him as the red corset he'd taken off her last night.

At least, he *thought* he'd taken it off her.

Jess strained to put the night in order in his mind. He distinctly remembered soft caresses and hot kisses that could turn a man to cinders. And he remembered laughing when Honesty spilled whiskey on his chest, then moaning when he made her lick it off . . .

It got a little hazy after that. Nothing more than sensations of heat and dampness and the most insane need to possess that he'd ever felt in his life.

The last thing he could recall with any clarity

was climbing atop her soft and willing body and hoping like hell he didn't explode before he buried himself inside her.

And then . . . nothing. Not even a glimmer to remind him what had transpired next.

"What . . ." He licked his lips, then glanced around for something to get rid of the chalky taste in his mouth. Half a glass of whiskey sat on the table. It was watered down and stale, but it was wet. "What happened last night?"

She paused in the act of tying her chemise to look at him. "Last night?"

For a split second, he'd have sworn she looked as confused as he felt. "Yeah. Did we . . . you know . . . finish?"

"What kind of question is that? Of course we did!" She bustled about the room, plucking her dress off the chair and a dyed black petticoat from the floor. "Twice, in fact! We might have gone for a third time, except you had me so plumb wore out . . . well, let's just say that had I known the extent of your talents, I'd have been more prepared. Have you seen my shoe?"

Something about the way her words gushed out and she kept avoiding his eyes struck Jesse as odd, but his mind was too damned fuzzy to sort it out. How much had he drunk? A few whiskeys? Surely not enough to wipe his mind clean. Hell, he could outdrink an Irishman.

"Gosh, I can't believe I fell asleep in your bed. First time I've ever done that."

It was the first time he'd ever *had* a woman fall asleep in his bed. That was one thing Jesse had always prided himself on, and what had always made him so good at his job: clearing himself of the scene before it became incriminating.

"By the way, you owe me three dollars."

"Three dollars!" he cried, then immediately regretted raising his voice when what felt like a thousand ice picks stabbed behind his eyeballs.

"Surely you didn't expect to spend a night with me for free."

No, but at that price he expected at least to remember it. How did he know he'd been given his money's worth?

Yet how could he prove he hadn't?

"Aw, hell and damnation." Jesse ripped his trousers off the floor and plunged his hand into the front pocket. Pulling out a handful of coins, he blinked, then narrowed his eyes. Was this all he had left?

She snatched the required amount from his palm so fast his head spun, then headed for the door. She paused with her hand on the knob. "Thanks, cowboy. You really were incredible."

At least one of them enjoyed it.

After Honesty left, Jesse dragged himself off the bed, got dressed, and went downstairs hoping a strong cup of coffee would help clear his head.

He found his hostess sitting at one of the tables, several books that looked like accounts spread open before her. From the frown of consternation on her face, the numbers weren't meeting with her approval. "Mornin', Scarlet."

She glanced up, then shut each book. "Well, good mornin', Mr. Jones." She leaned back in her chair and gave him an appreciative once-over. "My, my, my, don't you clean up nicely?"

He rubbed his hand self-consciously along the short bristles that replaced the bushy beard. "I feel like I've been rode hard and put up wet."

Amusement glittered in her eyes as she gestured to the empty chair across from her. "Enjoyed yourself last night, did you?" she asked after he lowered himself into the seat.

"I'm told I did." At her strange look, he confessed, "It's all a bit fuzzy right now."

"Well, from all the ruckus those bedsprings were making, the two of you were having a grand ole time."

Jess couldn't stop his jaw from dropping. If they'd been so . . . obvious . . . that even Rose knew how they'd occupied the evening, how was it that his mind remained so blank?

Something was beginning to smell rotten in the Scarlet Rose, and this time it wasn't him.

Jesse leaned back in his chair and feigned casual interest. "A woman of Honesty's talents must be quite in demand."

Again she looked Jesse up and down and grinned. "She seems to have a certain . . . effect on men."

That she did. "How long has she been working for you?"

"A few weeks. Poor thing wound up working in one of the mining camps after losin' her family. Diphtheria, I think she said."

A common occurrence, and no reason to question it, Jesse thought. He'd been in enough mining camps to know that they were prime breeding grounds for disease. It also explained why she was so sensitive about that ring from her father. Still, Jesse couldn't rid himself of the niggling feeling that there was something missing in the story. "Why didn't she just get married? Men are a dime a dozen and it isn't as if she's hard on the eyes. I doubt she'd have had any trouble finding a husband."

Rose made a sound of disgust, leaned back in her chair, and folded her hands over her stomach. "You think I didn't try convincing her of that? When she showed up on my doorstep, I told her she should find herself a good man, settle down, have a couple of young'uns . . . she looked at me like I'd asked her to drink poison.

She was bent on workin', so I figured she'd be safer here, where I could watch out for her, than in back in one of those camps."

As much as he hated to admit it, Rose was right. Honesty was a grown woman, fully capable of making her own decisions. If she chose to make her living this way he supposed she was a lot better off doing it here than in some filthy camp with a bunch of desperate miners.

Jesse frowned. Maybe that's what bothered him: why would a woman who made her living off men choose to work in a dying town that saw so few of them?

"You're awful curious about a girl you've only known a night," Rose remarked. "You aren't thinkin' on stealin' her away, are you?"

Jesse's head snapped up. "Hell, no!" Just the thought of getting involved with another woman sent a shudder down his spine. "I just wondered why a girl as pretty as her would choose this kind of life, that's all."

"Most of the men who show up at my place don't care why. They only care how soon and how much."

She had a point. He'd never given any thought before to what made women turn to whoring; why concern himself with it now? So it still nettled that he couldn't recollect spending the night with a woman as lusty as Honesty. He should count himself lucky that memory loss was all he'd suffered for his moment of weakness. Greater prices had been paid for smaller follies—Miranda had taught him that lesson well.

Yep, best he put the little firebrand upstairs out of his mind and start focusing on the person he really wanted. Deuce McGuire.

Chair legs screeching across the floor cut through his thoughts as Scarlet rose. "How about some biscuits and gravy, Mr. Jones? You've probably worked up quite an appetite—"

"It's Jesse—and thanks for the offer, but don't go to any trouble on my account. In fact, I think I'll see how my horse is faring this morning so I can be on my way."

"So soon?"

"I've been here longer than I planned." He got to his feet, reached into his pocket, and tossed several coins atop Rose's ledgers. It was twice the amount she charged, but he figured she could use it more than he could. "In case I don't see you again, take care of yourself."

"You, too, Jesse. I hope you meet up with your friend."

"Oh, I will. You can count on it."

He'd not sleep until he did.

Twelve dollars. Honesty stared in despair at the pile of coins, gold nuggets, and bank notes she'd dumped across her bedspread. That was all she had to show for three months of hard scraping, conning, and outright cheating. At this rate, she'd never get to Galveston. She'd be lucky if she got out of Colorado.

Her fingers went to the ring around her neck. For a moment she swore she could still feel the heat of Jesse's fingers brushing her skin. She closed her eyes and her mind filled with images of him as he'd been last night, lying in the tub wearing nothing but soap suds and a smile . . . standing in a ray of red-gold sunlight, all slicked and bronzed and glorious . . . sprawled across her stomach in drugged oblivion . . .

Oh, God. She still couldn't believe she'd fallen asleep in his bed. What had she been thinking? She *hadn't* been thinking, and that was the problem. Never, in all the times she'd forced herself to endure a man's groping, waiting for him to fall asleep so she could slip out with him none the wiser, had she ever been so swept away that she'd forgotten herself.

But last night had felt neither like groping nor endurance. With Jesse's flesh pressed against hers, his breath hot against her breast, his hands tangled possessively in her hair, sensations had kindled inside her that she hadn't thought herself capable of feeling. If he hadn't passed out when he had . . . her heart picked up speed when she realized how close she'd come, how tempted she'd been, to finish what they'd started in his bath.

Shaking the ludicrous thought from her mind, Honesty let the ruby fall and returned her attention to her small cache of savings and the map spread across her bed. A line of stars marking a dozen years of travel cut a diagonal path through Colorado, into New Mexico, then down through Texas to the Gulf.

The truth is hidden in the flowing stones.

Honesty shook her head, as perplexed now by her father's last words as she'd been the day she'd heard them. The truth about what? And where were the flowing stones? *What* were the flowing stones? A river? A canyon? A gold mine? Oh, the possibilities were endless.

Well, the only way to solve the riddle he'd left her was to find the flowing stones. *Go back the way we came.* She'd narrowed down that part of the riddle at least, and had memorized the name of every place she and Deuce had ever been between Denver and Galveston.

Twelve dollars wouldn't get her very far, but at least it would get her somewhere. If necessary, she supposed she could sell the ruby and buy herself a train ticket, or a seat on a south-bound stage . . .

No. She'd not sell the ring unless she had absolutely no other choice. It was all she had left of Deuce. That, and a puzzle she had yet to understand.

So now, the only thing left to do was to find a suitable escort.

She certainly couldn't ask Jesse, not after last night. The journey would takes weeks—even months! She didn't doubt for a second that he would expect her to indulge him whenever the mood struck. And given the way she turned to mush every time he so much as looked at her . . . well, that was just asking for trouble.

Who else was there, though? Honesty wondered, fighting back discouragement. If she could make the journey on her own, she would. Unfortunately, Deuce's vagabond lifestyle had taught her early on the perils a woman faced in a world ruled by men. And since his death, she'd learned firsthand that traveling alone was just plain foolish. As much as she wished otherwise, she needed protection. She needed a *man*. Someone strong enough to keep danger at bay, yet manageable enough to control. Jesse was strong enough, that she didn't doubt. But manageable? She shook her head. He didn't strike her as a man anyone easily controlled.

Or was he?

If only she knew more about him—where he was from, what he did for a living, what kind of friends he had . . . what did she really know of

Jesse Jones, other than that he had the face of an angel, the charm of the devil, and a body as inviting as sin?

Maybe he was just a rambler, as he claimed; he had that look about him. Yet there was something more, an unleashed power, an untamed aura she couldn't define . . .

Oh, her decision would be so much easier if the man wasn't so much a mystery.

Or so much a temptation.

A sudden rumbling in her stomach rescued her thoughts from venturing once again into forbidden territory. Knowing that Rose would be expecting her to help with the midday meal, Honesty folded the map, capped the money jar, and returned both to their hiding spot before venturing out into the hallway. Her steps slowed as she passed by the open doorway to Jesse's room. The bed was neatly made, the clothes gone, his saddlebags missing.

With a curious frown she sought out Rose and found her sitting alone in the main room of the saloon, scratching on a tablet with a pencil. "Where's our guest?"

"You just missed him," Rose answered without looking up. "He left about ten minutes ago."

He'd left? The bottom dropped out of Honesty's stomach. "Where'd he go?"

"Said he was goin' to check on his horse."

"Is he coming back?"

Rose shrugged. "He didn't say and I didn't ask."

A strange emptiness spread through her, which made no sense. She should be glad he was gone. It had been hard enough waking up beside him; seeing him after her story of unbridled passion would not only have been awkward, but downright foolish.

"He seemed mighty taken with you, though," Rose said with a smile in her voice.

Honesty glanced quickly at Rose's bent head and fought a surge of panic. "Did he say something?"

"Nope. But he was askin' all kinds of questions about you." She peered up at Honesty and her mouth twitched, as if holding back a grin. "I don't know what you did, but it sure left an impression on him."

Honesty averted her gaze. She didn't want to think about what Rose would do if she ever learned how she'd "handled" Jesse. And if Jesse ever found out how she'd duped him . . .

A sliver of guilt crept into her conscience. Drugging a customer, then playing it off afterward hadn't bothered her any other time she'd been forced to do it; why should it bother her now? She'd been trained to play on human weakness; it had been ingrained since she could remember. The one time she'd given in to a

weakness of her own, she'd paid the price—
with her father's life.

Fresh grief welled up at the memory, and
Honesty pushed it to the back of her mind, then
slipped into the chair across from Rose. Strands
of her golden-red hair had escaped their pins
and fell about her shoulders. Honesty couldn't
tell if Rose had recently woken up or if she'd
not gone to bed at all. "What are you doing?"

"Trying to turn coal into gold," Rose said,
scribbling something in one of the books before
her. "That damned Eli Johnson is going to be
the end of me yet. First he steals my girls, then
he steals my customers, now he's about to steal
my livelihood."

Contrition instantly rose up inside Honesty.
Lately, she'd been so focused on her own problems that she hadn't given much thought to the
struggles Rose faced in keeping the saloon's
doors open. Eli Johnson owned the Black
Garter, a bordello that sat directly on the stage
route a few miles east. He'd been sweet on Rose
once, but when she didn't return his affections,
he swore he'd make her regret spurning him.
Evidently, it was working. "Are things that
bad?"

"Put it this way—if I don't figure out some
way of drumming up business soon, I'll be
closing my doors."

Sometimes Honesty wondered if maybe that

wouldn't be the best thing. Her father always said, "Life is like a horse race: sometimes ye draw a quick mount that'll take ye far, and sometimes ye draw a plug. If that happens, ye don't waste time kickin' a dead horse; ye look for a fresh mount." She supposed that was why they never stayed in one place very long. He'd always promised that they'd settle down one day, but the promise only lasted until a fresher, faster horse came along. And before Honesty could unpack her bags, they'd be off again.

It used to be exciting—new horizons, fresh adventures, greater opportunities . . . it never mattered where they went, they'd had each other. If over the years she'd found herself yearning more and more often for a place to call her own, she only had to remind herself what would happen if their illicit past caught up to them.

And one of the things she admired about Rose was her determination to stay in the race, no matter how high the odds stacked against her. Now, though, Honesty wondered if the woman wasn't kicking a dead horse. "Rose . . . don't you ever dream of something more than this?"

The pencil froze in mid-scribble; she glanced up from her books. "More than what?"

"Being here. Living like this. Not that there's anything wrong with the Scarlet Rose," Honesty hastened to add. "But haven't you ever dreamed of something more?"

"What do you mean?"

Honesty shrugged. "I don't know. Sometimes I dream of a place. It's green, and blue, and so beautiful it takes my breath away." Unbidden, an image of Jesse rose in her mind, his eyes green as a meadow one moment, stormy blue the next, and glittering with such raw, naked hunger that the memory alone had the power to clench her stomach and quicken her heartbeat. That look, that longing, had awakened a curiosity she'd buried long ago—what would it be like to share herself with a man? To give herself to him heart, body, and soul, from first breath to last?

"Sounds like paradise," Rose said.

Abruptly Honesty shoved the foolish whimsy aside and leaned forward, clasping her hands on the table. "I've never been there, that I can recall. I can feel it pulling at me, though, in my dreams . . . calling my name . . ."

"But something holds you back."

Honesty nodded.

"I used to have dreams like that all the time," Rose softly admitted. "Mine were like fairy tales. Prince Charming, castles in the sky, people throwing flower petals at my feet . . ."

"Don't you have that dream anymore?"

An unladylike snort blew through the air.

"Dreamin' is for pretty young skirts like your-self, not frayed old garters like me."

"You're not old, Rose."

"I'm twenty-five, and I've done a lot and learned a lot and lived a lot in those twenty-five years."

More than most, Honesty suspected. Though Rose was only five years older, life had hard-ened whatever soft edges she might once have had. Once again, Honesty was reminded of how much her father had protected her over the years. "What about love, Rose? Did you ever love during those years, too?"

She looked suddenly ancient and weary. "More than any woman should have to, dar-lin'."

Again sympathy nearly choked her. Rose once told her she'd gotten into the business after becoming involved with a man of ques-tionable reputation. When he'd left her, she'd turned to the only means of survival available to her at the time—working in the Black Garter for Eli Johnson. When silver was discovered in the nearby hills, Rose used every penny she'd managed to save over the years to buy a plot of land and build the Scarlet Rose. For a while, Last Hope and the Scarlet Rose had thrived.

"Maybe there's a reason business isn't what it used to be," Honesty suggested. "Maybe Fate is giving you a chance to reach for your dream, but you have to give up the Scarlet Rose to get it."

"Oh, no." Her jaw took on a familiar stubborn set. "I helped found this town, and I built the Scarlet Rose with my own two hands so I'd never be dependent on a man again. I'll be damned if I let some no-account like Eli Johnson force me into giving up this place without a fight."

Honesty refrained from pointing out that whether Rose wanted to or not, her success depended on men—for without them and their baser needs, there would be no reason for places like the Scarlet Rose to exist.

But she was hardly in any position to judge, when she was sitting on the same two-edged sword. Wasn't she counting on a male to keep her safe in her quest to find the truth?

"Is there anything I can do to help?"

Rose laughed. "Start prayin' for a miracle—or we're both sunk."

No sooner were the words out of her mouth than the front doors opened and Jesse filled the room with his presence. "Ladies, it looks like you'll be stuck with me a bit longer than planned."

Chapter 4

❧◦◦◦◦◦◦◦

"**W**ell, look what the wind blew in," Rose drawled. "I thought we'd seen the last of you."

"So did I."

"That horse of yours still gimpin'?"

"Unfortunately. It's not too serious, but I'd rather not take any chances."

"Well, the two of you are welcome to stay as long as you need. I'll even have Honesty put clean sheets on your bed," she added with a wink.

His gaze slid to the woman sitting next to Scarlet, her hands clasped tightly in her lap, those glossy dark blonde curls he'd buried his fingers in last night tied with a ribbon and falling freely down her back. From the moment he'd walked into the saloon, she'd avoided looking at him; the expression on her face puzzled him. Was she hoping he'd stay, or praying he wouldn't?

"Honesty, would you mind dishin' up Mr. Jones a plate of those biscuits and gravy I left on the stove? The man's bound to have worked himself up an appetite."

As if waiting for any excuse to escape, Honesty jumped up from her seat and fled to the kitchen.

"So how long you think you'll be staying with us?" Rose asked after he'd taken a seat in the chair Honesty had vacated.

"It's hard to say. I do need to send a telegram, though. I'm running a bit short on funds and if I'm going to stay here, I'll need to wire for more."

"Not from around here, you won't. The telegraph office closed down six months ago, the hotel a month before that, and the post office burned down last year when Skeeter Malone decided to see for himself if gunpowder really did explode."

Wonderful. A lame horse, less than two dollars in his pocket, and no way to wire the agency for more. At Rose's prices, he had enough to cover lodging for a night or two, but that would leave him nothing for supplies. Even if she could afford it, his pride wouldn't allow him to ask for a room on charity. "Then I'll just have to find myself a job. I'm good with cattle and horses. Good with my hands, too."

"I don't doubt that," she countered with bawdy humor. "Unfortunately, there's not much call around here for a man of your abilities."

"What about here? Maybe you've got something that needs doing?"

"Sorry, sugar." She dashed his hopes again. "I've already got more hired hands than I do jobs. My uncles, Joe and Jake, take turns coming down from the mountain to help with the heavy work, and Honesty handles the day-to-day chores."

His shoulders slumped. Normally he wouldn't have given a second thought to sleeping on the ground under the stars, but the weather was turning ugly. And the prospect of that soft bed upstairs had just been too appealing to resist. He refused to consider that a particular brown-eyed beauty might have anything to do with his longing to stay here.

As if thinking about her could make her appear, she emerged from the kitchen, a cup of coffee in one hand, a plate piled high with fluffy white biscuits smothered in white gravy in the other. Jesse didn't realize how hungry he was until she set the food in front of him. When was the last time he'd sat down to a meal?

"I'll be upstairs if you need anything, Rose."

And before Jesse could thank her, she was gone.

"I wish I could help you out, Jesse, but the truth is, I'm scraping the bottom of the barrel to get by as it is. The only thing I need is more business, so unless you've got piano playing in that bag of tricks—"

He stopped in mid-chew, swerved around, and for the first time noticed a dusty black object tucked in a corner by the stage. The bottom seemed to fall out of his stomach, and an old, familiar resentment flared in his gullet.

"Do you play?"

Years peeled away in Jesse's mind. He'd been five years old the day the piano had arrived for his mother, and he'd sat down, felt the keys beneath his fingers, and played Mozart. No one, least of all him, could explain how or why he was able to play an instrument he'd never set eyes on before, or to recognize the notes of his mother's favorite song. The music instructors his father hired soon after called him a prodigy. A musical genius.

Jesse hadn't realized then that it had just been a curse.

He swallowed a mouthful of biscuit and it hit the bottom of his stomach like a bar of lead. "Not anymore," he answered bitterly.

"But you *can*."

Fifteen years had gone by since he'd last set
fingers to keys, and another fifteen could go by,
for all he cared. But yes, he could play. Jesse set
the fork down and pushed the plate away, his
appetite gone. "It's been a long time."

"Maybe we can make a trade."

The glitter in her eyes sent a sudden shiver of
foreboding up his spine. "What did you have in
mind?"

"Let's see what you can drag out of the old
ivories. Then we'll talk."

The instant Honesty made it to her room, she
shut the door tightly behind her and pressed
herself against it. Her heart thundered in her
chest, her hands trembled. Oh, heavens. When
Rose said to start praying for a miracle, surely
she hadn't meant Jesse! Why had he come
back? Surely he wasn't planning on staying. Or
was he?

She started pacing the floor and nibbling on
her thumbnail. Shoot, she hadn't thought to see
him ever again! What if he expected her to . . .
what if he wanted . . .

Oh, dear. Just the thought of him touching
her the way he had last night sent a rush of heat
into her cheeks. Getting away with her ruse for
one night was possible. But for two?

Or more?

Or what if he discovered that she'd lied about it, and that he'd forked over three dollars for nothing? What would he do?

Well, she wasn't about to stick around and find out. Men did not like being made out to be fools; some even thought it an offense so great, they were willing to commit cold-blooded murder.

Spurred on by the thought, Honesty made a beeline for the armoire in the corner, threw open the doors, and dragged out a carpetbag that had seen more travels than Gulliver. She'd wasted too much time in Last Hope, anyway. A suitable escort was not going to show up, no matter how much she wished it. If she hoped to find someone willing to help her search for the flowing stones, she'd have to go elsewhere.

After tossing the carpetbag on the bed, Honesty began clearing her belongings out of the armoire. She didn't know how she would tell Rose. After their conversation this morning, the thought of leaving her to shoulder the burdens of her situation alone just didn't feel right.

But what else could she do? She'd spent almost three weeks in Last Hope and was no closer to solving the riddle her father had left her than she'd been the day he died. She couldn't hide out here forever. Surely the men after her would either have found her by now or given up the chase.

As she swept her arm across the bottom of the cabinet for any garments she might have missed, the red satin evening costume she'd worn last night fell to the floor. Honesty paused, then bent to pick it up. Thoughts she'd kept at bay all afternoon came rushing back as the scents of patchouli soap and a manly essence that was Jesse's alone rose up from the fabric. She buried her nose in the scent and closed her eyes. Once again she felt Jesse's strength wrap around her, could almost feel the power of his arms and the bliss of his touch . . .

Honesty swallowed the lump of regret in her throat. She should have let him bed her when she'd had the chance.

Oh, now, there's a sensible thought. Yes-siree, just give yourself to the first man who turns your head. She didn't have much anymore, but she still had her virginity. If she ever *did* give herself to a man—and that was a very big if—it would be to one who put a ring on her finger, not coins in her palm.

She almost laughed at the irony of it. Working in a saloon, playing the part of a well-versed doxy, and here she was, worrying about being ruined before the "I do's". But she had no intention of marrying for marrying's sake. The only way she'd ever consider tying herself to a man was if she found one with honor, courage, and unwavering devotion. Someone she could trust never to hurt her or use her. Someone who could make her heart laugh and her soul sing.

A man like her father.

Good cow feathers, this was ridiculous. She was acting like a smitten fool, and it had to stop. Her life was complicated enough without throwing some devilish drifter into the mix.

She crumpled the dress into a ball and tossed it into a corner of the armoire. The last thing she needed to take with her was any reminder of her folly.

She finished shoving the last of her garments into the bag and was just about to buckle the strap when a sweet tinkling sound drifted up the staircase. She froze, then lifted her head.

The piano? Who on earth . . . ?

With a puzzled frown, she slipped out her door and went down the hall to the balcony overlooking the main room. An angel sat at the piano—an angel with streaked golden hair spilling past a set of broad shoulders . . .

Jesse?

Astonished, she could do nothing more than gaze down at him as his long fingers glided over the dingy keys. It took her a moment to recognize the tune, but once she did, it knocked the breath out of her.

"Lorena." One of Deuce's favorites.

Honesty closed her eyes against the swell of bittersweet memories. Of riding with her father across windswept prairies, of roasting chestnuts over a mountain lodge cookstove. Of curling up in his big arms on a cold November night, his deep voice lulling her to sleep.

Of their own will, the words of the second stanza slid from her mouth. "A hundred months have passed since, Lorena, since last I held that hand in mine, and felt the pulse beat fast, Lorena, though mine beat faster far than thine . . ."

She hardly noticed when Jesse's playing slowed, but she knew the instant he turned his head in her direction. Their eyes locked, and as she sang the lyrics of a lover who'd lost his one true love to duty, their connection became a tangible thread, drawing her down the staircase. Memories of her father dimmed. In Jesse's eyes, she watched last night replay itself, and felt as if he were seducing her all over again. Not with his eyes and hands and mouth, but with his music, melody and harmony blending together in a mating of such poignancy that it pierced her to her soul.

With the last note still fading, they continued to stare at one another. The air hummed with an awareness that transcended the physical attraction she'd felt last night, a longing bordering on pain. Her eyes shimmered, turning the interior of the Scarlet Rose into shades of green and blue. And in the back of her mind, she could hear a small voice calling out her name . . .

Clapping broke the spell. Honesty swung toward the bar, where Rose was slapping her hands together with such enthusiasm that it made her cheeks burn.

"That was the most beautiful thing I've ever heard in my life," Rose declared, then dabbed her eyes with a handkerchief. "Honesty, why didn't you tell me you could sing? With a voice like that, you could make a for—" She gasped. "That's it! Oh, I knew if I waited long enough, the solution would drop into my lap!"

The solution to what? Honesty wondered.

"How long did you say you planned on staying, Jesse?" Rose asked.

"I'm not sure. A couple days, a week, maybe. Depends on how long it takes my horse's leg to mend. Why?"

Absently Rose tapped her lips with steepled fingers. "That don't give us much time . . ."

"Much time for what?" Honesty asked.

"Why, to rehearse, or course!"

"What are you talking about, Scarlet?" Jesse asked.

Dread curled up Honesty's spine as Rose turned to him with a calculated gleam in her eye. "I want you and Honesty to perform for the Durango-Denver passengers this Saturday."

Stunned silence fell on the air like iron notes.

Honesty's attention swung from Rose to Jesse, then back again. "You can't be serious!" she declared, once she found her voice.

"Serious as an April blizzard. Between your singing and Jesse's playing, folks will be lining the street, beggin' us to take their money!"

Her and Jesse, performing together? In public? She struggled to catch the breath caught in her throat.

"Hold on there, Scarlet," Jesse interjected. "Playing for you is one thing; playing for a bunch of strangers is something else."

"Look, you wanted a job, I'm offering you one."

"This was not what I had in mind."

"Maybe not, but you just said you couldn't leave till your horse mends, so what's the harm? The way I see it, you've got nothing to lose."

"What about her?" he countered, gesturing toward Honesty. "Has she ever even sung for a crowd before? How do you know she can do it? What if she gets up on stage and freezes?"

Honesty didn't know whether to laugh or cry at his attempt to help her. If he had any idea how many times she'd literally had to sing for her and Deuce's supper . . . but she hadn't done so since that horrible night when her world had crumpled at her feet.

"Honesty, not be able to sing for a crowd? This girl was made for the stage!" Rose crossed the few feet between them and clasped the girl's hands in her own. "Hon, you know the position I'm in. If I don't do something to attract business, it'll be the end of the Scarlet Rose. I'm not asking for much—just one night. And in return, I'll cut you both in on ten percent of the profits."

Honesty looked into the pleading gray eyes and felt her resistence crumble. She knew what Rose was doing, giving her a chance to seize her dreams.

But at what cost?

She thought about the packed valise waiting on her bed, the measly twelve dollars trapped in an old mason jar, and a worn map that hid a mysterious truth somewhere in its crooked lines. More, she thought about how Rose had opened her doors to a frightened orphan on the run, with no questions asked.

And Honesty knew the battle was lost before it had begun. "All right," she sighed. "I'll do my best."

After rewarding her with a blinding smile, Rose turned to Jesse. "Now, what about you, Jesse?"

Honesty waited for his answer with bated

breath. His eyes glittered like chips of ice, and his jaw was set so hard she wondered that he didn't break his teeth. He reminded Honesty of a trapped animal, waiting for the doors of a cage to open so he could spring free. Oh, how she knew the feeling.

"If I'm busy banging out tunes, who will keep an eye on your customers if they get too rowdy?"

"Oh, me and Honesty'll handle the customers. You just provide the music."

He turned to Honesty then, and stared at her in silence for several long, tense moments. She had no idea what he was thinking when he looked at her like that, but the grim set of his mouth told her louder than words that he didn't much care for what he saw.

"Yes," he finally said in a flat tone, "I'm sure the customers will be well satisfied."

Chapter 5

❧〜❧

Jesse strode outside to the porch, feeling as if he'd barely survived a twister with his hide intact. In the space of twenty-four hours, two women had taken control of his well-laid plans and turned them upside down. And all because he'd set out to repay a debt he owed to a man who'd saved his life.

What the hell kind of trouble had this cursed assignment landed him in now? More important, how was he going to get out of it? He didn't have time to dally away the next week in this two-bit town.

Unfortunately, damsels in distress had always been his weakness.

Propping the bottom of his foot against the

wall, he leaned back and scanned the darkened town with cynical distaste. Mountains loomed before him, capped peaks shimmering in a haze of setting sun. Shadows crept along the ground from the trunks of aspens and bounced off the sides of rocks in every shade from sand to rust. Far in the distance, a train whistle blew.

Rebirth? Hell, Scarlet wanted a miracle. Oh, Last Hope had been a grand place once, that was evident. In its heyday, it had probably never known a moment's peace. He imagined raucous laughter pouring from the eight saloons, and dance hall trulls calling out their wares; merchants conducting business on every corner, and bankers discussing the latest hike in ore prices. There may even have been a few ladies strolling down the boardwalk, parasols shading their delicate skin as they passed by shops with hats, dresses, children's toys, and hand-made furniture, while miners, the backbone of the community, led their pack-laden mules down the center of the road and traded nuggets for new handles, pans, and picks.

Yeah, Last Hope had probably been a grand place once. Now it was just tired and dreary, a broken-down poverty-stricken skeleton of what it once had been.

Much like he felt.

When had it happened? he wondered. During the Appleton Stagecoach heists? While chasing the James Younger gang? He couldn't pinpoint the exact moment, but it had been creeping up on him for some time now. And that last job . . .

If anyone had told him he'd tire of being a Pinkerton Agent, he'd have laughed himself loony. Twelve years ago, fed by noble intentions and an outrage at injustice, Jesse had packed his boots, his hat, and his horse and walked out of his father's upper-crust Chicago house. He'd been young and rash and reckless—hell on hooves, McParland used to say. No assignment was too dangerous, no subject too elusive. He'd spent every waking moment racing from one end of the country to the other, rooting out the bad seeds of society, and he'd loved every blazing moment.

Until the day obsession for the job gave way to passion for a woman, and landed him six months in the deepest bowels of hell.

That had been the beginning, Jesse thought. What he felt lately seemed to go beyond tired, though. He couldn't explain it, couldn't define it, yet he felt it sucking at him like quicksand around his ankles, draining the life out of him. He'd spent so long immersed in a world of deception and intrigue, pretending to be someone he wasn't just to expose the criminals, that he didn't even know who he was anymore. As soon as he found McGuire and took him back to Denver, he wanted to . . . to . . .

Hell, he didn't know *what* he wanted. But it sure wasn't to stick around this pathetic excuse for a town, or use a rusty talent he'd rejected years ago just to entertain a bunch of traveling drunks.

Jesse sighed and stared up into the overcast sky. Damn Scarlet for manipulating him with her sad story and bartered solutions.

And damn Honesty, too, for touching something inside him with her voice that hadn't been touched in years. Not since the day he'd discovered his father's duplicity had he allowed music to bond him with another soul. But for a moment there, he'd felt closer to Honesty than he'd felt toward anyone in a long, long time. Hadn't he learned his lesson?

Obviously not, or he wouldn't have gotten himself involved in another woman's problems.

Well, he'd play for Scarlet; he'd given his word. At least he'd have a soft bed to sleep in each night and a hot meal in his stomach each day. And considering his pockets were emptier than a dead man's eyes, he needed the extra cash to restock on supplies.

But then he was out of here.

And in the meantime, he'd keep as far away from Honesty as the situation would allow.

As if to mock his decision, the door opened and she stepped out onto the porch. She gave no sign of noticing that he stood a few short feet to the left, in the shadow of the overhang. Jesse opened his mouth to make her aware of his presence, then held his tongue. He really had nothing to say to her; she was part of the reason he was in this mess.

Then she stepped off the porch and made a right turn down the boardwalk, her head bent, her step swift, and the chance was lost anyway.

Jesse started to go after her, but stopped himself and leaned back against the post with his thumbs plugged into his waistband. Where Honesty went and what she did with her time were her business. Still, she was obviously upset about something, and he had a good idea what it was. He couldn't forget her expression the instant Scarlet brought up performing for the passengers; her creamy complexion had gone a ghastly gray shade, the luster in her eyes vanished, and her shoulders lost a measure of their proud carriage.

One of the things that drew him to Honesty was the almost regal aura she had about her, her way of taking command of a situation without saying a word. But at that moment she had seemed to shrink before his very eyes. Why she'd be so reluctant to share that beautiful voice with others, Jesse couldn't figure. Talent like that shouldn't be kept in a bottle.

Yet the emotion in her eyes was beyond simple reluctance. It had bordered on panic.

What was she so afraid of?

They'd find her for certain.

The thought pounded through Honesty's brain in tempo with her footsteps, drowning out the hollow clack of her heels on the boardwalk. She couldn't remember what excuse she made when she walked out of the Scarlet Rose, but it must have sounded reasonable, because neither Rose nor Jesse made any move to stop her. Nor did they come after her, much to her relief. Rose had wasted no time diving into plans for the inspired event, and Jesse . . . she didn't know where he'd taken himself off to, nor did she give a tinker's care. If not for him playing that cussed piano, she'd not be in this predicament. Word would get out, and once it did, the shadows she'd acquired soon after her father's death would reattach themselves to her backside. And this time, Honesty feared she wouldn't be able to shake them.

Oh, why had she agreed to sing for the passengers? Had she lost the last ounce of common sense she'd been born with? She empathized with Rose, but she hadn't sung in public in months—not since that horrible night of her father's murder.

Even now, the memory had the power to make her throat tighten and her stomach pitch. They'd only been in Durango a few days when Deuce made himself a regular customer at the Miner's Delight, a fancy dance hall and gambling parlor all in one stick. As was their ritual, he ingratiated himself with the management and soon convinced them that their profits would increase tenfold if they allowed Honesty to sing. Little did they know that Deuce had been using the same ploy for as long as Honesty could remember: while she acted as a decoy and distracted the audience, he worked the crowds—picking pockets, playing with stacked decks, selling deeds to mines that didn't exist . . . mostly penny-ante stunts that did little harm, but that often led to quick escapes deep in the night.

On a particularly dismal evening after one of her performances, Honesty found him slumped over a table, sotted out of his senses. They'd taken rooms only a few doors down, but Deuce was a brawny man, and there was no way she'd have gotten him home if not for the assistance of Robert Treat.

In retrospect, Honesty should have guessed Robert's true character right off, but at the time she'd been too smitten to notice. Any girl would have been, she supposed, for he cut a slick and dashing figure in his fine frock coat and silk bowler, and his courtly manners could make a pauper feel like a princess.

It took Honesty only a week to realize that the man she thought her Prince Charming was nothing more than a blackguard in disguise.

She fought off the memory as she wandered through the deserted streets and alleyways, but it did little to ease the constriction in her chest or the knot of anxiety in her middle. As she stepped off the boardwalk and onto the packed dirt road by the crumbling foundation of the former bank, a gust of moist air hit her full in the face. Honesty wrapped her arms around herself. The weather had been the last thing on her mind when she'd left the saloon; now she wished she'd thought to bring a wrap. There was a sharp bite to the wind, even for June, and the scent of coming rain lay heavy in the air.

But the weather didn't have as much to do with the chill settling in her bones as the memories haunting her. The evening of Deuce's murder had begun like any other evening. She wore a low-cut, high-hemmed gown designed to keep the audience's attention on her. Thick smoke hovered above the heads of two dozen rowdy spectators; the crowd, made up mostly of miners and merchants, with a few cowboys from the outlying ranches thrown in, voiced their approval of her performance with shouts and whistles that Honesty accepted with practiced grace. The attention always made her uncomfortable, but she'd learned to deal with it.

During the second stanza of "Johnny Sands," Honesty spotted Robert approaching her father's table. The two spoke for a moment, and though the conversation appeared amiable, her father's stiff-jawed expression told a different story.

"What did he want?" she asked, going to Deuce's side after the song was over.

He brightened immediately at the sight of her. "Ach, nothing to worry your bonny head aboot. Now, get back onstage, me sweet Honesty, and sing for our supper."

Honesty barely remembered getting through the rest of her show. The room seemed to have shrunk tighter than wool in hot water, and each step on the stage felt like a path to the gallows. Something was terribly, terribly wrong; her father's brogue was hardly noticeable unless he was bothered by something. But Robert and Deuce had become quite the pals, and a dispute—especially in so public a place—just didn't make sense, so she charged the uneasiness to the unusually wild crowd.

She wished now that she'd listened to her instincts.

During the last number, all hell broke loose.

The front window exploded into tiny shards, then the chandeliers within. People screamed, ducked, and dived beneath tables, while others returned the gunfire. Dodging the barrage of bullets, Deuce pushed his way through the frenzied crowd, flying glass, and choking smoke to reach her. He all but shoved her off the stage and out a back door she hadn't known existed.

They ran until Honesty thought her lungs would burst, and Deuce finally dragged them into an alley.

"No matter what happens, lass, remember that I love ye with all me heart."

"Oh, Papa, what have you done?"

"I canna tell ye now, but ye'll know all there is to know soon enough. Should we be parted, run as far away as ye can and I'll find ye. Go back the way we came and do no' trust a soul, ye ken? *Trust no one.*"

She wanted to demand he tell her what was going on, but the urgency in his tone compelled her only to nod.

Then Robert appeared at the mouth of the alley, blocking their escape. "Thought you'd get away with it, didn't you, McGuire? Thought you could sneak off, welch on our deal, and I'd just forget about it?"

Honesty remembered staring at her father in

surprise. Few knew his real name; it was safer that way. Why would he have told Robert?

"I'm not sneakin' off. I told ye inside, I don't have it with me. I have to go get it."

"And you expect me to believe you'll return?"

"I told ye I would, didn't I?"

"Your word is worthless, McGuire. Honesty, come to me," Robert coaxed in a silky tone that sent shudders down her spine.

Her father's grip on her arm turned bruising. "Ye're not gettin' the lass, Treat."

"You think not?" Robert raised his arm, and moonlight glittered off the pearl-handled pistol gripped in his hand. "Send her to me and no one gets hurt."

"What's this about, Robert?"

"Perhaps you should ask your father."

"Papa?"

"'Tis nothin', lass."

"Nothing?" Robert barked. "Your father and I had a gentlemen's agreement and he is trying to break it. You are my insurance. When he holds up to his end of our bargain, I'll release you."

Deuce instantly pushed Honesty behind him and withdrew his pistol. "You'll take her over me dead body!"

Robert smiled then. "That can also be arranged."

Her memory grew vague after that. The crack of bullets, the acrid stench of gunpowder, and the sight of Robert lying lifeless on the alley floor while Honesty and her father ran for the train station and jumped the first car leaving Durango . . . It wasn't until they'd sunk against the car's plank walls, and she caught sight of his blood-soaked shirt front, that she realized how prophetic his words would be.

"Papa? Oh, God . . ." She scrambled to his side and gathered his bulky form in her arms.

"My sweet Honesty, there's somethin' you must know . . ."

"Don't talk, Papa." Frantically she tried to stem the blood that gushed from his middle. "We've got to get you to a doctor."

He caught her hand in a frighteningly feeble grip and whispered, "Listen to me, lass, there isna much time."

Her breath caught on a sob.

"I done ye wrong, and I pray ye can find it in yer heart to forgive me."

"Papa, please . . ."

"That's what I must tell ye." His head lolled to the side, and the light in his blue eyes dimmed. "The truth is . . ."

"What?" she asked, unable to catch his fading words.

". . . Hidden in the flowin' stones . . ."

And he was gone.

Honesty swiped at her damp eyes. God, how she missed him. His gruff voice, that gravelly brogue. His thick arms and long flame-red hair with the balding spot at the crown . . .

Oh, curse Jesse for playing that song! Curse him for coming to Last Hope in the first place. She'd kept a low profile since that fateful night, making her way north, town to town, mine to mine, saloon to saloon, searching for the secret he'd taken to his grave. She hadn't sung since.

Until this morning.

And because of it, because of Jesse and his resurrection of days best forgotten, she was once again committed to putting herself on public display.

She should have left town the minute she'd woken up in his bed. No, she should have left town long before that, as she'd originally planned. She'd managed fine without anyone's help before.

But somehow she hadn't been able to bring herself to abandon Rose. And now . . .

"You shouldn't be wandering out here alone."

Honesty jerked, startled as much by the sound of Jesse's voice as the sight of him. She glanced around, aware for the first time that she'd circled back to the saloon. Her attention returned to him, where he leaned against the outside doorframe, knee bent, heel propped behind him. Despite his casual pose, she sensed a restless energy inside him.

Honesty ignored the traitorous leap of her heart and tossed her hair back over her shoulder. "I don't see that it's any concern of yours."

"When I see a young woman putting herself in possible danger, I make it my concern."

"Danger from whom?"

"Any scoundrel who finds his way into town."

Honesty gave him a scathing once-over. The remark hit too close to home. "The only scoundrel I see about is you."

"Really?" His brow lifted in mock surprise. "Just this morning I was the most incredible lover you've ever had."

Honesty grimaced. She should have figured he'd throw her own words back in her face. "What else would you call a man who rides in and worms his way into a job for reasons I have yet to fathom?"

"I'd hardly call being backed into a corner worming my way into anything."

"You could have told her no."

"Why? I needed a job, she needed a piano player." He shrugged indifferently. "Besides, I didn't see you turning her down."

"That isn't always as easy as it sounds. Rose helped me when I needed help. Singing for her for one night is the least I can do."

AN UNLIKELY LADY   91

"Whether you want to or not."

The words brought an unexpected sting of tears to her eyes. He sounded so . . . protective. So compassionate. How often, when she'd been young and naive enough, had she dreamed of finding someone with those qualities? "Your concern for my welfare is touching, cowboy, but it's also misplaced. I've been taking care of myself for quite some time now, so I would appreciate you keeping your thoughts to yourself."

Fearing her emotions would get the better of her, Honesty tried to push past him but found herself halted by his grip. She glowered at the long fingers wrapped around her wrist, then at his face. His eyes, a compelling swirl of green grasses and blue skies, glittered with a demand for answers. "Let go of me."

"Not until you tell me why you're so upset with me."

Because you're here. Because you're too handsome for your own good. Because against all wisdom, I'm attracted to you, and when you touch me, I forget everything that's important. She locked the words inside, refusing to give him more power over her than he already had. "Because if you hadn't played that stupid song, I wouldn't have been manipulated into singing."

His own temper leapt up a notch. "Look, I don't like this situation any better than you, but I gave Scarlet my word. So you and I are just going to have to make the best of it."

"Fine. But that doesn't mean I have to like it."
Just in case he could read the truth in her eyes,
she flung away from him and headed for the
doorway. Abruptly, she paused on the threshold. "Oh, and one more thing, *Mr. Jones*—I
might have to suffer your company for the next
few days, but that's as far as it goes. Don't expect me to tend to your bath—or any other duty
that requires bodily contact. If you feel another
whim"—her gaze dropped to the bulge at his
crotch—"arise, I suggest you direct it elsewhere."

As she disappeared up the stairs and out of
his sight, Jesse waged an inner battle between
laughing at her spunk and grinding his teeth in
frustration. Never had he met such a contradic-
tory, unpredictable female: one moment
provocative and eager, the next, stiff and
proper. And never had his emotions been riled
into such a frenzy.

He fished in his shirt pocket, found a bent
cigarette that he saved for emergencies, and
struck a match to it. Then he sank back against
the rough plank wall and willed the night air to
cool the fever raging in his bloodstream.

How did she do it? That's what he couldn't
figure out. There was just something about
Honesty, a blend of brassy boldness and furtive
vulnerability that aroused his curiosity and his

desire in a way no woman had done since. . . . No, not even Miranda had intrigued him this much.

Maybe he'd deserved the lambasting she'd given him; where she went was none of his damn business. Hell, he'd put in his time trying to protect the innocent, and look where it had gotten him. Not that Honesty was innocent, he thought with a snort. Far from it. Yet sometimes he'd catch glimpses of softness, like when she sang the old southern song, or spoke of Rose helping her. And he couldn't decide which was the true Honesty: the haughty princess, the reluctant siren, or the mesmerizing performer.

Even more dangerous was the temptation to find out.

Chapter 6

After a night of fitful slumber, the sound of rain sprinkling on a hot tin roof drifted into Honesty's subconscious in a pattern of aching familiarity. She lay still, heavy nostalgia filling her for a place only in her dreams, where the grass sparkled like emeralds and the sea like sapphires, and the sun glittered like gold. She didn't know why she continued having the same dream. She saw it so clearly that it was almost as if she'd been there before. She hadn't, of course. Her entire childhood had been spent traveling from one end of the western states to the other, searching for that fabled pot of gold at the end of the rainbow. Yet no place she'd ever been compared to the mysterious place that so often beckoned to her at night.

She stared at the filmy window curtains and listened, a wistful longing spreading through her for something she could neither define nor understand. Even as the lilting melody opened the door to an aching sorrow, it wove threads of comfort around her, filling an emptiness she'd carried around inside for as long as she could remember, and she savored the sensation the way a convicted man savored the notion of freedom—

Until a sour note and mild curse snapped her to awareness. Silly girl, she chided herself, the sprinkling music had come not from her dreams, but from the piano downstairs.

Jesse was playing again.

With a sigh, she swung her legs over the side of the bed and rubbed her eyes. When she'd returned to her room last night, it had taken all the self-discipline she could muster not to slam the door behind her. *A man of his word.* Any other time she'd have considered that an admirable quality, but at that moment, she felt his honor wind around her like a black widow's web.

As tempting as it was to avoid rehearsing with him today, cowardice had never been in her nature, nor would dallying get anything accomplished. She hadn't exercised her vocal cords in months. If they were to be ready for Saturday's performance, she needed to practice.

A few minutes later, dressed in an old but

neat calico dress, Honesty shoved one last pin into her hair and went downstairs, determined to keep her composure no matter what Jesse said or did.

Her resolve splintered the instant she saw him, and she paused on the bottom step with one hand on the banister. He wore his streaked blond hair tied back with a strip of leather. The silky tail flowed past his shoulders like heaven's path and slid along his gunmetal blue shirt as he bobbed his head in time to the music. The anger she'd felt toward him last night dissipated like frost on warm steel. It was so unfair that someone so beautiful could be so forbidden.

As the last note died away, Rose entered the room from the kitchen.

"Oh, good, I'm glad I caught the two of you together!"

Honesty froze. Jesse swung around to face her, surprise on his face. As his gaze swept over her, that peculiar buzzing again suffused her blood. For a moment, she thought she saw the same longing in Jesse's eyes that she'd woken up to a short time ago.

"Am I interrupting?" Rose asked.

Jesse jerked his head away and Honesty self-consciously patted the up-sweep of her hair, then dropped her hand when she caught a glimpse of Rose's sly smile. Let Rose make of her momentary bout of vanity what she would, Honesty thought, lifting her chin. She simply didn't like feeling dowdy in the face of such beauty.

"I found somethin' you might be able to use."

"What are they?" Honesty asked as Rose handed several books over to Jesse.

"Song books."

"Where'd you get these?" Jesse asked, thumbing through one of them.

"From an old suitor. He used to serenade me each night. Beautiful voice, lousy lover . . . anyway, I found them in one of my trunks and figured the two of you might find them useful." She tugged on a pair of black gloves and flipped a cape around her shoulders. "The pantry is lookin' pretty pitiful, so I thought I'd carry myself over to Wentworth's and see if Sarah is expecting any shipments soon. There's biscuits and gravy on the stove, if you're hungry."

"Thanks, Scarlet," Jesse said.

"Call me Rose, will you? All my friends do." She patted him on the shoulder, then sailed toward the door. "Be back in a bit."

After she left, an awkward silence stretched between Honesty and Jesse. Usually she didn't have to think about how to act in any given situation, she simply slipped into a role. A girl didn't spend all her life with the greatest con man in the West without learning to adapt. But Jesse had a way of rattling her to the bone, making her feel awkward and unsure and completely out of her element. She didn't like the feeling. She didn't like it at all.

"That song you were playing . . ." she finally said, if only to break the tension. "It was lovely."

"I didn't realize you were listening."

She almost told him that she'd practically crawled inside the music, but bit her tongue at the last minute. "Who wrote it?"

"I did. A long time ago."

If he had written it, then she couldn't possibly have heard it before. So why did it sound so familiar?

"What's it called?"

He turned and pinned her with a merciless stare. " 'Tell Me No Lies.' " A flush crept into her cheeks, and Honesty couldn't help but wonder if Jesse suspected how often she'd been false with him. "Well, you have an amazing talent. Where did you learn to play?"

"I didn't. I just sat down one day and played." Honesty realized then that she'd touched some hot spot, for he turned on the bench, signaling an end to the conversation. "If you're ready, I thought we'd warm up with some scales."

"Fine by me." Honesty shrugged as if it made

not a whit of difference and stood beside the upright while Jesse spread his fingers on the keys. Closing her eyes, she focused all her energy into the range of climbing notes in an effort to block out the man beside her.

Once she'd warmed up with a few octaves, Jesse opened the first book Rose had given them, flipped over a couple of pages, then once again set his fingers lightly upon the keys. A sprightly tune she hadn't heard before filled the saloon. Drawn to Jesse by a force beyond her control, Honesty moved closer to him and tried to make sense of the black dots on the page, but they could have been crows on a barbed wire fence, for all the meaning she got from them. "That book tells you to play that?"

"You don't read music?"

"No, I just sing what I hear."

"It's quite simple, actually. There are different symbols for different notes, and each symbol represents a sound."

"Did you just sit down and read music, too?"

"Not hardly," he replied with a grimace. "As soon as Father realized I could play, he hired instructors to teach me everything there was to know about classical music."

Father. Not Pa, or Papa, as she'd called Deuce. And from the stiffness of his tone, they hadn't had a close relationship. She thought that a shame. "Yet here you are, playing in a saloon."

"We all have our vices. Would you like to try?"

Honesty hesitated, then nodded.

"The keys have the same pattern of notes repeated across the keyboard," he said after she'd taken a seat beside him. "Each pattern is an octave. The middle key is a C." He hit a key in the center of the board, then pointed to a black circle hanging on a middle bar in the book.

As he explained the effect of whole notes and half notes, Honesty tried to concentrate on his instructions, but found it nearly impossible when his voice flowed through her like melted gold. Gone was the rough saddle-tramp who'd wandered into town a couple days ago; in his place sat a more educated, more polished, more . . . elite Jesse than she'd ever dreamed existed.

He glanced at her now and again, sometimes he even smiled, but mostly his gaze remained fixed on the page.

Hers remained on him. On his face. The way his hair pulled back from a smooth, high brow. The angle of his jaw, lightly bristled.

The curve of his lashes, gold tipped and thick; the slope of his nose, straight and narrow without being sharp. The shape of his mouth. Lips firm and ambitious, yet soft and seductive.

A liquid warmth pooled low in Honesty's belly; her mouth watered.

Her gaze dipped down to where his collar lay open at his throat, lingered on the smooth, sun-darkened skin, then drifted down to his hands where they rested on the dingy white keys. He had such fine hands. His fingers were long and tanned, the knuckles slim yet strong. Flexing. Bending. Stretching again and again to touch keys just out of reach.

Those same fingers had been on her. Touched her. Stroked her. Played her like the instrument now filling the room with song. Who was this entrancing man? And what had he done with her ire-provoking scoundrel?

"You keep staring at me like that, and I'm likely to think you want a repeat of the other night."

Honesty's gaze snapped to his eyes, and she found the old Jesse looking at her with undisguised amusement. A flush of embarrassment crept into her cheeks. Denying it when he'd caught her all but drooling over him seemed not only futile, but pointless. "You'd have to earn the privilege first," she quipped.

A grin tugged at Jesse's mouth. One minute seducing him out of his senses, the next spurning him like a saintly virgin—he didn't know from one moment to the other what to expect from her.

Throwing down a challenge of his own, he launched into a bawdy tune. She slid off the bench and gave him a wicked smile. The temperature in the room had already spiked a good ten degrees; now the blood in Jesse's veins started to simmer.

As she sang the old range parody, she held his gaze over her shoulder, swished her hips to and fro, and taunted him with the lyrics to "The Juice of the Forbidden Fruit."

Jesse's groin hardened and sweat beaded his brow. Images he'd tried to forget flashed in his mind: of naked skin and lilac perfume, of swollen lips and tousled hair . . .

Damn, he wished he could remember the rest of that night.

He abruptly shut the book and got up from the bench. "That's enough practicing."

"But I was just starting to have fun!"

Yeah, he'd bet she was, the little minx. The look of mock innocence on her face told him that she'd known exactly what she was doing.

He felt like a coward, escaping from the saloon like a two-bit bandit with six-guns barking at his heels, but a man could take only so much.

He stopped at the edge of the porch and sucked in a deep draft of air, patting his pocket for a smoke. He didn't know how she did it. It wasn't as if she'd been wearing that should-be-illegal red dress, or even that black-lace-lined corset. She'd been wearing faded calico that covered her from neck to ankle, for God's sake, and still she managed to set him on fire. His only chance of surviving till Saturday was to take her in small doses.

When his search for an emergency smoke came up empty, he dug into his pocket, found a nickel, then scanned the town. It had rained sometime during the night and the rich scent of damp earth rose up from the ground. Already the early summer sun was drying up the puddles left behind, and birds swooped down from the trees behind skeletal buildings in search of worms.

A door opened across the street and a woman emerged from the old general store, her shoulders hunched, a white bib apron tied around her portly belly. Jesse watched her set a broom to swinging across planks that never seemed void of dirt. She was eighty if she was a day, with hair a rich silver color piled atop her head in one of those intricate knots women seemed so partial to, and wrinkles that populated her face like briars in berry patch.

She caught sight of Jesse in mid-swing, stopped, and shaded her eyes with her hand.

Hoping she might keep makings on her shelf, Jesse pushed away from the wall and cut across the road at a leisurely stroll.

She leaned against the handle of the broom and watched him approach. "You must be the tall drink of water staying over at Rose's," she said when he reached the step then gave him one of those up-and-down inspections he'd come to expect from the opposite sex.

"For the time being."

"She always could snag the good ones." She struck out her hand. "Name's Sarah Wentworth. I own this heap of spit and boards."

"Jesse Jones," he said, returning the introduction. He glanced behind her into the storefront window. The glass was spotless and Jesse could see that pickin's were running awful slim. "You don't by chance carry tobacco and papers, do you?"

"Are you ever in luck—I think I've got some Georgia Fine left over." She picked up the broom and carried it inside the store.

Jesse followed her waddling steps, absently taking in the empty shelves behind the counter, the scanty supply of canned goods and fabric, the utter lack of wares, period. "How long have you been here, Mrs. Wentworth?"

"First to arrive, last to leave. And call me Miss Sarah. Aha, I knew I had bit left." She set a pinch of tobacco onto a piece of paper and rolled it into a tube, folding the ends. "So I hear you'll be playing the piano for the stage passengers come Saturday night."

"News travels fast."

"It doesn't have far to travel around here," she replied with a reedy laugh. "Rose was just in, gloating about her catch. She said you came in looking for work." She added a packet of papers to his purchase and shoved both across the counter top. "I'm surprised you didn't head over to the Black Garter. Everyone else did."

A puzzled frown pulled at his brow. "The Black Garter?"

"A saloon over in Poverty Gulch, a few miles east of here. It sits on the main route, so it gets a steady business, and Eli Johnson is always looking for helpers."

She leaned over the counter and looked both ways, as if someone might overhear. "Back in the days when Rose worked for Eli, before she built the Scarlet Rose, he fell for her like a load of iron ore. Rose didn't return his affections, though, and I can't say as I blame her. The man's got a temper like a keg of explosives. One spark, and *phooosh!* When she spurned him, he swore he'd make her pay." She gave a succinct nod. "He's doing a fine job of it, too. First he lured her girls away, now he's set on stealing her business. It does my heart good to see her fighting back with both barrels."

Now he understood Rose's dogged determination to see the Scarlet Rose succeed.

Still, she could have told him about the Black Garter when he'd asked her about a job. What other tidbits of information might she be keeping from him? He'd had no reason not to believe Rose when she'd said she hadn't seen McGuire; what if McGuire detoured through Poverty Gulch?

"Do you know if this Eli Johnson ever hired himself a big Scotsman?"

"It's possible, I suppose. Foreigners have been swarming these hills ever since the Leadville strike. Of course, most of them wind up going bust and packing it on home, but it might be worth checking out."

That it was. "I appreciate the tip, Miss Sarah."

"Just don't tell anyone that I sent you over there. If Rose finds out, she'd skin me alive and roast me over an open fire."

Jesse gave her his most charming smile and winked. "My lips are sealed."

More than likely it would turn out to be another long shot, Jesse thought as he left but at this point, a long shot was better than nothing.

The rest of the afternoon passed in a flurry of preparations and frenzied cleaning. Not a smear existed on the drinking glasses, not a speck of dust remained on the woodwork, and freshly washed sheets hung on the line out back.

Honesty didn't like to think she was using her chores as an excuse to avoid Jesse, but ever since the morning's rehearsal, she'd been plagued with a restless energy she could neither explain nor expel. She wished she could blame it all on anger toward him for getting her riled, or for evoking sensations she'd vowed not to feel again, but the truth was, he frightened her. Just when she thought she had him pinned, he changed on her, smashing her perceptions of him to smithereens.

Which was the real Jesse Jones? The shiftless drifter, the torrid lover, or the aristocratic pianist?

Honesty played tug-of-war with a northern wind for the last of the towels on the line, then dropped them into the basket at her feet. Like every other man she'd met, he made no bones about what he wanted. Unlike every other man she'd met, he had at least a measure of honor, proved in the way he'd dedicated his time and talent to helping Rose. And that's what drew her to him more than anything; more than his looks, more than his smile, more than his sensuality.

Scoffing at herself for finding something good in the scoundrel, she picked up the clothes basket laded with sun-dried towels and carried them to the back door. She had to get this . . . attraction for him under control. Just before stepping inside, she caught sight of Jesse's horse grazing in the paddock. Its front leg wore a red and blue paisley bandage, and the animal kept its weight off it. Jesse had been telling the truth about the horse's injury, at least. Not that she'd doubted him, exactly; she just couldn't seem to rid herself of suspicion.

She glanced around, searching for the animal's owner. The sun hung low in the horizon, burning the land a deep, brilliant orange. It occurred to her that she hadn't seen his ornery hide all day.

With a puzzled frown, she carried the basket of towels into the kitchen and set it on the table. "Rose?"

"In here."

Honesty wiped her hands down the front of her apron and sought out Rose, who stood by the stage with a sketch pad and pencil. "Have you seen Jesse?"

"Not since this morning."

A peculiar combination of relief and disappointment churned in her middle. The relief she understood. The disappointment didn't make any sense. "What are you working on?"

"Plans for Saturday night. I figure if I drag out some of those old hurricane lamps, it'll give the room a soft glow and keep the fellows tame."

"Do you always draw out your plans?"

"Reckon I do."

"Why?"

"Don't know, really. I suppose I have to see something on paper to know if it'll work."

Honesty hadn't seen Rose so alive in all the

weeks she'd known her. She took a seat on the stage and said, "I never know if anything will work. I always have to try it to find out."

"Impulses like that can get you into trouble."

"Don't I know it," Honesty grumbled. But anytime she planned something, it fell apart. Spontaneous moves, on the other hand, seemed to gain results.

Honesty went suddenly still. Was that the problem? Up until Deuce's death, she'd lived for the moment, grabbing opportunities as they came with little thought to the future, holding fast to his faith that all would work out for the best in the end.

These last few months, though, all she'd done was plot and plan her search for the truth—from mapping out every place she and Deuce had ever been, as far back as she could remember, to amassing money in every manner conceivable and searching for an escort . . .

And look at the results.

What if she simply threw caution to the wind? What if, instead of finding fault with every prospect that showed up, she simply took a chance on the next one to walk in and see what happened? Lord knew she couldn't be any worse off than she was now.

Just then the front doors flew open, and Jesse was shoved into the room by a pair of men half his size and twice his age. Honesty's mouth dropped open. *No.* When she'd decided to take a chance on the next man to walk in the doors, she hadn't meant *Jesse.*

"Caught this varmint sneakin' around our claim," one of the geezers declared, aiming a stream of chewing tobacco into the brass spittoon nearby.

Jake, Honesty quickly deduced. Rose's uncles were mirror images of one another: in their late fifties, with the same receding hair line and pale blue eyes, the same stoop-shouldered build from years of bending over stream beds in search of the elusive fortune. Only two things set the brothers apart: Joe had a milder disposition than his twin, and Jake chewed tobacco.

Another shove from the pair nearly sent Jesse to the floor. He glared at the men flanking him, bony hands gripping Jesse's arms as if to prevent him from escaping. Rose's uncles had to know as well as Honesty that Jesse had only to flick his wrists and they'd wind up flying through the window behind him. To his credit, though, he remained calmly in their hold.

"Scarlet, I can explain—"

"You'd best do it quick," she said, folding her arms under her breasts. "Joe and Jake don't take kindly to claim jumpers."

Jesse flicked a glance at Honesty, who watched the exchange with unabashed curiosity and—he would swear—amusement. Enjoying this, was she? Jesse scowled and turned his attention back to his waiting hostess. "I wasn't jumping their claim." Hell, he hadn't even known there *was* a claim. He'd merely been returning over the mountain when the pair jumped him from behind.

But he couldn't tell Scarlet that he'd just wasted half the day at the Black Garter. Considering her history with Eli Johnson, who was everything Sarah had said he would be—a loud-mouthed, arrogant braggart with more bitterness in his heart than good sense—he'd find himself run out of town on a rail.

If he'd learned anything over the last dozen years, it was to trust no one and make no enemies. You never knew when you'd be put in a position to need them again.

"Jesse, you might as well tell her—she's bound to find out anyway."

Jesse's attention snapped toward Honesty, as did that of the others in the room. She stood a short distance behind Rose with her hands clasped loosely at her waist.

"Tell her?" Tell her what? How could Honesty know what he'd been doing?

Honesty nodded. "I know you wanted to keep it a surprise, but since the cat's out of the bag . . ."

What the hell was she doing? he wondered, staring at her through narrowed eyes.

She stared back at him, beseeching him to play along. "Jesse didn't mean any harm, Rose; he was only trying to figure a way to catch the stage driver's attention before he reaches the Black Garter. A diversion, so to speak. Otherwise, we've no guarantee that he'll be willing to travel off the main route to come here. I expect that's what he was doing on Joe and Jake's mountain," Honesty finished. "It does have the best view, after all."

Rose looked first at Joe, then at Jake, who were both studying Jesse with dumbfounded expressions. "Is that true, Jesse?"

He was in too deep to back out now. "Like she said, it was supposed to be a surprise."

"That's brilliant! We *do* need a way to bring the stage into town." She crossed the room to cup Jesse's face in her hands and planted a whopping kiss on his lips. "Jesse, you are amazing." Grinning ear to ear, she said, "Looks like we got us more than just a piano player here."

"Yes, it looks like it," Honesty agreed with a sideways grin that had alarm bells ringing through Jesse's head.

"Uncle Joe, Uncle Jake, I'm glad you two showed up. We've got a big night coming up and I could sure use your help," Rose began.

As she prodded her uncles toward the storage room door, Jesse released a relieved breath. That had been a close call. One of the first rules of being an operative was to set a consistent pattern in case a subject ever checked into your background; that had been drilled into him before his first assignment. Yet he'd almost botched it. If not for Honesty's intervention . . .

His eyes suddenly narrowed on her. "Why did you do that?"

"Do what?"

"Make up that cockamamie story?"

"It was the first thing that popped into my head." She set the lamp on the table and fussed with the red place mats. "I felt sorry for you. I mean, you've been shot once already; I didn't want to see you taking another bullet. Do you think I should put dried flowers around the lamp bases, or would that look too feminine?"

"They'll catch on fire." He crossed his arms and tilted his head, telling her without words that he wasn't buying her reason. Honesty always tried to change the subject when she wasn't telling the truth. "What do you want, Honesty?"

"What makes you think I want anything?" She continued to carry the lamps to each table, more to avoid looking him in the eye, Jesse guessed, than to decorate the saloon. "Can't a girl do something nice for you without you second-guessing her reasons?"

"Not you. I may have been here only a couple days, but that's long enough to know that

Rose has trained you well. You don't do anything—nice or otherwise—unless you stand to gain something in return."

She swung around to face him with a righteous expression. "I'm thinking I should be insulted by that."

"Think whatever you want. Just tell me why you felt the need to come to my rescue."

He could practically see the gears whirring in her head, and if he didn't want the truth so badly, he might have laughed.

"Maybe I was afraid Rose would send you packing," she finally said. "She is fiercely protective of things that belong to her, including her uncles. If she thought you were out to steal from them, you'd be a goner."

"I'd think you'd be glad to see the last of me. You've made it quite clear where I rank on your list of favorites." Jesse unfolded his arms and strode toward her with a flat smile. "So why don't you tell me what you really want?"

Chapter 7

Honesty hated that he could see through her so easily. She'd always been adept at hiding her emotions, so Jesse's ability to see more than she intended left her feeling vulnerable.

"Tell me what you really want."

Did she dare?

Wisdom told her to forget this foolish, impulsive notion; it was too risky; he couldn't be trusted, there was too much at stake.

Desperation insisted that whether she liked it or not, Jesse was the best man for the job. He blended in well with his surroundings, could take on several roles, and all in all, he seemed relatively harmless. Not since that first night had he made any demands on her body or expected more from her than she was willing to give. If anything, he boasted a protective streak that she found both irritating and comforting.

As she wandered about the room, trailing her fingers along the tabletops and filtering through her thoughts, Jesse's gaze followed her, unblinking, unwavering. His intense study made her feel warm all over and sort of . . . shy. Honesty almost laughed. Why, she didn't have a shy bone in her body! Her father used to say she'd been born under a brazen moon.

She cast a glance over her shoulder. Jesse hadn't moved from his spot near the door and he continued to watch her with wary contemplation. What did he think when he looked at her like that? Did he see the scared little girl she tried to hide? The bold and independent lady she wanted to become? Or did he see the woman she saw when she looked in the mirror—a lying, deceitful wench who would use anyone and anything in her hunt for the truth?

She turned to him and tried to gauge his thoughts. Dirt smeared his cheekbone, his hair had come loose from its ponytail, and strands flanked his jaw to brush the tops of his shoulders. Even his scuffed boots and rumpled, dusty clothes bore the proof of an afternoon spent outdoors—doing what, she hadn't a clue.

No, she *did* have an idea where he'd been and what he'd been doing; she just didn't want to admit it. Jesse was a virile man, and if he couldn't get what virile men sought here at the Scarlet Rose, naturally he'd go elsewhere. Hadn't she all but told him to do just that?

But other than an unyielding quest for answers, she saw nothing in his eyes to give her any hint as to what went on in his mind.

"All right. I want you," she blurted before she lost her courage.

His eyes widened; tawny brows shot up.

"Don't look so surprised. You're strong, you're healthy, and you're not completely intolerable to be with. You and I would make fine partners."

He conceded the point with a slanted nod. "Except for one little detail—you hate my guts."

It was Honesty's turn to regard him in surprise. "I don't hate you. I find you a bit overwhelming, and maybe a tad arrogant, but I don't *hate* you. As a matter of fact, I find you quite . . . fascinating." She punctuated the compliment with a brilliant smile.

He shifted from one foot to another, then raked his fingers through his hair, pulling several more strands loose from his ponytail.

"Look . . . Honesty, I'm flattered, but . . ." He gave an awkward little laugh and shook his head. "I'm afraid the prices around here are a bit too rich for my blood."

"But I would pay *you*."

"Is that so? Forgive my confusion, but yesterday you couldn't stand to breathe the same air as me. Today you want me and *you're* willing to pay. Why the sudden change of heart?"

Put that way, she realized her behavior did seem somewhat erratic. She swallowed roughly and confessed, "Because you're my last hope."

"Ahh, I see," he said, though it was obvious that he didn't see at all. "I've heard some outrageous propositions before, but this one beats all. What makes you think I even want to go to bed with you?"

Honesty's mouth dropped open. "Go to— good cow feathers, who said anything about going to bed? I want you to help me, not have sex with me!" Although the idea wasn't all together distasteful. That night she'd spent with him was still so fresh in her mind that she could practically feel him on her skin.

Jesse's face paled, then flushed. A curse singed the air. "I don't need this."

"Wait!" she cried, rushing toward him as he moved to leave. His voice had gone tight as a whipcord, and she realized that he thought she'd purposely misled him into thinking she was inviting him into her bed. "Just hear me out, will you?"

He folded his arms across his chest. He hardly looked interested, but at least he seemed willing to listen.

Battling a sudden attack of nerves, Honesty resisted the urge to wring her hands. "I want to hire you to help me find something."

"And that would be . . . ?"

"First you must agree and swear loyalty to me."

A shake of his head sent a few more blond strands swinging across his shoulders. "No deal. I don't do anything without knowing what I'm letting myself in for."

Honesty felt a trap of her own making closing in around her. Jesse didn't strike her as a man who would agree to travel untold miles looking for something even she couldn't define. What could she say? *Jesse, I need you to safeguard me while I canvass a thousand miles looking for God-knows-what, God-knows-where?* She needed to give him something tangible. Something that would appeal to his honor.

"I want you to help me find my family." Honesty didn't know where the words came from; they just spilled out. But as she said them, she realized it was the perfect quest.

Unfortunately, Jesse wasn't so easily convinced.

"I thought your family was dead," he said with narrow-eyed suspicion.

Honesty started in surprise. "Where did you hear that?"

"Rose mentioned it."

Honesty licked her lips and averted her eyes. "It's true that both my parents are now gone. My mother died when I was too little to remember, and my father . . ." She swallowed heavily. "My father was killed a few months ago. But I have a brother." *Yes, that's it.* "He's a traveling actor. He doesn't even know our father is gone. Surely you can understand how important it is that I find him."

He seemed to mull over the information. "What's his name?"

"George," she said without hesitation. "George Mallory." Deuce had used the name once down in Texas; it would be easy to remember.

Jesse repeated the name under his breath. "George Mallory." He frowned. "Where have I heard that name before . . . ?"

Pride in her quick-thinking immediately gave way to apprehension. "It's a common name. You could have it heard it anywhere!"

If he heard her, he gave no indication. The frown remained, even as Jesse gave his head a swift shake, as if to dislodge the name from his mind. "Do you even know where this brother of yours is?"

She paused for a heartbeat. "Uhm, not exactly. But I've got an inkling that he's headed for Galveston."

"An inkling. You want me to give up God-only-knows how many weeks of my time for an *inkling*?"

Put that way, it did sound a bit eccentric, but, she was running out of choices as well as time. "You would be handsomely rewarded," she added brightly.

"Oh, really?" he drawled. "With what?"

Good question. Men could usually be swayed by only two things. She doubted he'd be impressed with the measly twelve dollars stashed in her pillow slip, and she wasn't willing to give him the other. The only thing she had of value was the ring her father had given her.

She lifted her hand to her throat and freed the ruby from beneath her blouse. Tears stung her eyes. She'd sworn she'd keel over dead before giving up the only valuable thing she owned, but now, faced with the choice of keeping the bauble or uncovering the secret Deuce had taken to the grave, she felt there wasn't much of a choice to make.

With a decisive flick of her wrist, she wrenched the chain from her neck and dropped the ring onto the table between them.

Jesse stared at it for several long, stunned seconds before looking askance at Honesty. "What's this?"

"Your reward. It's well worth your time."

Silence lay thick in the air as she waited for his decision, and she watched as his eyes went from a hard green to a turbulent blue. The shift in color sent a jolt of alarm through her, for it came dangerously close to the shades seen only in her dreams.

Finally he relaxed his obdurate stance, but just when Honesty thought he would agree to take the job, he dashed her hopes.

"I don't think so, Honesty. Find another pigeon."

"You're refusing? Just like that?"

He quirked one brow. "Never had anyone turn you down before?"

"Not with such haste." Or such vigor!

"Look," he sighed. "As much as I sympathize with your wanting to find your brother, you're barking up the wrong tree with me. I've already got a job."

"Surely you don't mean here!"

"No, but now that you mention it, I do have a commitment to Rose. Then first thing Sunday morning, I'm kissing this town goodbye."

"But that's when I would want—"

"*Alone.*"

And before Honesty could stop him again, he spun away and climbed the stairs.

She clenched her hands into fists. Why was he being so difficult? Her request was a simple one, yet he swatted it off as if she'd asked for the moon.

Fighting the temptation to go after him and

demand he reconsider, Honesty sat hard in an empty chair, slammed her arms in a fold across her breasts, and blew out an aggravated breath. So much for her spontaneity theory. Now she'd have to endure the rest of the week knowing he'd gotten the upper hand.

Just as suddenly, her mouth curved in a naughty grin. She still had three days. She was Honesty McGuire, and in the proud words of her father, she'd been born with the creativity of a thespian, the resilience of steel, and more tenacity than a pack of timber wolves. And if she'd learned anything during her time with Rose, it was that there were ways of bending a man to her will—even a man as inflexible as Jesse Jones.

Over the next three days, Jesse couldn't decide whether to choke the life out of Honesty or drag her upstairs and show her the danger of pushing a man too far. She catered to him as if he were the Prince Royal, serving him breakfast, drawing his bath, seeing that his clothes were kept freshly washed and pressed. She also teased him during rehearsals, praised his music, and laughed at his stupid jokes.

Though he knew that she was only pursuing him for her own benefit, he couldn't help but compare her lively, even seductive, efforts with Miranda's "helpless maiden" manipulation—

which he'd fallen for hook, line, and sinker, and barely lived to regret.

And against all wisdom and reason, the initial temptation to take Honesty up on her offer grew until he could hardly bear it. The thought of her all alone, searching for the last of her family . . . God knew, she'd not have an easy time going down that road.

But he already had enough on his plate.

He thought about demanding that she quit her nonsense, but two things stopped him: he hadn't been this pampered since childhood, and he wanted to see how far she was willing to go.

By Saturday, Rose's plans had become a reality. The saloon sparkled from top to bottom, thanks to Honesty; Rose had cajoled Jesse into cutting down a few trees to block the path of the stagecoach, so they'd be forced to take the detour; a sign the size of a barn wall had been painted by Rose and Sarah Wentworth; then Joe and Jake had hauled the monstrosity up to their mountaintop and planted it well. It read, SWEETEST SONGBIRD IN THE WEST! PERFORMING SATURDAY, JUNE 12, SCARLT ROSE SALOON, and could be seen for miles. If all went well, not only would the blocked road force passengers to the Scarlet Rose, but any traveler looking for a bit of entertainment would see the sign and make his way to Last Hope.

Joe and Jake came in early to stock the shelves

with liquor. They hadn't given him any trouble since the day they'd caught him near their claim, but they continued to keep a watchful eye on him, as if waiting for any excuse to thump his skull. Jesse'd had enough skull-thumping in the last week to last him a lifetime, and he avoided them as much as possible.

After helping Rose with last-minute arrangements that morning, Jesse slipped out back to check on his horse. Gemini pranced around the split rail paddock, head high, tail raised, almost parading his prowess to the sorry mule grazing nearby. Spotting Jesse, he cantered to the fence for his daily ration of oats.

Jesse scratched the shank of black hair between Gemini's eyes. "Itchin' to hit the trail, aren't you fella?"

Gemini whinnied and pawed the ground.

"Yeah, me, too."

Jesse led him into the stall and hung a bucket of feed from the top rail. A quick examination of Gemini's leg put a satisfied smile on Jesse's face. Though the wound was still visible, the gash had closed to a healthy pink seam, and the swelling had receded after the first day.

Only one more day. Then he'd kick the dust of this two-bit town from his heels.

Prickles at the back of his neck warned him he was no longer alone. He turned slowly, and the sight of Honesty hit him like a blow to the sternum.

She stood in a beam of sunlight, wearing a frothy pink gown that fit her like a dream. The silk fabric was drawn tight around her figure, emphasizing the length of her legs, the flare of her hips, the fullness of her breasts. A draping of fabric hemmed in white lace fit snug around her stomach. A sash sewn with baby roses crossed from right shoulder to left hip, while the other shoulder had been left bare, revealing flawless peaches-and-cream skin.

"Do you like it?" She whirled in a circle.

Jesse's mouth went dry. His gaze traveled up her slender neck, past lush, pouty lips, to the snub of her nose and the rich coffee brown of her eyes. She'd piled her hair atop her head, and a wreath of silk roses sat upon the mass of loose amber ringlets at her crown. A fire kindled in Jesse's veins and sent the blood rushing to his groin.

He clutched the rag he'd used to polish his saddle tightly in his hand and brushed past her to reach for a bridle on the wall. "What are you doing out here?"

"I came to ask your opinion. I can't decide which outfit to wear tonight. What do you think? Soft and alluring?" She paused a moment, then flipped the red and black lace dress she'd worn his first night in town in front of her, and pulled the wreath from her hair. The pale mass tumbled down her shoulders and back. "Or bold and brazen?"

Was she trying to kill him?

Every memory he'd retained of that night ambushed him in vivid detail; the lush curve of her body, the heat of her skin, the sultry promise in her eyes and in her smile. Sensations he'd fought to ignore this past week blazed through his system like wildfire, searing through his chest, his loins.

Damn, he wished he could remember being with her.

"It wouldn't matter if you went out there in sackcloth and ashes," he said gruffly, turning away before she noticed his arousal. "You'll have that audience so wowed, they won't know what hit them."

"You're no help." She chuckled.

It grew quiet then, with nothing but the occasional stomp of a hoof against packed ground, a twitter of sparrows nesting in the rafters, and the dim bark of orders from inside the saloon to break the silence.

Jesse knew it was too much to hope that she would leave him to suffer in peace.

"That's a fine looking animal."

He glanced over his shoulder as she sashayed toward Gemini.

"Have you had him long?"

Jesse tore his eyes away from the fluid swing of her hips and cleared his throat. "Since he was a colt."

"I'll bet he cost you a pretty penny."

"He was a gift."

"You must be quite talented."

Jesse's hands froze on the bridle. Realizing she'd thrown his remark back in his face, he turned to her in shock. Her impish grin told him she'd done it on purpose. "I'm not changing my mind, Honesty."

"Why, Jesse? You're leaving tomorrow anyway. And I won't be any trouble, I promise."

"Look," Jesse sighed. "In a few hours, you'll have a whole bevy of protectors to choose from. I guarantee that you'll be able to convince one of them to help you."

"But I don't want one of them. I don't even know them."

"You don't know me, either," he reminded her.

"I know you're honest and reliable and decent. And I know that I would never come to any harm with you. I don't have that confidence in anyone else."

The faith she placed in him weighed on his shoulders like medieval armor. *Honest. Reliable. Decent.* Hell, he was even better at his job than he thought.

Jesse raked his fingers through his hair, as frustrated with the burden she put on him as his own desire to be the man she professed him to be. "Honesty, I admire your ambition to track down your brother, but if you ask me, you'd be a whole lot better off staying here with Rose and hiring a professional to find him."

"You mean, like a detective?"

"Why not?" Though it galled him to encourage her to remain in the lifestyle Rose provided, he sure as hell couldn't cave in to her request, no matter how tempting it seemed. "I'm sure there are some who specialize in finding people."

For a moment he could have sworn he'd seen panic flash across her face, but it disappeared so quickly that he wondered if his suspicious nature was running amuck. She gave a flippant wave of her hand. "You're right. I don't know why I didn't think of it before. So, which is it?" She lifted the dress in front of her again. "The red or the pink?"

Jesse frowned. He might have accepted the abrupt change of subject if the blinding smile she gave him reached her eyes. "What's wrong, Honesty?"

"What makes you think anything is wrong?"

"Your hands are shaking."

She dropped her gaze. "I'm a little nervous about tonight, I suppose. Sometimes the audiences get a bit rambunctious."

Again, a logical answer. "You've got nothing

to be nervous about," he countered gruffly. "I'll be right there."

"You will?"

"I have to be. I'm the piano man, remember?"

Her crestfallen expression snaked around his heart. He tipped her chin in the air and stared into worried brown eyes. "I'll be right there. I give you my word."

She closed the distance separating them with two swift steps and wrapped her arms around his neck in a bruising grip, not seeming to care that her fine costumes were being crushed between their bodies.

Jesse closed his eyes and let her hold on, but he didn't embrace her back. God knew he wanted to, though.

Just when he thought he'd lose his self-control, she pulled back and kissed his cheek. "Thanks, Jesse."

As she picked up her skirts and hurried back to the saloon, Jess touched his fingers to his cheek. It was a damn good thing he was leaving tomorrow, because if he had to spend one day more in her company, he feared he'd might do something really stupid.

Like fall for the devious minx.

Despite her efforts to banish their conversation from her mind, it stayed with Honesty

throughout the afternoon and into the evening
as she dressed for her performance. *Hire a detective.* A reasonable solution if not for one minor
fact: Detectives had been hunting her father off
and on for as long as she could remember.
Deuce had once confessed they were after him
due to a con gone awry years ago, but he'd
never revealed the details. It must have been serious, though, or else he wouldn't have feared
them. She hoped that they would learn of his
death and drop their search. Unfortunately, she
feared the opposite—that if they learned of his
death, they'd redirect their hunt to her. She had,
after all, been part of his schemes . . .

"Honesty, are you ready? We've got a crowd
down there clamorin' to hear the 'Sweetest
Songbird in the West.' "

"I'll be down in a sec," Honesty called to
Rose through the closed door.

With brittle precision, she set the brush on
the vanity, then stood and smoothed her skirt.
She'd chosen the pink gown, for the way it had
made Jesse's eyes light up, and for the roses that
promoted the saloon. Then she adjusted the
wreath in her hair and left her room.

Conversational murmurs from the crowd
mingled with a rising layer of cigar haze. Rose
had recruited Sarah Wentworth's help for the
evening and the two wound their way around

tables and chairs, serving drinks and exchanging banter, while Joe and Jake manned the bar and the gaming table.

Hollow dread curled in Honesty's stomach. The last time she'd sung before an audience her world had crumbled, and anticipation of all hell breaking loose again had her palms growing damp and her tongue swelling.

She managed to hang onto her fragile composure by forcing herself to concentrate on placing one slipper in front of the other instead of thinking of the men watching her descend the stairs. Curiosity had drawn a good majority of them from the Black Garter, and the stagecoach passengers—a dozen men and two women—were scattered about the room. The ladies sat close to the door and looked to be related. The younger of the two stared in wide-eyed fascination at Honesty while the elder one glared at her with undisguised disapproval. Honesty would have bet her white silk garters that if there had been any other place in town to bed down, the woman would have braved a wall of fire to get there. The picture might have made her laugh if she hadn't been so darned petrified.

Then she heard Jesse whispering her name like a caress. He stood at the piano, lighting up the room with his presence, an angel in disguise, an answer to a prayer.

Their gazes met and held for endless seconds. Awareness of him sped through her every nerve ending: the way his borrowed black coat hugged his broad shoulders, the contrast of his white shirt against his tanned complexion, the aura of confidence he wore with the same ease as the gun belt around his waist. She sank into the warmth of his blue-green eyes, drawing strength.

Then he winked.

The heavy coat of anxiety she'd been wearing slithered off her shoulders, and she gave him a wobbly smile of thanks. While he took a seat on the bench, she climbed the stairs to the stage, then waited for her cue.

Miraculously, the audience disappeared. Honesty sang to him and him alone, songs they'd practiced so many times that she often found herself humming them in her sleep. Saucy numbers, jocular ditties, bittersweet ballads.

Though she was dimly aware of the claps and whistles around her, the world had narrowed down to the two of them.

Then Jess keyed in on the first sweet notes of "Greensleeves," and Honesty's voice carried to every lonely heart in the saloon. By the time the last sweet note faded to silence, warm tears tracked down her cold cheeks.

Even Jesse's eyes looked suspiciously shiny.

And Honesty had never felt closer to another human being in her life.

A movement to her left broke the spell as a man got up from his seat and instantly went to Rose. After a brief conversation she took his hand with a compassionate smile and led him upstairs to the rooms above. The exchange didn't go unnoticed by the elder lady; she clapped her hand over the younger girl's eyes, then ushered her out of the saloon with an imperious tilt of her nose.

Jesse didn't miss the exchange, either. He turned to Honesty, pinning her with a gaze so hot and accusing that her heart jumped into her windpipe. The ferocity in his eyes and the disapproving line of his mouth made her feel low and dirty and cheap.

A touch at her elbow drew her gaze to a flannel-shirted man in his late forties. With a stiff smile, she took him by the hand, and, as Rose had done, led her customer upstairs.

Jesse lost count of how long he spent at the piano with a bottle of whiskey for company, but it was long enough to make fuzz grow on his brain and turn his muscles into jelly.

He knew he shouldn't be drinking himself into oblivion, but it was the only thing he could do to blot his mind of the sight of Honesty heading upstairs with yet another lovesick customer. Having Honesty all to himself the last few days, he'd almost been able to forget how she made a living.

Tonight had been a cutting reminder.

One after another, he'd watched through increasingly bleary eyes as men came stumbling down the stairs. Most of 'em would still be buttoning their shirts and carrying their boots in their hands. And all of 'em, every damned, stinking, thievin' one of 'em, would be wearin' a shit-eating grin.

Thick loathing pooled in Jesse's gut to join the excessive amount of liquor he'd consumed. He took another deep swallow of whiskey to wash it away. It didn't help. The thought of her lying in one of those beds, her amber hair spread across the ivory sheets, her mouth parted in ecstasy as hands cupped her breasts, had printed itself in his mind so deeply and so permanently that he could have painted the son-of-a-bitch.

Not just any hands, though.

His hands.

Jesse pounded the keys with a heavy fist. Joe glanced up from behind the bar, and the broom in Jake's grip stopped its motion. Everyone else had either left, fallen asleep at one of the tables, or found a bed upstairs to catch a few winks before the stage left the next morning.

Jesse ignored the lot of 'em and downed the

last bit in his glass, then slammed it atop the piano and grabbed the bottle, only to find it empty, too.

Why the hell couldn't he remember being with her? Had he been as incredible as she'd claimed, or had he been just one of the many besotted fools who'd paid for the privilege of her body and her praise?

The thought made him scowl. At least the other men she'd taken to her bed would remember the hour spent with her, all soft and sinuous one minute, hot and wild the next. And it wasn't friggin' fair. When he rode away from here tomorrow he wouldn't even have the memory of the night to carry with him.

Well, damn it, there was only one way to fix that. She owed him. He'd paid for her, by God; the least she could do was see to it that it had been worth it.

The room spun as he got to his feet, colors blurring into one big blob as he stumbled toward the stairs. Several chairs and a table jumped into his path and tripped up his feet. He kept his gaze trained on the steps that would lead him to his sweet firebrand's arms.

Just as Jesse reached the banister, laughter at the door brought him to a halt. He let out a mild curse under his breath, partly at the interruption, partly at the identity of the latecomers entering the saloon.

Roscoe Treat was the taller and dimmer of the two, with a huge black nose and the yellow remnants of a pair of black eyes, and he wore a bulky buffalo-hide coat as if he'd just walked in from a blizzard instead of a mild June summer night.

His brother Robert, older, shorter, and ten times neater, sported a pinstriped coat and matching creased trousers. A pearl-handled pistol was strapped to his hip; both men were walking loads of trouble.

What the hell were they doing in Last Hope? Last time he'd seen them, they'd been breaking rock down in an Arizona penitentiary.

"Evenin', fellas," Joe called.

"The sign on the hill says 'Sweetest Songbird in the West,'" Roscoe bellowed. "I don't see no 'songbird.'"

"Performance is over for the night. But if you're lookin' for other entertainment, take a seat and one of the ladies will be down shortly."

Jesse ground his teeth together. He didn't want to think of either the mule-skinner or the dandy laying hands to Honesty—or even Rose, for that matter. But mostly Honesty. She was his tonight.

Roscoe looked none too happy at being asked to wait, but a nudge from his brother prompted him toward a table. "Forget it, Roscoe. Don't you remember the last time you

let your pecker rule your brain? You're lucky
McGuire stopped at breaking your nose."

The name penetrated through Jesse's mud-
dled brain. He cursed himself for drinking himself senseless and tried to haul his mind back to
sobriety.

"The son-of-a-bitch got in a lucky shot, is all.
He won't be so lucky when we catch up to him,
though."

"We won't ever catch up to him if you insist
on detouring to every liquor stop between here
and the border."

"Oh, we'll catch up to him. And when we do,
I'll make him sorry he was ever born."

"Not before we get our money."

Jesse caught sight of Jake heading toward
the table with a bottle of liquor and a couple of
glasses. He glanced up the stairs, then back at
the men. The decision shouldn't be so hard: an
hour between the sheets with a woman, or a
lead on McGuire. This was the break he'd
been waiting for, so what the hell was his
problem?

Gritting his teeth against Honesty's pull on
him, he turned his back on the stairs, relieved
Jake of the bottle with a tight "I've got 'em, old
man," and joined their newly arrived customers.

"Evenin', boys." Jesse set the bottle in the
center of the table. "This round's on me."

* * *

The moon hung low and full and sad in a sky as black as tar. With her latest victim snoring obliviously in the bed, Honesty slid her legs off the mattress and onto the floor, then bent to gather her discarded robe. She pushed one leaden arm through a sleeve, then the other, then sat at the edge of the bed, her head bowed, the heels of her hands pressed tightly against the mattress.

She couldn't do this anymore.

Deuce had always said, "If ye lose the edge, lass, get out o' the game."

She hadn't just lost the edge, she'd plunged right over it. Drugging men, then duping them into believing they'd shared a couple dollars of passionate sex, used to bring her a sense of empowerment. Now, it just left her feeling empty and pathetic. The only thing that had gotten her through the evening was the image of a golden-haired man and a song of the future, but now the dull ache of loneliness she'd felt all night had grown to a painful cramp.

She had to change Jesse's mind.

In just a few hours, he'd ride out of Last Hope and out of her life, and Honesty knew with certainty that he'd be taking more than her best chance at finding the truth.

With renewed strength, she gathered her clothes quickly, then spent the next twenty min-

utes in her own room, touching up her lashes
and rouge. She'd bring him here tonight. She'd
never allowed a man into her room before; it always felt like such an invasion. But she wanted
this evening to be special. She refused to think
of the sacrifice. Trading her virginity for the
truth seemed a small price to pay.

With one last brush of color to her lips, a pat
to her freshly coifed hair, and a tug of her
corset, she left her room, pausing at the top of
the stairs to search the area below. Most of the
lamps had been extinguished and nearly all the
chairs were empty save a few near the bar,
where sleeping bodies were slumped over the
table.

Finally, she spotted Jesse standing near a corner table just below the stairs, where two men
sat, one lean, one bulky. She couldn't make out
their features in the dim lighting, but she hoped
they weren't waiting on her—because if they
were, they'd be waiting all night.

She belonged to Jesse now.

Honesty lifted her chin and squared her
shoulders, and just as she prepared to descend
the stairs, the glow from a nearby lamp illuminated the features of one of the men. Honesty
gasped. She wrenched herself back into the
safety of the shadows and pressed her spine
against the wall. *Oh, my gosh. Robert? It wasn't
possible—he was supposed to be dead!*

"Do we know you?" she heard him ask in a voice of such cultured familiarity that it sent chills skittering down her arms. Honesty peered around the corner to assure herself that it was indeed a flesh-and-blood man below, and not a ghost. Her stomach knotted at the vision of slicked-back hair, narrow chin, trim mustache. Oh, God. What was he doing here?

"Not that I'm aware of," Jesse replied. A chair scraped across the floor as he pulled it free from the table and straddled it. "I couldn't help but overhear your conversation."

"Yeah? So?" The sarcasm came from the deeper, gruffer voice of Robert's companion.

"It appears that we're looking for the same man."

"What do you want with him?" *Robert.*

"I reckon that's my business." *Jesse again.*

"Word has it that he was headin' up to Leadville."

"That lyin' son-of-a-bitch. He told us he was headin' south to Tex—"

"Shut up, Roscoe. Where'd you hear that, mister?"

"Same place I heard that the two of you together didn't have enough brains to blow your nose." From the holster at his side, he withdrew a Colt revolver and aimed it at the bigger man. With a smile that sent shivers down Honesty's spine, Jesse said, "Now, here's the deal—you tell me where I might find Deuce McGuire, and I might just let you live another day."

For a moment, Honesty was too stunned to breathe. Never had she seen Jesse draw his weapon; never had she heard such cold determination in his voice.

Then his words registered.

Honesty sank against the wall, every nerve numb, Deuce's name on Jesse's lips a blade of betrayal stabbing through her heart. Oh, God, how could she ever have thought him harmless?

He was far more dangerous than she'd ever imagined.

Chapter 8

An hour later, Honesty scanned one side of the hallway, then the other. Moonlight from the window at the end of the hall cast a beam of light on the plank floor. Shadows touched the paper roses that once probably looked real enough to smell, but now wilted against the wall in aged dejection.

Assured that the path was clear, she stepped out of her room, then shut the door behind her. She winced at the soft click that echoed in the silence and gave the dim hallway another quick inspection. At half past three in the morning the chances of anyone being up and about were slim, but she didn't dare risk those men or Jesse catching her.

Jesse.

x

143

Just the thought of his name brought a fresh surge of contempt twisting inside her. She couldn't believe she'd almost asked him to help her. How could she have been so stupid to think she could trust anyone? Hadn't she seen, over and over again, that men were faithless, traitorous creatures who used any means at their disposal to get what they wanted from a woman? Even Jesse had proved himself no better; after he'd gotten what he'd paid for, she was of no further use to him.

Jesse's betrayal hurt more, because she'd walked in with her eyes wide open and she'd still come out the fool.

Well, no more, she thought, tiptoeing toward the stairs. She was a clever, resourceful woman, capable of finding the flowing stones all by herself. So what if she'd rarely traveled alone before? Hadn't she managed on her own for the last three months, despite the dangers? She had no choice but to risk it again.

Honesty straightened her spine and strode down the hall with confidence. Downstairs, a light shone under the door of Rose's bedroom. Honesty raised her fist, and after the briefest of hesitations, gave the door three short raps.

At the call to enter, Honesty stepped inside. Of all the rooms in the Scarlet Rose, this one was undeniably the plainest—and the loneliest. Not one picture hung on the walls, not one piece of bric-a-brac cluttered the top of bureau tucked in the corner, or the desk below the window where Rose sat, and there was not a single red item in sight. In fact, everything was pristine white, from the curtains and bedspread to the furniture and the walls, almost as if by wiping the room clean of any shade, Rose might forget for a time the soiled life she led.

Upon her entrance, Rose glanced up and gave Honesty a beaming grin. "Honesty, you won't believe this. We've made more profit in this one night than we have in the last three months!" She clutched a wad of money in her fist and shook it in the air. "And I have you and Jesse to thank. Playing 'Greensleeves' was a stroke of genius. Those men were so homesick and love-struck, I swear they'd have sold their mothers for comfort. Next time—"

"There won't be a next time, Rose." Honesty glanced down at her hands. "I'm leaving."

Taut silence stretched into the corners of the tiny room. "Leaving?"

Honesty could hardly bring herself to look Rose in the eye, but the woman deserved that much, and more. She nodded.

"When?" Rose asked.

"Now."

Honesty could almost hear the questions churning in the woman's mind, but she asked not a one.

Instead, she said, "Well, I'll admit I expected it to happen one day. Just not this soon. Do you know where you're goin'?"

Honesty nodded again. "I have an idea. I have a favor to ask, though."

"I'll do what I can."

"I need transportation." She opened her hand and let the ruby fall on the desk. "It's all I've got, Rose. It's well worth your mule."

"Hon, that cantankerous critter isn't worth a tenth of this rock! You could buy a dozen mules with this!" She cast Honesty a speculative glance, then pushed the ring back toward her. "Just put that back in your pocket."

"Please, Rose. It's . . ." She swallowed the thick knot of emotion in her throat. "It's very special to me. I'll have to sell it sooner or later anyway, and I'd much rather you had it than some stranger."

"Why don't you just buy a ticket for the stage with your earnings? It'll be leavin' in just a couple hours and it's a whole lot more reliable."

It was also heading north; she needed to go south. Besides, the stagecoach would naturally be the first place anyone would search. "I prefer the mule, if you're willing to part with him."

"Believe me, I've been wanting to part with that sorry plug since I got him dumped on me. But hon, I won't take your ring—it just don't feel right."

Honesty swallowed. How was she going to get out of Last Hope now?

Again she endured searching examination from her friend. "I don't suppose there's anything I can say to change your mind?"

"No," Honesty answered.

She issued a resigned sigh. "Then take the mule. Take this, too—you earned it, and you'll need it wherever you're going."

Honesty took the money Rose handed her and turned away with a stab of guilt. Yes, she'd earned it, but it didn't feel right, considering all that Rose had done for her. Nor did it feel right leaving her stuck here to fend for herself. "Come with me, Rose," she invited on impulse.

"And leave all this?" Rose gestured to her surroundings, then shook her head. "No, Honesty. You go on. Find your dreams."

"What about you?"

She smiled a watery smile. "I'll be fine. Last Hope ain't 'Lost Hope' yet."

Knowing how stubborn Rose could be, Honesty swallowed, then folded the bills Rose had given her and tucked them and her ring between her breasts. She'd tried. It was the best she could do, she thought, and started for the door. As she put her hand on the crystal knob, Rose's soft query brought her to a stop.

"Honesty?"

She turned back.

"I hope you find whatever it is you're lookin' for. But if you don't, you know where to find me."

Tears threatened to choke Honesty as she looked at the woman who had been there when she'd needed someone most. She'd been scared and tired and grieving when she'd stumbled into Last Hope a few short weeks ago, with nothing to call her own save a worn carpetbag and a few dollars in her shoe.

But Rose had never asked questions or demanded anything Honesty hadn't been willing to give. She'd simply offered her food, shelter, and a place to lick her wounds while she planned her next move.

"Thanks, Rose. For everything."

Then, before her emotions got the best of her, Honesty walked out of Rose's room, passed the piano where she and Jesse had spent so much time together with steely resolve, and then went through the kitchen.

Outside, darkness lingered and the chirp of crickets filled the air. Honesty paused on the stoop, attacked by a fleeting moment of panic. Though staying here was even more dangerous than setting off into the great unknown, what if her plan was just a fool's errand? How did she even know the flowing stones existed? No one knew Deuce McGuire better than she; he'd been a notorious schemer, a gypsy thief.

He'd also been comforting arms on a difficult night, a soothing voice in a frightening storm, a loyal friend when she'd needed someone to talk to.

No, she thought resolutely, she'd not let doubt or cowardice stop her from seeking whatever "truth" he wanted her to find. Not the pair of ruffians downstairs, not Jesse, not even Rose would stop her from finding the flowing stones.

As Honesty took a determined step toward the paddock, she felt a sudden clamp around her arm just before she was wrenched back against an unyielding body twice her size. A meaty hand clapped over her mouth and muffled her shriek. The sour odors of whiskey and sweat filled her nostrils, along with the more familiar scent of expensive cologne.

"Lookee here, 'Bert. We didn't have to go huntin' songbirds. The sweet little dove came flyin' straight to us."

Breathing heavily, Honesty felt her fearful gaze dart between the two faces leering at her, unable to decide which posed more of a danger—the bigger man's brute strength, or Robert's mental cunning.

"Well, well, well," he said, "if it isn't my long-lost love. As fetching as ever, isn't she, Roscoe?"

She tried to shy away from the hand reaching

out to stroke her hair, but the brute's tight grip prevented her from moving more than an inch.

"Yep. Feisty, too." Coarse laughter sizzled up her spine. "I knew that low-down piano man was tryin' to hide something from us."

Robert acknowledged the remark with a flat smile. "Yes, but a beauty such as she cannot remain hidden for long. Now, Honesty, when my brother removes his hand, you will not scream or run if you know what's good for you, is that clear?"

As soon as she nodded, Robert flicked his hand and the muzzle fell away from her mouth. Honesty sucked in a deep breath and licked her lips, which had gone numb from the pressure against them. "I thought you were dead," she said when she could finally speak.

"Yes, I'm sure that distresses you greatly, but as you can see, I am alive and well—no thanks to your father."

She wouldn't give him the satisfaction of a reaction. "How did you find me?"

"Why, we followed the signs! 'Sweetest Songbird in the West'—that could only be you."

Oh, God. She'd known the stupid performance would bring nothing but trouble.

"Now, if you just tell us where your father is, I might be persuaded to let you go."

"My father?" Obviously neither of them was aware that Deuce had died from their shoot-out. She had no idea what they wanted with him, but instinct told her to keep that bit of information to herself. "I don't know where he is. He left me just outside Durango. I haven't seen him in months."

Her jaw was suddenly seized in a brutal grip. To Honesty's shame, tears of pain and fear burned at the back of her eyes.

"Don't lie to me, Honesty, I'm in no mood for your games. Either tell me where McGuire is hiding or I'll have to resort to measures neither of us wants."

She had not a single doubt that Robert meant what he said. The look on his face when he'd shot at them in the alley was as fresh in her mind today as it was the day it had happened. "He's gone, I tell you. And he won't be coming back."

"What are we gonna do now, 'Bert?"

"What we should have done in the beginning." Robert released his grip on her jaw and glanced at his brother. "Fetch the horses. We're taking her with us."

"I'm not going anywhere with you."

"Oh, yes you are. Your father and I had an arrangement, and he welched on it. But once he learns that we have you, he'll either come to his senses and tell us where he hid the money, or we'll kill you."

Money? Honesty's stomach sank. *Oh, Papa, what have you done now?* "What money?"

"The million dollars McGuire told us he stashed away," Roscoe hissed in her ear.

Honesty's eyes bulged and she almost laughed at the absurdity. "A million dollars? Surely you didn't believe him!" Honesty didn't know what shocked her more: her father's outrageous claim or Robert's gullibility. Suddenly her eyes narrowed. "Is that why you were so nice to me? Because you thought my father . . . that he . . . ? Great goose eggs, Robert, Deuce McGuire never had more than two nickels to rub together. And when he did, it was gone almost as soon as got it. He *swindled* you! Just as he has swindled countless other buffoons in his lifetime."

Honesty realized too late that she'd stepped on a nerve; Robert's face turned a mottled red and she feared that he would take a swing at her.

"I am *not* a *buffoon*. Nor am I a man to be trifled with. Either you tell me where McGuire is, or you tell us where the money is hidden. Otherwise . . ." The pale blue eyes she'd found so alluring long ago turned to ice and he smiled coldly. "Well, let's just say that Roscoe here hasn't been with a woman in a good long while."

The image painting itself in her mind sent dread through each nerve ending, and a chill broke out along her arms. Her father had one significant flaw: a penchant for exaggeration. If Robert was to be believed—and she had no reason yet to doubt his story—Deuce had entered into some sort of agreement with Robert that involved, of all things, a hidden fortune.

And they expected her to produce it.

The truth is hidden in the flowing stones.

A shocking thought occurred—what if it wasn't one of his numerous exaggerations? What if the truth he wanted her to find was indeed a fortune? The notion seemed too ludicrous to consider, but at the same time, it would explain why she'd been the object of a hunt these last few months.

At this point, though, it didn't matter whether the money existed or not; Robert and his brother believed it did, which left her in a precarious situation. She could continue to deny any knowledge of her father's whereabouts and leave herself at the mercy of the hulking brute, or profess to know where the money was hidden—which might persuade them to let her go, but would also leave room for retaliation once they realized she'd sent them on a wild-goose chase. Neither option held much appeal.

Think, Honesty, think! If only she could buy herself some time . . . "All right, I'll take you to my father."

"No, you'll tell us where to find him."

"No, I will *take* you to him. And if you or your brother lays one hand on me before we get there, I'll see to it that you never find him."

An hour before dawn, Jesse awoke to a herd of longhorns stampeding through his skull. Gingerly he sat up, slid his legs over the edge of the mattress, and cradled his pounding head. He gave up trying to figure out how he'd made it into his own bed; at least he hadn't gone to Honesty's room last night and made a complete fool of himself. And he'd managed to earn an unexpected break on McGuire. Not that he much cottoned to the idea of traveling to Texas on the word of two bad seeds, but he didn't see that he had much choice. Right now, it was the only lead he had on McGuire's whereabouts.

Every sound, every movement, every breath sent excruciating waves of pain through his head as he dragged himself out of bed with ag-onizing slowness, but he figured a hangover was the least he deserved for being stupidly over-indulgent. He managed to dress himself without throwing up, then collected his saddle-bags and hat. As soon as he settled up with Rose, he and Gemini would quit this place.

As he passed Honesty's closed door he briefly considered telling her goodbye, then thought better of it. The farther he stayed from the little firebrand, the sooner he'd forget her, and the better off he'd be. He'd kept his word to Rose; his debt was paid. Time to kick the dust of this one-horse town from his heels.

With grim determination, he descended the stairs. None of their overnight guests were up and about yet and he'd managed to chase off the troublesome duo in the wee hours of the morning, which left the main room empty and hollow. Hard to believe that only last night, the place had been nearly busting at the seams with people. He hoped Rose had made enough profit to tide her over for a while.

He found her in the kitchen, taking an enameled pot off the stove. The glare from the window drove blinding shards of pain through his brain and his system rebelled at the pungent odor of brewed coffee. "Mornin', Scarlet," he whispered gruffly.

"Mornin' Jesse. You're up early, and lookin' a bit green around the gills." She poured him a cup of coffee and after adding a generous dose of whiskey, set it on the table. "Here, drink this. It'll make you feel better."

Just the thought of putting one more drop of liquor down his gullet, turned his stomach. "No thanks, Scarlet. I think I'll just be on my way."

"I expected as much." She set the pot on the stove and claimed the cup for herself. "In fact,

I'm surprised you haven't gone after Honesty sooner. Any fool with eyes could see that the two of you were taken with each other."

It took several seconds for the remark to register. "Wait—did you say Honesty left?"

" 'Bout ten, fifteen minutes ago. You didn't know?"

He shook his head, then regretted it when the longhorns stampeded again.

"But I thought she was . . . Well, I guess it don't matter now what I thought. Fact is, I was wrong, and I don't mind tellin' you that I don't like the idea of her goin' off on her own," Rose said.

He didn't much like it, either. For all her gutsy determination, she didn't have a clue about what dangers she might face chasing after that gypsy brother of hers.

Maybe he shouldn't have been so quick to reject her request . . .

Nope, nope, nope. By God, he'd let himself get sidetracked too many times to let it happen again. Honesty was a grown woman. He'd told her already that he had a job to do, and by God, he'd not let her or anyone else delay him another second.

No sooner did Jesse draw his pay from Rose than a ruckus outside brought the pair of them to the window. Clouds of dust rolled between the saloon and the horse stalls, obscuring the source of the noise.

Jesse threw open the back door and raced outside with Rose not far behind, and shaded his eyes from the choking dust. In the distance, he could barely make out the shapes of three riders heading for the hills: two men and one woman.

Honesty.

On his horse.

"Hey! She stole my horse!"

Rose clutched his arm. "Jesse, she wouldn't do that."

"She just did, goddamn it!" And no doubt the conniving little wench had been planning this since he'd turned down her request: grab the first two suckers she could find, and charm them into helping her find her brother. But if she thought he'd let her get away with swiping Gemini, she had another think coming.

Jesse plugged two fingers between his teeth and gave a sharp whistle. Gemini skidded to a stop and reared, and Jesse's heart dropped as Honesty rolled off the mustang's back end. Instantly, she picked herself off the ground and started running toward the saloon. The bigger of her companions seized Gemini's reins, while the other man swerved around and headed her off.

"Oh, shit," Jesse whispered, the blood draining from his face as he watched Honesty get plucked up into the second man's saddle.

It took only a second for him to recognize the men: his no-account informants from the previous night. He had no idea why they'd come back to Last Hope after he'd chased them off, unless . . .

Shit. They couldn't have figured out that it had been *his* testimony that had helped send them to prison six years ago. His hair had been shorter and dark, and a waxed mustache supported the impression of the wealthy railroad investor he'd played at the time to catch them for fraud.

But one thing was abundantly clear: Honesty was not with the Treat brothers of her own free will. The question was, why had they taken her?

A string of female curses punctured the air. "Jesse, do something!"

"What the hell am I supposed to do?" he bellowed in helpless fury. "They've got my horse!"

Rose abruptly pushed him toward the stalls. "Take Bag-o'-Bones."

"That pitiful plug? I'll be lucky if I can get him out of the stall!"

"Well, you've got to try. He's slow but he's steady, and he's better than nothing."

Rose was right. He couldn't just let Honesty be stolen out from under their noses, and as much as it galled him, the mule was his only chance of rescuing her.

Chapter 9

By the second or third day on the trail—Honesty was starting to lose count—she began to despair of ever getting away from Robert and his brute of a brother. Though they left her alone for the most part, they kept Gemini's reins tied to one of their saddles to avoid a repeated attempt of the animal's escape, and both watched her like beady-eyed hawks with a mouse in their sights. Even trips to the bushes were monitored with humiliating attention.

With nothing to occupy her time as she rode between the men and waited for one of Deuce's famous opportunities to present itself, her thoughts strayed more and more often to Jesse. Part of her, the part that found such pleasure in his smile and excitement at his touch, longed for him with an intensity that bordered on a physical ache. The other part of her, the part that felt used and battered and betrayed by his duplicity, hoped he'd take a running jump off a high cliff.

How could she have been so stupid, not once, but twice? As hard as she tried not to let it affect her, his mysterious interest in her father weighed on her mind like a black cloud. She'd sensed from the beginning that his arrival in Last Hope hadn't been as innocent as he'd wanted her and Rose to believe, but never in her wildest dreams had she imagined he might have been after her father.

And therein lay the big mystery—why? Did Jesse believe in the fabled fortune, too? If Deuce had told Robert of the stashed million, what would have stopped him from telling others? Not a gosh-darn thing. So it wasn't beyond the realm of possibility that Jesse might have caught wind of the tale, and like Robert, believed that she was the key to finding the money.

On the other hand, she supposed that Jesse really could have been stranded in Last Hope, had no idea she was Deuce's daughter, and had truly stayed at the Scarlet Rose to help a woman in need. His interest in her father could involve something completely unrelated to her. Deuce had been swindling people for years, after all, so it was possible that Jesse, for all his apparent astuteness, had been duped by him, too. Hadn't she managed to convince him that they'd shared a night of passionate love-making?

Oh, she could drive herself daft trying to find answers to the questions, and it wouldn't change anything. Jesse had still been dishonest with her, she was still the captive of a pair of greedy fortune seekers, and until she figured out a way to elude them, she'd never learn the truth about anything.

Including how she could possibly pine for a man she'd known only a few days, and whom she couldn't trust as far as she could throw him.

With a sigh, she directed her attention to the narrow path ahead. They'd long since left behind the tiny valley that nestled Last Hope, and were now descending a mild, evergreen-studded slope between snow-capped peaks. Robert's constant vigilance wouldn't allow her to give any creeks they crossed more than a cursory exploration, nor did she dare sneak off on her own. Robert had already promised to strip her of freedom completely if she tried anything stupid. At least her hands weren't bound, and a little freedom at this point was better than no freedom. She'd get her break; she simply had to wait for it.

By midday they hit a wide, gently rolling meadow at the base of the mountains. The morning chill had long since given way to an unrelenting heat; sweat had her clothes sticking to her, her throat was parched, and grime coated every inch of her body like a second skin. Having learned the hard way that complaining only resulted in being gagged, Honesty kept her discomfort to herself. Robert and Roscoe would stop when they decided to stop, and not before.

She sent up a silent prayer of thanks when they did just that a few minutes later near a tiny mountain stream. Robert dismounted first, then Roscoe, but Honesty remained in the saddle, her muscles so weary that she didn't think a charging herd of bighorn sheep could persuade them to work.

For the hundredth time in the last few days, Honesty fought the urge to weep. How was she ever going to keep up the pretense of knowing where to find Deuce? Already, Robert's impatience was beginning to reveal itself. If a miracle didn't happen pretty darn quick, she was going to find herself in a deep pot of hot water.

"Howdy, fellas; we meet again," came a diabolical drawl from high above.

Robert and Roscoe froze. Honesty's gaze snapped upward.

Her mouth fell open and her heart gave a traitorous leap at the figure sitting high on a branch of an old oak tree, swinging his legs, appearing for all the world like a man taking innocent pleasure in a midsummer day.

"Jesse?"

One tawny brow winged upward. "Expecting someone else?"

Honesty could only shake her head in disbelief. She hadn't been expecting anyone, least of all *him*!

Then a curse from Robert singed her ears, and her heart stopped as Roscoe reached for his gun. Before it cleared the holster, Jesse flipped backward on the branch with breathtaking agility and hung suspended by his hands as he laid a mighty kick to Roscoe's face.

Roscoe dropped the gun with a cry and grabbed his nose; the gun went off, a wild shot that made the horses bolt, save Gemini. With a twist of his body and another swing from the branches, Jesse clubbed a charging Robert in the chest, then dropped to the ground between the downed men. "What are you waiting for, Honesty? Get the hell out of here!"

"I can't just leave you!"

"I'll catch up. Now, *go*!" And before she could object further, he smacked his horse on the rump and sent him into a flying gallop.

Wind tore at Honesty's hair and stole the breath from her lungs as she tried to bring the animal under control, but even away from his master, Gemini refused to obey. His muscles bunched and flexed with every powerful stride, and Honesty, bouncing in the saddle, held onto his mane for dear life.

Several miles later, she finally managed to bring Gemini to a halt. Her limbs shook so badly that she could barely hold herself upright in the saddle and her breaths came in harsh gasps. Honesty kept her gaze trained on the horizon and wavered between waiting for Jesse and going back for him. What if he *died* trying to save her? What if Robert shot him, just as he'd shot her father? Could she ever live with herself if she didn't at least try to help him?

Just as she grabbed the reins, she spotted him in the distance trotting toward her on Bag-o'-Bones, unharmed except for a trickle of blood near his eye.

Honesty slid off the horse, her knees so weak with relief that they nearly buckled, and stared at him in wonder as he closed the distance between them. His body bounced in time to the mule's quick gait, his hair had come loose from its ponytail and hung about his shoulders in reckless disarray, whiskers once again covered the lower half of his face, and the soiled, rumpled state of his shirt implied that he hadn't changed clothes in days.

And still he was the most beautiful sight she'd seen in her life.

As he stared back at her, making her keenly

aware of her own less than pleasing appearance, Honesty couldn't decide whether to hug him or run from him.

The fierce glitter in his eyes and forbidding set of his mouth warned her against doing either.

And so she waited where she stood, a sense of foreboding stealing into her bloodstream.

"What the hell did you think you were doing?" he ground out when he reached her. "Didn't I warn you about wandering around alone?"

She didn't make the mistake of acting as if she didn't know that he meant her flight from Last Hope. "I wasn't *wandering*, I was leaving. They ambushed me outside the Scarlet Rose. Are you all right?" She lifted her hand, wanting to erase the blood dribbling from the gash at the corner of his eye.

"You're lucky you're alive to tell the tale," he said, rearing back from her concern. "Mount up."

"Where are we going?"

"I'm taking you back to Rose's."

She shook her head. "I'm not going back."

Jesse stared at her for an interminable moment, then slid out of the mule's saddle. Two long strides brought him to her side, and he wrapped his fingers around her arm in a firm grip. "Now is not the time to argue with me,

Honesty. I've been to hell and back looking for you, and I'm in no mood to take any guff. You're going back to Rose's, and that's final."

Honesty dug in her heels. "I'm *not* going back. I was only working there to make traveling money, and now that I've got it, I'm going to look for the—my brother," she amended quickly.

The blunder earned her a searching study from Jesse. Honesty tossed a tangled lock of hair over her shoulder and lifted her chin in silent daring. If he planned on taking her back, he'd do so with her kicking and screaming the entire way.

Then his hand fell unexpectedly away. "Fine. If you're so damned determined to go after that brother of yours, let's go."

"Thanks, but no thanks. I don't need you. I can protect myself."

"Oh, that's right. Two men steal you away with God-only-knows what intentions, but of course you were perfectly safe. My mistake."

Honesty's eyes narrowed as he turned toward his horse. "Is this a trick?"

"It's no trick. We're both headed in the same direction anyway, so we might as well ride together—at least to the Texas border. If we find your brother before then, great. If we don't, then we'll find you another escort and you can go your way and I'll go mine."

Yesterday she'd have been overjoyed at the prospect of having Jesse along. But that was before she'd overheard his conversation with the Treat brothers. "Why the sudden change of heart, Jesse? Three days ago I asked you for your help and you couldn't be budged with a pick-ax. In fact, your exact words were, 'I already have a job.' So why the sudden insistence on being my protector now?"

He stared long and hard at her, making her feel somehow ashamed for asking, as if she'd ventured into forbidden territory.

"Because maybe if I'd agreed in the first place, you wouldn't have suffered at their hands today."

Her mouth went slack. Jesse? A guilty conscience? Why on earth should he feel to blame for Robert and Roscoe stealing her away? Unless . . . "What are you, an outlaw?"

"Where did you get that notion?"

She could hardly tell him that no one with an ounce of respectability had anything to do with men like the Treat brothers. "Well, you're not a miner, and you're certainly no cowboy. It seems a logical assumption about a man who professes to gamble when it suits his purposes."

"Do us both a favor; don't try getting logical." After swinging fluidly onto Gemini's back, he turned to face her. "So what's it going to be, darlin'? Do you want my help or don't you?"

"Not particularly."

"Fine. Don't say I didn't offer." He turned his horse away.

And Honesty suddenly panicked.

She hadn't a doubt that he'd leave her to suffer whatever miseries fate decided to throw at her. Going on her own would not only leave her at the mercy of every scoundrel in the Rocky Mountains, but vulnerable to Robert and Roscoe. Accepting Jesse's help would put her at the mercy of a shameless and totally unpredictable drifter.

Of the two, Jesse seemed the lesser of two evils. She couldn't trust him any more than the next person, but she could not dispute the need for protection. Deuce was dead, men like Roscoe and Robert—and possibly even Jesse himself—were focusing on her in their hunt for her father's "hidden million," and there wasn't a soul on earth she could turn to or trust with her secret. And Jesse had saved her . . .

"All right!" she called out to his departing form. "You can ride with me—but just until we reach the Texas border."

She should be safe with him until then. Provided he never learned the truth about her relationship to Deuce.

* * *

The first order of business, Jesse decided, was
to trade that bow-backed waste of skin and
bones Honesty rode for a decent mount. He
didn't dare push Gemini faster than a leisurely
walk for fear of losing Honesty, who lagged behind on a mule that knew nothing of the term
canter and seemed to care even less. If they'd
made ten miles today, Jesse would count them
lucky.

Honesty didn't appear bothered by the plod-
ding pace, though. She looked around her in
avid interest, soaking in the sights as if she'd
never before seen the steep granite walls of the
Royal Gorge or the rushing waters of the
Arkansas River. She insisted, too, on stopping
near the base of every waterfall they came
across as if they had all the time in the world.
While Jesse couldn't deny the falls cascading
down hundreds and thousands of feet of sheer
rock were spectacular, the turtle's pace frayed
his temper.

"Can't you make that animal go any faster?"
he finally snapped during a long stretch of trail.

"Not unless we hit a downward slope. Bag-
o'-Bones was not created for speed."

No kidding. He'd learned that during the
two days it had taken him to track down the
dim-witted duo.

"Do you think they're following us?" Honesty asked, as if reading his thoughts.

A picture of the pair he'd left tied to a tree brought a derisive smile to his face. "I doubt they'll be in any position to follow anyone for a long while."

She fell silent for another moment, then said, "I don't think I ever thanked you for coming after me."

"Don't flatter yourself. I was after my horse."

A heartbeat passed before he heard a solemn, "I see."

Jesse waited for her to come back with some shrewish complaint. Most women did. Hell, Miranda had been an expert at laying guilt on him to distract him from her own.

But Honesty didn't complain. In fact, she didn't say much of anything for the rest of the day. Jesse should have been grateful; he didn't often have a traveling companion, and it felt odd enough having her along as it was.

Except, with nothing but the gentle breath of the wind or the rush of the Arkansas River or an occasional hawk's cry to break the quiet, Jesse found himself regretting his careless remark and longing for conversation. Something more than the silence that had been his mate for longer than he cared to remember.

He glanced over his shoulder to make sure

she was still there. It seemed almost impossible to believe that the woman riding a horse-length behind him was the same woman who'd sashayed about the stage in pink roses a few days before, crooning to a roomful of hungry men. The same woman who'd cooly descended a staircase wearing a sizzling red dress. The same woman who turned him inside out with sultry eyes and a winsome smile.

Now those eyes were glazed with fatigue and her smile seemed to have been left behind in the abandoned mining town.

Jesse faced forward and frowned. She'd had a harrowing few days of it, and though she tried to hide it, it showed not only in the tired lines of her sunburned face, but in her sagging posture. They'd have to make camp soon; she'd not last much longer.

Once again he damned the sense of honor that had not only possessed him to go after her, but compelled him to travel with her as her guard. One of the traits that had gotten him into the agency and made him a top operative was his dogged focus on any case he'd been assigned. Yet here he was, traipsing across the country with trouble in the flesh after a man he wasn't even sure existed.

Yet he couldn't help but feel responsible for her. The Treat brothers had wanted something, and if they had the slightest inkling who he was, that something had very likely been a way to get to him.

Well, he'd get her as far as Texas; that should keep her out of the Treats' reach. If they didn't find her brother before then, he had a couple of trusted connections across the border who would see her safely to Galveston.

They left behind the mountains of green velvet, and before them lay mile upon mile of prairie land, as golden and rippling as an angel's hair. Aspen, oak, and cottonwoods lined a calm stretch of the river, and a pair of mule deer loitered near the timberline.

Jesse pushed forward, knowing that they needed to find shelter someplace less open. An hour before dark, he spotted a narrow stream lined with trees.

"We'll make camp up ahead."

"Already?" Honesty cried in astonishment. "It's not even dark yet!"

"It will be soon. Besides, the animals need to rest, and I'm hungry."

Now that Jesse mentioned it, Honesty realized her stomach felt a bit pinched, too. Still, now that she was actually on her way, she was in no hurry to stop. And there was the little matter of sleeping under the aspen boughs with Jesse. This was the first time she'd been truly alone with him since the night they'd spent together. Always before, she'd known that help was only a holler away if she needed. There was no one about now—just a few crows roosting in the branches, and they'd hardly offer any protection should Jesse get it in his head to take advantage of their isolation. Though he wasn't a huge man, he possessed a wiry power to be reckoned with, and she wasn't sure she had the strength to fend him off.

It gave her small comfort to see his stiff dismount. Then he rolled his arm in its socket, and a sliver of sympathy cut through her anxiety. "Is your shoulder paining you?"

"Sometimes the weather stiffens it up." He shrugged off her concern and flipped his saddlebags over one shoulder. "Did you pack any food in that bag?"

Food? "Uhm, I think I have a few biscuits left."

His drawn out sigh made her realize how ill equipped she was for this venture. She'd left with little more than a few changes of clothing and her money jar. "I wasn't expecting to feed an army on this trip, Mr. Jones. I brought just enough to tide me over until I reached Canon City."

"We aren't going to Canon City."

Honesty paused in mid-dismount. "Not going to—but it's on the map!"

He turned and pinned her with a narrow-eyed look. "What map?"

Oh, blast it! She'd never meant for him to learn of the map she'd coaxed a peddler into drawing soon after Deuce's death, for that might lead to more questions. Now that she'd let its existence out of the bag, she couldn't very well hide it. "The one I got off a troupe of actors," she improvised, then reached into her skirt pocket for the folded slip of paper. "They said they saw George with another troupe headed for Galveston."

"What are all these stars?" he asked, pointing to the marks that indicated Canon City, Rocky Ford, and the old Dripping Gold Mine.

"Their stopping points."

Jesse raised his gaze and studied her face with an intensity that made Honesty squirm. "Who else knows about this map?"

"Only the man I got it from."

Then he gave her a grim smile. "Sorry to disappoint you, darlin', but we aren't going to any of these places. In fact, we're going to avoid towns altogether for a while. We'll head south, then hitch up with the first train into New Mexico."

"But how am I supposed to find my brother if you plan on avoiding the places he might be?"

"The train will take us to Trinidad. If his troupe was there, we'll hear about it, and cut over into Texas. If he hasn't shown up yet, we'll hole up there till he does."

Honesty seethed. "I don't recall agreeing that you would be the one to call the shots. If you expect me to pay for your protection, then you'd best take me where I want to go."

"Fine. As long as it isn't Canon City."

She resisted the childish impulse to stomp her foot. "What do you have against Canon City?"

"It's the second place they'll look."

Honesty felt the blood drain from her face. She didn't need to ask who "they" were. "What's the first?"

"Last Hope."

Oh, God, she'd known he'd say that.

A sudden horrifying thought occurred. "Do you think they'll hurt Rose?"

"She's a tough lady. She can take care of herself."

The implication that Honesty couldn't made her bristle.

"I'm going to see if I can scare up a few trout. Go ahead and set up camp if you think you can manage it, and while you're at it, try to get a fire started. Keep this with you just in case." He tossed her the Colt from his holster. "Don't shoot yourself."

As he walked away, she curled her lip and mimicked, "Don't shoot yourself." *Arrogant ass.* She'd pitched so many camps and started so many fires, she could do it blindfolded. Just because she hadn't expected to be accosted by a pair of murdering fortune-seekers, and hadn't packed enough food to feed a blasted army, didn't mean she was completely incompetent.

And, by God, she'd prove it.

Chapter 10

Jesse stared grimly into the ripples in the stream, his thoughts on Honesty and that map she'd produced. The marked route closely resembled the trail he'd set for himself, stretching from Colorado through New Mexico and across Texas to the coast.

She said she'd gotten it from a troupe of actors. It was a logical explanation, considering George Mallory was a traveling thespian, and one he might have bought hook, line, and sinker if his nose wasn't itching up a storm. Honesty was lying, and for the life of him, he couldn't figure out why. What was she hiding from him?

He'd bet his boots it had something to do with George Mallory. Damn, but he wished he could remember where he'd heard that name before. In Denver? Leadville? Down in Durango? No, for some reason, he felt it hadn't been in recent months.

Well, maybe someone at the agency could shed a little light on the mystery. It had been weeks since he'd sent in his last report to McParland, so as soon as it was safe to slip into a town, he'd wire him an update on the McGuire case and tack on an inquiry about Honesty's brother.

In the meantime, Honesty was like a child's puzzle with too many pieces missing, and the pieces he did have just didn't fit. The harder he tried to make it happen, the more it fueled his appetite for answers.

Forty-five minutes and two scaled trout later, Jesse headed back to camp. He found Honesty sitting on the ground in front of a pile of dried logs, a saddle blanket around her shoulders to ward off the chill.

"Why didn't you start the fire?" he asked.

She glared at him over her shoulder. "You didn't leave me any matches."

Jesse's shoulders slumped. Jesus, this was going to be a long trip. He reached into his pocket with a sigh, dug out a small tinderbox, and tossed it to her.

She caught it one-handed. "Nice box. Where'd you get it?"

"My mother gave it to me last Christmas."

"You have a mother?"

"Of course I have a mother! Did you think I sprouted from the ground?"

"I don't guess I thought much about it at all. I just never pictured you as a man with ties."

She was right on that mark. Few agents he knew had ties with anyone.

"Well, I do. My mother used to sing. You sound a lot like her."

"Why did she stop?"

He paused for a moment to choose his words. "Reckon she couldn't hear the music anymore."

Honesty studied him closely, and Jesse turned away lest she see more than he wanted her to and start asking more questions.

It wasn't until she turned the tin box over that Jesse remembered the symbol etched into the bottom. He lunged forward and swiped the tinderbox from her grasp before she could see it.

Honesty gasped and cast him a startled look. "What did you do that for? I was just trying to figure out how it opened!"

"The catch sticks sometimes," he answered shortly. He made a show of popping the clasp, then presented her with the flintstone and steel stick inside, making sure to cup the bottom of the container in his hand.

Honesty took the items with a disgusted

shake of her head, then struck the flint and the steel against each other. After several unsuccessful tries, she handed the items back to Jesse with a grimace. He bit the inside of his cheek to keep from grinning.

"Your mother," she said, sitting back on her heels to watch while he took over the chore. "Where is she now?"

"Probably still raising hell in Montana with my grandmother." Sparks flashed from the tinder as Jesse struck the flint against the rock. "Last I heard, they'd joined up with a bunch of women lobbying for their right to vote. If I know my mother, she'll be leading the pack."

"I never knew my mother."

"Did she die?"

"When I was very young. My father never talked about her. I think it was too painful."

Holding the tangled strands of her hair out of the way, Honesty leaned forward and blew gently on a mound of dried grasses, fanning not only the glowing embers, but a banked memory of those pursed lips beneath his, and her soft, willing participation. His stomach twisted into a tight knot and as the tinder burst into a tiny flame, Jesse became painfully aware that unless he was careful, the same thing would happen to him.

He tore himself from the spell Honesty was winding around him, whether by accident or design, and strode toward his saddlebags to fetch a frying pan. If he hadn't already agreed to escort Honesty to the Texas border, he'd have kept right on walking.

When he turned around, he found Honesty waiting with her hand outstretched toward him.

"What?"

"The pan," she said. "You caught the fish; I'll cook them."

Jesse laughed and shook his head.

"Look, I might not have gotten the fire started, but I think I can manage to fry a couple of fish."

A few minutes later, much to his surprise, she presented him with a plate of trout cooked so tender that it melted in his mouth. He finished off his share quickly, then closed his eyes in bliss. "That was the first decent meal I've had since leaving Last Hope."

"See? I'm not completely helpless."

"I never said you were."

"You didn't have to."

A sliver of guilt once again crept into his conscience. Had he really been that hard on her? Recalling his behavior since her escape from the Treat brothers, Jesse realized she'd taken more off him than she deserved. What kind of man yelled at a woman, drove her past her endurance, then treated her like an imbecile after an ordeal such as the one she'd endured?

"Look Honesty, I know you've had a rough few days of it, and I probably haven't made it any easier—"

A soft snort told him he'd get no argument from her there.

"—but we'll find your brother."

"Soon, I hope."

No sooner than he did.

Jesse leaned back and patted his pocket for a cigarette. After lighting it with a twig, he leaned back against his saddle and rested his hand on an upraised knee. "Have you given any thought to what you'll do when we find him?"

She lifted her head.

"He's a traveling actor, right?" he asked. "Do you plan on traveling with him?"

The question caught her noticeably off-guard. "I guess I never gave it much thought. I suppose I'll decide that when I find him."

If they found him, Jesse thought, but kept it to himself.

"It must have been tough losing your father."

She shoved a bit of flaky trout into her mouth. Eating was never a function Jesse considered evocative, but by God, that was before he'd seen Honesty do it. She took delicate bites, pushing each morsel partway into her mouth, drawing the rest in with her tongue, then licking her fingers. One long, slender finger at a time. Then she'd repeat the process.

Oh, damn.

He shook his head and crossed his legs at the ankles to conceal the growing bulge between his thighs. "How did he die again?"

"He was shot."

"I thought he caught a disease."

Her fingers stilled on the last bite of trout and her gaze snapped to his. "Who told you that?"

"Rose. She said you went to work in the mining camps after you lost your family to diphtheria."

She glanced away and wiped her hands on her pant legs. "You probably misunderstood. Are you finished with that plate?"

There she went again, trying to veer away from the subject. "What part did I misunderstand? You working in the mining camps, or the way your father died?"

"Since when is my personal life any of your business?" she snapped. "Do you hear me flinging questions at you left and right? Do you hear me prying into your affairs? No, you don't. So unless you're willing to spill all your little secrets, don't go drilling for mine."

She got to her feet and strode down to the stream. Jesse watched her, fighting an insane urge to go after her and apologize. Why, he couldn't figure. She'd done nothing but turn his life upside down since the day he'd met her. If anyone needed to apologize, it was her. She was the one dragging him into her problems, keeping secrets, delaying his own mission.

Even if he did owe her an apology, he wasn't sure he could find the words. Apologies had never come very easily to him—maybe because he'd spent so many years turning off his conscience to get the job done, that he found it hard to believe he had a remorseful bone left in his body.

She was right, though. He'd agreed to be her protector, not her interrogator, and he had no right digging up her secrets unless he was willing to make her privy to his. The day he'd been carried out of that old coal mine on a corpse's cot and discovered Miranda had sold him out, he'd sworn never to make himself that vulnerable again.

So why did he feel as if he was in the wrong?

It must have been about three o'clock in the morning when his dozing senses came wide awake. He thought he'd heard a sound, but it was quiet as a lullaby, with only an occasional cricket's chirp and the lonesome babble of the stream. Nothing out of the ordinary, nothing he wasn't used to.

Just the same old quiet he'd dealt with every day of every year since he'd been seventeen.

There wasn't a part of the night he didn't call friend. Often he'd felt as if he were the only one in the world.

Except tonight he had company.

His head angled toward Honesty's still form across the fire. He couldn't see her clearly, with the night wrapped around her as tightly as the woolen blanket around her shoulders. But he was aware of her. Her scent. Her shape. Even her heartbeat.

He looked up through a tunnel of branches to the diamond-speckled sky. Was she the reason for his waking up at such an ungodly hour? It was possible. It felt strange, having someone share his blanket of stars. Strange in a disturbing, comforting kind of way.

Hell.

He rolled onto his side and closed his eyes. *Just go to sleep, Justiss.* This regrettable little venture was complicated enough without him letting his thoughts drift down a road he hadn't traveled in years.

Again the sound came, the barest of whispers, a muffled whimper. Jesse's eyes snapped open and he strained to listen. Was she crying? Dreaming?

With an impatient sigh, he flipped off the blanket and rolled to his feet. Three steps around the fire pit brought him to her side. The embers cast a red glow against her creamy cheek and turned the golden brown strands of hair around her face an auburn hue.

Again, she shivered. Jesse frowned. It was colder than a well-digger's ass out here, and all she'd brought to cover up with was a woolen blanket that had more holes in it than a gold panner's sieve.

"Honesty . . . are you all right?"

No answer.

The gentlemanly thing to do would be to give up his own blanket. But he was no gentleman, and she'd proved herself no lady. It wasn't as if she had a reputation to compromise, he told himself as he slid in next to her and settled his own blanket over both of them. Besides, a romp on the frozen ground wasn't his idea of a good time.

He'd just warm her up and stop her teeth from chattering. Otherwise he'd never get any sleep.

His decision justified, Jesse laid his head on his left arm, his right arm resting in the dent of her waist.

Damn, she smelled nice. And she felt like heaven. He'd forgotten how good it felt to hold a woman. Not just in the heat of passion, but to lie with her curves tucked snug against him. He tightened his hold around her, and she curled up against him with a sigh.

Jesse closed his eyes and swallowed a groan.

Determined not to do anything but hold her, no matter how good she felt, or how good she smelled, or how hard he got, he lay with his eyes shut and his hands idle.

Then she rolled over against his chest. Moon kissed the delicate angles of her face, and her lashes lay in innocent repose on her cheekbones.

His lungs quit working. His nerves stretched tight. He only meant to smell her hair, but somehow his lips had other ideas and pressed against her temple . . . then her cheek, where it met her ear lobe. Then another to the curve of her jaw. And somehow his hand wound up on her hip, his fingers curving into the soft flesh of her bottom. The heat he'd tried to keep banked burst into flame when he pulled her closer, and her mound touched the ridge of his erection.

A little voice inside his head warned him that he was dancing with a lightning bolt, but his body didn't care. He moved slightly away, then pulled closer in a primal rhythm. The heat built, as did the pressure in his loins. His clothes started to shrink on his skin. The blanket he'd thrown on top of them felt like lead. He wanted to see her wearing nothing but the moonlight, to touch her with nothing between them but passion.

As the fire burned hotter, his mouth grew bolder, seeking the smooth column of her neck, and his hands broadened their exploration, moving around to cup her backside, pulling her flush against him.

And Honesty pressed herself closer to the warmth against her front, snuggled deeper into the hardness beneath her cheek, aware only of an unbearable need to absorb into herself the glorious scents of fire smoke, old leather, and man.

She tensed suddenly. Her eyes popped open. Man?

She reared back. "Jesse?"

"Expecting someone else?" he countered in a strangled voice.

"What do you think you're doing?"

"What does it feel like I'm doing?" His hand skimmed down the outer slope of her thigh, then up again. "Your teeth were chattering loud enough to shake the leaves loose. I'm just warming you up."

She smacked at his hand and scooted out of his reach. "I don't recall inviting you to touch me."

Even in the darkness, she recognized the glaze of desire in his eyes. Good Lord, how long had he been pawing at her? How long had she been *letting* him?

"I didn't realize I needed an invitation."

Outrage at his gall and irritation at herself roiled in her middle. "I knew this would happen."

"What?"

"That just because I'm here, you'd think I was yours for the taking. And sure enough, the minute I turn my back, you're all over me."

His dumbfounded expression gave way to one of bruised male pride. "You weren't so prudish the first time I touched you."

Why did he have to bring up that night? She'd only just gotten the memory of it out of her head.

Almost.

She clasped her collar to her throat and tipped her chin. "That was different."

"What's so different about it? I want you. You want me. Just name your price."

Her cheeks flamed with outrage. "The difference *is*, I don't work for Rose anymore. I won't be a body to use for your own pleasures, no matter how much you offer, because I'm not for sale. Not for you, not for anyone, and not for any price."

As she rolled onto her side and clutched her blanket close to her breast, she refused to consider that only yesterday, she'd been willing to trade her virginity for his help.

Darn. She was cold. She was tired. She was scared.

And she was much too aware of the man lying a short distance away. Part of her wanted to punish him for taking such liberties while she'd been asleep, for awakening sensations inside her no man had roused before. Yet another part wanted to demand he do so again. And still another part of her wanted to run as far away from him as she could get.

She squeezed her eyes shut against the tears burning at the back. She'd gotten herself caught between the devil and the deep blue sea, Deuce would say, and left herself open to more trouble than she could handle.

It was time she admitted that she'd made a big mistake.

And find some way to get rid of him.

"Get up, Honesty. It's time to hit the trail."

Honesty's eyes cracked open, blinked at the blackness, then shut again. "Go away. It's not even light out yet."

"It will be by the time you're dressed. I'd like to hit New Mexico sometime before the new year, so you'd best get up, or I'm leaving without you."

She rolled onto her stomach and crunched her carpetbag beneath her head. She felt as if she'd just gotten to sleep, and even if she wanted it to, she doubted her body would obey any order to rise. "Go ahead. I'll catch up."

"Suit yourself."

At the recess of her mind, Honesty heard footsteps, a rustling, a creak of leather . . .

Then all went quiet.

Too quiet.

Her sense froze and Honesty snapped upright, frantically searching the area.

"Lookin' for me?"

She whipped around and spotted Jesse leaning against his horse, his elbow propped on the saddle. But it was the smug grin on his face that set off sparks of outrage. "You . . . you . . . scoundrel! Don't ever do that to me again. Your job is to protect me."

The grin slowly disappeared from his face and his eyes turned to the color of slate. "Then you'd best learn to drag your lazy fanny out of that bedroll before noon. I realize it's quite a stretch from your normal routine, but make no mistake: if you can't be up and ready to ride by dawn, I will leave you behind."

She tossed her tangled hair over her shoulder. "Then I'll fire you."

He laughed a humorless grunt. "If only I could get so lucky."

She glared at his back as he strode toward his horse.

He'd been in a foul mood for two days now, and she wasn't so innocent that she couldn't discern the cause. One of the things she'd learned of men was that sexual gratification— or frustration, in Jesse's case—played a large part in their mood. "Can I expect this tantrum of yours to wear itself out, or do you plan on being an ass till the day we part?"

"If you're not happy with the rules I set, then find another patsy."

"Maybe I will."

His snort told her what he thought of her chances in that arena. Worse, he was right. If there had been anyone else, she certainly wouldn't have chosen *him*.

After dressing, Honesty made her way to the edge of the creek she and Jesse had decided to camp by. The rising sun sent a shimmering reflection across the surface of the water. Honesty knelt at the bank, and just as she went to dip her hands, blinding speckles across the creek captured her notice. Brows drawing together in curiosity, she shielded her eyes and peered closely at the natural fall of rocks a few feet upstream on the opposite bank. They looked as if they'd been welded together, and formed a dripping shelf over, then into, the water's edge.

Suddenly Honesty's mouth went slack. Her breath caught in her throat. Her veins hummed with excitement.

The truth is hidden in the flowing stones.

Could this be it? Could she actually have found Deuce's hiding spot? For nearly three months she'd explored every gold vein and waterfall she'd come across with no success, and the few streams and creeks she'd traveled had held no better results.

But what if this one *was* different? What if her hunt ended right here, right now?

She cast a glance over her shoulder and spotted Jesse kicking dirt over the fire pit. He'd be mad as a hornet that she was taking so long, but she couldn't let this possibility go by without at least *trying*.

Quickly unbuttoning her shoes and rolling down her stockings, Honesty scrambled to her feet. She gasped in shock as the current tumbled around her ankles. Cold cut through her skirts and into her skin, to the bone.

Knowing that she didn't have much time before Jesse came looking for her, she forged on. Only twenty-five feet of shallow but frigid water separated her from the opposite bank. If the truth that Deuce spoke of was found beneath the glitter, she could call off the search and send Mr. Do-Things-My-Way-or-Else on his merry way.

The pebbled stream bottom gave way to sandy loam that sucked at Honesty's feet as she closed in on the granite rim. Her legs were numb and burning from cold from knee to toe. The glitter she'd seen from the other side had dimmed; still, she couldn't turn back until she'd explored the pitted banks. She ran shivering fingertips along the formation, searching for any clue to the puzzle Deuce had left her to figure out. If only she knew what she was looking for! A message carved into the rock? An object? A container?

Soon the hum of excitement gave way to leaden disappointment. Honesty whimpered and gave the shelf a final inspection before finally accepting that there was nothing hidden here. It was just a bunch of stupid rocks.

Shoulders slumped, Honesty fought back tears of anger and frustration. She should be used to disappointment by now, but for a moment, she wondered if she shouldn't just give up the search.

No, she thought, pushing the notion away as soon as it formed. Feeling sorry for herself would not accomplish anything. Even if it took the entire journey to Galveston, she'd find the flowing stones. Difficult or not, it was all she had left.

But as she twisted around and started for the opposite bank, she discovered her feet wouldn't obey the command her brain had given them. The harder she tried to pull herself free, the deeper she seemed to become entrenched. But it wasn't until she started sinking that confusion gave way to climbing terror.

"Oh, my God . . . Jesse! *Je-sseeeee!*"

Chapter 11

His name echoed in a cry of such terror that Jesse's blood ran cold and his entire body went rigid. He threw down the bedroll he'd been about to strap to her mule and tore off across the camp site, scattering ashes and charred wood in his wake. "Honesty, where are you?"

"Help me, please!"

Racing in the direction of her voice, Jesse fought the tangle of knee high grasses separating himself from the creek where he'd last seen her. Had she run into one of the wildcats that sometimes came down out of the mountains? Had the Treat brothers found her? Possibilities spun through Jesse's mind in bone-chilling succession. Damn it, he never should have pitched camp in such an exposed area!

He reached the bank and frantically searched the place. A strip of a creek cut a winding swath through rocky banks sparsely lined with cottonwood and brush. Catching sight of Honesty standing still in water up to her breasts, Jesse's whispered, "Oh, sweet Mary . . ." Even from twenty yards away, the terror was visible in her wide eyes.

Wasting not a second more, Jesse jumped into water up to his waist, oblivious of the frigid temperature as he forded his way to Honesty. A strong current in the middle of the creek slowed his progress, muck sucked at his boots, and the pressure in his chest built so he could hardly breathe. Yet on he forged.

"Please hurry," she called feebly. "I'm sinking."

"Just don't move." Trying to discern where the quicksand formed, Jesse avoided the calmest waters and the widening circle of murkiness that indicated danger, and waded upstream, before cutting to the opposite bank.

He reached the other side and heaved himself up over the grassy edge, onto dry ground. His boots pumped water as he loped the rest of the distance to where Honesty waited.

She stood five feet from the bank, just out of reach, eyes wide with terror.

"Don't let me die."

"I won't." Surrendering her to the quicksand

would deprive him of the pleasure of killing her himself when he got her out of there. "Stay still," he commanded, frantically searching the area for dead fall. "As long as you don't struggle, you won't sink." Damn—there was nothing he could use.

His gun belt!

Cursing himself for taking so long to think of it, Jesse tossed the sodden Colt out of his holster and fumbled with the buckle. Once he had it free, he dropped onto the bank as close to the water's edge as he could get without slipping in. "Now listen close, Honesty." Her blue lips and glazed eyes worried him. He feared her system had either gone into shock or wasn't far from it. "Are you listening?"

She finally nodded.

"I'm going to toss the belt out to you. Grab hold of it tight, then lift your arms over your head, lie flat on your back, and relax as much as possible."

"But I'll drown!"

"No, you'll float. Quicksand will hold you up better than water. You're going to have to trust me."

She finally nodded, and he threw her one end of the belt. She caught it, then let herself fall back into the water. Her legs bent at an awkward angle and the water rose up to lap against her cheeks, but as Jesse had told her, she didn't sink.

"Now hold on tight," he said. "I'm going to pull you out. While I'm pulling, I want you to free your legs, one at a time. As soon as you get one foot loose, let it drag behind you. Whatever you do, don't struggle, and don't let go. Understand?"

When she nodded again, Jesse sat on the ground with his feet braced against the earth. The belt went taut, and her arms nearly came out of their sockets as he dragged her toward him inch by agonizing inch.

Hours seem to pass before her hands finally came within reach. Jesse wrapped his fist around her fingers, then her wrists, then finally curled his hands beneath her arms and pulled her up the muddy bank, onto dry ground. Honesty climbed across the front of his body in a mass of sodden skirts and grasping hands and seized his neck in both arms. Jesse fell back, his breath coming in heavy gasps, and closed his arms around her shuddering frame. How much was due to fear and how much to cold was hard to say.

Until this moment, he hadn't realized how small and fragile she really was. Like a child afraid of the dark, she held him as tightly as if she wanted to crawl into his skin. A fierce tenderness welled up inside him, so strong and powerful that his throat swelled shut. If she hadn't called for him, if he hadn't found her in time . . .

No, he wouldn't think of that. Not while his emotions lay so close to the surface.

At last, her shuddering abated. Jess pressed his mouth to her temple, then whispered, "Let's get you back to camp." Still holding her, Jesse awkwardly rolled to a stand, then with a supporting arm around her waist, led her upstream.

She tensed the instant he started into the water. "No! I don't want to go back in there."

"There's no other way to reach the horses, Honesty."

Her head shook frantically back and forth; her nails bit through his shirt into his skin. "I can't."

"Yes, you can. I've got you, darlin'. Just hold onto my neck and don't let go."

When she turned those wide, rich brown eyes on him, and he saw the soul-deep fear, his heart melted. "Do you trust me, Honesty?"

She swallowed, then finally bobbed her head.

Jesse brushed his damp fingers along her cheek and smiled. He wasn't sure if she really trusted him or if she was just putting up a brave front, but the girl had guts, he'd give her that.

When they finally reached the campsite, Jesse led her to a rock and helped her sit, then immediately scrounged the area for whatever dead fall they hadn't burned during the night. Soon he had a mound of tinder piled atop the charred wood and fresh logs, and a small fire flickering.

"You'd best get out of those clothes."

She nodded with jerky movements and lifted blue fingers to her blouse. Jesse watched her fumble with the buttons, a strange loss spreading through his chest at her blind obedience, as if the quicksand had sucked all the spirit out of her body.

She managed to pop one button through its hole, then reached for another and whimpered.

Jesse cursed.

He unfolded his body and gently brushed her hands aside. "Let me do that."

Drops of water clung to her lashes. Her ruby lips had turned a deep purple. Each button he unfastened revealed more of her skin; blue veins ran through the creamy flesh he'd admired from the first moment he'd clapped eyes on her. The swells of her breasts became visible, the mounds goose bumped from cold, the nipples tight and hard. Jesse swallowed, and cursed his body's reaction to her nudity. What kind of lecher was he, to get aroused by a woman in her condition? "Did you bring other clothes?" he asked over the roughness in his throat.

"In m-my b-b-bag."

He tore himself away from her and fished

through the worn brocade carpetbag for several moments before releasing a frustrated curse and dumping the contents on the ground. No weapons, no provisions; only a couple extra shirts, skirts, and a set of plain cotton unmentionables. He'd seen tin-horns better prepared for travel. He grabbed a full change of clothes, not caring if they matched, then collected his duster and a shirt from his own bags to dry her off.

After fastening the duster around her cape-fashion, he managed to strip her without once looking at the body that so often haunted his dreams. Another log on the fire sent up a shower of sparks and soon blazed away the chill of the morning. Jesse led her closer to the fire and set her beside it. "Can you dress yourself, or must I do it for you?"

"I think I can manage."

Her teeth weren't chattering as badly, at least. Her lips had begun to regain their normal color, and her voice sounded calmer, too. She still shivered, but even that seemed to be abating. Once she got into the dry clothes, Jesse felt sure she'd make a full recovery.

He wished he was that sure about himself.

He grabbed the coffee pot from his packs and strode to the stream. There he dropped to one knee and bowed his head, barely aware of plunging his hand in the water. His own limbs started trembling uncontrollably. With rage. With relief. If he hadn't heard her hollering his name, if he'd gotten there a few minutes later . . .

He ripped his hand from the stream and returned to the campsite, his throat and chest tight with an emotion he could neither identify nor wanted to examine.

Honesty was sitting next to the fire with her hands stretched out to capture the warmth. She gave no sign of noticing as he scooped grounds into the pot and shoved it on a flat rock jutting over the fire. For a long time, she said nothing. Silence stretched tight and dense between them.

"It seems I owe you my life again."

The fear he'd fought so hard to deny manifested itself in fury. "What the *hell* did you think you were doing?"

She flinched. "Trying to get to the other side. I saw something glitter and I wanted to get a better look. I thought I might find gold."

"The only gold you'll find in this stream is fool's gold."

"I realize that now."

Her feeble answer took some of the fire out of his temper. "We'll stay here for the day. Let you rest up—"

"We can't stay! What if the men have picked up our trail?"

Damn, how could he have forgotten? By now, the Treat brothers would have untangled themselves from their trusses. And though they'd be too sore to do much traveling, Honesty did have a point. The wisest recourse was to keep moving. "Are you sure you're ready to travel?"

"As ready as I'll ever be."

La Veta was one of those overnight towns cut into the edge of the mountains to accommodate the rapid expansion of the railway. A mix of native lumber and stone, the buildings rose against a backdrop of lofty pines and scrub-coated hills. Even though it was well into June, patches of snow clung to the sides of the barren hills.

Honesty guided her mule out of the path of an oncoming team of six. She didn't even care that La Veta wasn't on her map. They'd ridden hard to find a place to restock on supplies, trade in the mule, and rest their weary bones. From the looks of the place, they'd have no trouble accomplishing their goals. She couldn't help but compare the town with Last Hope. The place teemed with activity. Rail workers, mostly Orientals with soot-stained faces and dungarees strode with heads down and shoulders stooped. Gentlemen gathered on the corners discussing business, and now and then Honesty spotted a lady leaving a store or strolling down the walk, peering into windows displaying everything from the latest fashions to children's toys.

The sight of them in their tight skirts, coiffed hair, and frilly parasols made her keenly aware of her own state. She hadn't washed her clothes or hair in days, and smelled of dirt, horse, and sweat, and the sun had baked her skin a pale brown.

"We'll get a couple rooms at the hotel yoder," Jesse said, pointing to a two-story brick structure on the corner near the center of town.

Honesty nodded. Since the mishap at the creek Jesse had been withdrawn, speaking only when necessary, and even then he kept the conversation terse and to the point. She couldn't quell the feeling that she'd somehow disappointed him. More, she'd failed herself. Protect herself? Ha. What kind of fool walked blindly into quicksand? If she let herself think about it, she could still feel the sand sucking at her feet, the heart-stopping terror of no escape. If Jesse hadn't come along when he had . . .

Honesty shook away the thought as they reached the hotel. Jesse pulled up in front the porch rail that wrapped around two sides of the structure, and Honesty watched in envy as he swung fluidly out of the saddle. He never appeared affected by the long days in the saddle or the even longer nights of sleeping on the cold, hard ground. She, on the other hand, ached in places she hadn't known could ache.

She braced herself for the strain on her muscles and prepared to swing her leg over the cantle when hands pressed against her waist from behind. Honesty's heart tripped over itself and an instant sizzle of awareness branded itself into her skin. She glanced over her shoulder into the swirling blue-green of Jesse's eyes and saw from the tense set of his jaw that he hadn't been unaffected, either.

Immediately after setting her on her feet, he strode to the hotel entrance. Honesty followed him into the lobby, empty save for a bill-capped youth behind the counter in white shirt and sleeve garters.

A few minutes later, Jesse escorted her up the stairs. His hand at the low of her back sent a funny little thrill up her spine. How she made it to the room without her knees giving way, she hadn't a clue. She clutched the hem of her waist-length jacket while Jesse unlocked and opened the door to a pretty little room papered in white lilies on a burgundy backdrop. Floral lithographs hung on the wall above a chest of drawers. A pair of Queen Anne chairs sat beneath the window, flanking a rounded table topped with a white doily and a prismed oil lamp. White eyelet lace pillows lay against plumper companions dressed in burgundy at the head of the floral spread.

Jesse set her carpetbag near the door, then stepped back with his thumbs hooked into the low-slung gun belt around his hips. "Do you need anything before I go?"

Honesty glanced at him in surprise. "You're leaving?"

"I have a few errands to run. I'll be back before supper."

"What am I supposed to do while you're gone?"

"You might as well relax. I'll see about having a bath brought up."

"A lot of good that will do. I have nothing clean left to wear."

"I'll see what I can do about some clean clothes, too, while I'm out. Do not leave this room, understood?"

Before she could answer, he slipped out the door. A strange emptiness invaded the room, and Honesty fought the impulse to call him back. To beg him not to leave her alone in this strange town, with these strange people. He'd been so distant with her since leaving the creek . . .

What if he didn't come back?

She knew what was happening. She was letting herself get too attached to the scoundrel. Letting her emotions get tangled up, letting her heart get involved. She knew better than to allow that to happen, yet she didn't know how to stop it. Or if she even could stop it.

He was abrasive and overbearing at times, but he was also irresistibly confident, infinitely gentle, and unquestionably exciting. And no matter what, he was *there*.

But for how long?

Jesse would not be with her forever; he'd made that clear from the start. She wasn't sure she even wanted him to be.

She wrapped her arms around her waist and wandered to the window. Shortly he appeared on the boardwalk below, scanned the length of the street in both directions, then propped his Stetson on his head and sauntered toward the depot in that long, loose-limbed stride that always sent her pulse racing.

He'd asked what she would do when she found what she was looking for. In truth, Honesty hadn't allowed herself to ponder her future. But now she wondered if maybe she shouldn't start thinking about what she would do.

There was a time when she'd dreamed of finding a man like her father, who could see past the facade she wore for survival's sake, who could make her heart sing, who could challenge the skills she'd acquired over her colorful lifetime. God, how she wanted someone to believe in, and who believed in her. Someone who would accept her for the woman she was and the woman she wanted to be—a woman of independent thinking, unconventional living, a woman who paved her own destiny.

Was Jesse that kind of man?

Once again she wished she knew what he wanted with her father. How she could ask him without giving away the fact that she not only knew McGuire, but that she was his only living relative? What would he do if he discovered that connection?

What would *she* do if Deuce had indeed stashed a fortune, and Jesse meant to take it? Or what if Deuce had left nothing, and Honesty was wasting all this time chasing after fool's gold?

Oh, she could play this game till the moon turned blue and it wouldn't get her anywhere. Until she found whatever Deuce had left behind, she had no future to plan.

She sighed and started to turn away from the window when a sign at the end of town caught her eye. LA VETA SURVEYOR OFFICE: LAND AND MINE HOLDINGS.

Oh, my gosh. Why hadn't she thought of it before? Didn't surveyors travel all over the area? Wouldn't they know better than anyone if there was a place of the flowing stones? It was a long shot, but if it could narrow down her search . . .

Wasting not another moment debating the issue, Honesty hastened to the bed and dug through her carpetbag for her money jar. Taking only the old map, she rushed to the door, pausing long enough to peek up and down the hallway, just in case Jesse was lurking nearby. After his reaction by the creek, she had no desire to rile his temper again; he might decide that she wasn't worth the trouble and pawn her off on someone else.

But he'd said he wouldn't be back until supper . . .

Honesty stepped into the hall and gave the door a tug shut behind her. She'd only be gone a minute. Jesse would never have to know.

Chapter 12

~~~~~~~~~~~~∞∞~~~~~~~~~~~~

He heard her long before he saw her.

Riding on the rusty notes of an out-of-tune piano came a voice of such seductive familiarity that Jesse would have melted on the spot if he wasn't so furious. Only one woman had a voice of such mesmerizing power.

And only one woman would dare use it as a weapon.

At first, he couldn't believe she'd be so foolish. Then he remembered who he was dealing with.

Fists clenched at his sides, he stormed down the center of Main Street toward the gaudy gold and black building set in the middle of town. Damn her ornery hide. If he had a lick of sense, he'd get on his horse and ride in the opposite direction as fast and as far away as the animal would take him.

Except he knew that a bunch of rowdy rail workers and gold seekers wouldn't settle for just a song from the sweet little liar's lips. As soon as she finished getting them hot and bothered with her saucy smile and sultry eyes, they'd storm her pedestal and make off with her faster than he could say "Eureka."

The closer he got to the combination bordello–dance hall, the clearer it became that his prophecy wasn't far from coming true. Shouts and whistles drowned out the lilting velvet of her voice. Hollow thumping on puncheon boards and raucous encouragement joined the clatter.

Reaching the batwing tongue-and-groove doors, Jesse stood outside on the boardwalk and peered in. There she stood, on a table in the center of the room, tapping one high-ankled shoe and flipping the hem of a drab, faded calico gown that showed the week's worth of travel in the torn hem and sleeve. Yet her bearing suggested she wore the finest Dresden silk. From her mouth spilled bawdy lyrics inviting each and every one of the shoulder-jostling, mouth-gaping, bug-eyed swains to her "parlor." A red haze crept through his bloodstream and blurred his vision. Pure primal reflex had Jesse reaching for his Colt, then cursing. What was he going to do—barge in there and shoot his way to her side? That would be something straight out of one of Ned Buntline's dime novels.

Oh, what the hell.

He drew his weapon and fired into the air.

Instant silence fell over the crowd. Plaster showered down from the ceiling.

"Jesse!"

"Show's over, boys," he announced. "Honesty, let's go."

She stared at him in gape-mouthed wonder, making no move toward him until Jess stretched out his other hand in silent command.

Then she smiled, and the world shrank to the two of them. Jesse's mouth went dry and his chest swelled as she gracefully swung herself off the table and pushed through the throng of men. Her blind obedience had his mind spinning back to a moment in the Scarlet Rose when she'd serenaded him with a ballad wrenching enough to send a pack of wolves retreating into their cups and their tears.

The memory made unexpected longing well up inside him, and he was seized with an urge to grab this woman, tuck her under his heart, and hold on for dear life.

Two steps away from him, a railroad worker the size of a bull stepped into her path. "Whaddya think yer do—"

The barrel of Jesse's Colt pressed between

the man's eyes. "This woman sings for no one but me."

He reached around her self-appointed henchman to grab Honesty's hand and draw her to his side.

"Thank God you came," she whispered.

"I wouldn't be thanking God just yet."

Before she could ponder the meaning behind that remark, he dragged her through the recovering crowd, out the front doors, and down the boardwalk, then up a back alley that sent shivers of déjà vu skittering up her spine. Any moment, she expected Robert to pop out at the end of the alley. She gasped for breath, as much from the crazy pace as from the memory, and tried to keep up with Jesse's long, strong strides.

She barely caught a glimpse of the young bellhop's startled expression as Jesse ushered her through the hotel lobby and up the stairs. It didn't occur to her to call out for help. In truth, Honesty had never felt so honored in her life as when Jesse appeared in that dance hall and demanded her hand in front of God and everyone. No man had ever looked at her with such ownership, and no man, not even Deuce, would have challenged a room full of rowdy men with such unwavering arrogance. For a moment there, Honesty knew what it felt like to belong to someone, and the experience filled her with such profound joy that she couldn't stop grinning like a simpleton.

Until back in her room, the door shut with an ominous click.

Jesse took a forbidding stance at the door, feet spread, arms folded tightly over his chest, bringing corded muscles into stark relief. Honesty's euphoria took a sudden plunge and she found herself trapped between the hard oak wall and six feet of fierce iron will.

"Why is it," he said in an uninflected drawl, "that the instant I turn my back, you take that as an invitation to defy me?"

"Jesse, I can explain."

"I'm sure you'll try."

Honesty licked her lips and wrung her hands. "I was on my way to the surveyor's office—"

"What, more gold seeking?"

"Of course not! I thought one of the clerks might have news of my brother. But as I passed by the saloon, I got stopped by a couple of men who said they'd heard me sing in Denver. I tried to tell them they were mistaken, but they wouldn't listen. The next thing I knew, they were carrying me into the place and standing me on top of the table."

"Now tell me the truth."

"You think I'm lying?"

"I think you're trying to. You're just not doing a very good job."

"Why would I lie?"

"Good question. People don't usually lie unless they're hiding something." In a conversational tone, he asked, "So what was it, Honesty? Did you have an itch that needed scratching? Did you think you'd find yourself a lover for the night?"

Her mouth fell open in shock. "You are vulgar and despicable. Good Lord, Jesse, do you think I *enjoyed* singing for those men?"

"You weren't putting up much of a fight when I saw you."

"That shows how much you know. You have no idea what it's like to stand on display and have men slobbering all over you."

"Seems it would beat the alternative. At least you aren't lying beneath them."

Tears scalded the back of her eyes at the callous remark. Worse, she knew she deserved the low opinion he had of her, because she'd given him that impression to begin with. But really, did she have a choice?

Honesty quickly regrouped and took a step toward him. "Oh, but I'm in control, then." She walked her fingers up his chest, and dropped her lashes and her voice the way she'd often seen Rose do. "You see, a woman has the power to be quick and exciting . . . or slow and torturous."

The satisfaction that bloomed when he

tensed, wilted in the next instant when he cocked his brow and said, "But a man has just as much power. Sometimes more." His blue-green eyes swirled with wicked promise. "You see, a man can also satisfy as well as torment."

A chill broke out along her arms. She swallowed and defiantly lifted her chin. "I've yet to meet that man."

"That's not what you told me back in Last Hope."

He just wouldn't let it drop, would he? "Jesse, Jesse." She shook her head and sighed. "Haven't you figured it out yet?" Honesty screwed her face into an expression of feigned ecstasy. "Ohhh. Mmmm. Yes, touch me there. It feels sooo good."

He paled, and once again, guilt tried working its way into her conscience. Honesty resolutely pushed it aside. He'd deserved everything he'd gotten. More, in fact. Because unlike every other man who had fallen for the ruse, this one had the power to make her want to cast off her own rules of survival. "It's a game, Jesse. I would think that a man of your experience would have recognized that."

His flat gaze remained fixed on her for so long that Honesty began to squirm.

Then he unfolded his arms and took a step toward her. "So you're saying that my touch does nothing for you?"

Honesty stepped back, fearing she'd pushed him too far with her taunting.

"That when I touch you here "—he placed his hand on her rib cage, just below her breast, and smoothed a deliberate path around her waist to her bottom—"you don't feel a thing?"

Against her will, her heartbeat escalated and her breathing quickened. "Not a thing," she denied, as much to herself as to him.

"What about here?" He brought her cold hand to his mouth and pressed moist lips to her palm. "Does that not affect you either?"

The tip of his tongue against the sensitive hollow sent shivers coursing down Honesty's spine. Her mind reeled; her knees went weak. It took all the strength she could summon not to melt at his feet.

"Or when I kiss you like this?"

He slipped his free hand beneath the heavy fall of her hair and curved his fingers around the back of her neck. Even as she watched his head descend, Honesty couldn't find the will to avoid the mouth swooping down on hers in a kiss potent enough to curl her toes. She set both her palms against his chest, intending on pushing him away before she lost complete control of her senses.

Instead, she gripped the edges of his vest and pulled him closer. Their bodies came together, breast to chest, rib to rib, thigh to thigh. Honesty found herself being sucked into a tide pool of sensation and wrapped her arms around Jesse's neck to keep from sinking.

The man was a skilled kisser, she'd give him that. Unlike other men who were either disgustingly sloppy or zealously rough, Jesse knew just where to slide his tongue within her mouth, just how much pressure to apply against her lips— and oh, heavens . . . the most glorious amount of suction on her tongue to draw a response from her.

A moan from deep in his throat penetrated the mist closing over her brain. Honesty stiffened, then broke the kiss and stared at him in breathless, wide-eyed wonder.

"Don't feel a thing, do you?" he asked, his voice an octave lower than normal.

She released her hold on him. "Damn you, Jesse."

"Curse me till the cows come home, sweet Honesty, but your body doesn't lie: you want me; you just don't want to admit it."

She raised her hand, consumed beyond reason to smack the smirk off his face. He caught her wrist in an unrelenting grip, and before she understood what he was doing, he'd wrapped the thong that he used to tie back his hair around her wrist. He tied the other end around his own wrist.

Honesty tried yanking herself free. "What are you doing?"

"Keeping you safe. Our train won't be leaving till mid-morning, and until then, I'm not going to take a chance of you bolting again."

"So you truss me up like a hog to slaughter? Get this thing off me!"

"Not on your life. A very dear and wise friend once told me the best way to keep a wild filly from running was to hobble her."

Frustration made her tear at the thong.

"The more you tear at it, the tighter the knot." With his hand around her elbow, he led her to the bed. "So you might as well get used to it."

"What's the matter, Jesse, is this the only way you can get a woman to stay with you? By chaining her to yourself?"

He gave the thong a pull to tighten the knot around his own wrist and smiled flatly. "No, sometimes I just pay her."

Jesse kept to himself the entire trip to Trinidad. Honesty had the window seat and spent part of it trying to engage him in conversation, and the other part staring out the window. If he wasn't so damned furious with her, he might have admired her ingenuity. He wouldn't have thought to inquire after a missing person at a surveyor's office.

Honesty had, though, and a quick visit while Honesty slept had given him a helluva lead. They'd never heard of George Mallory; they had, however, heard of Deuce McGuire.

Three or four years ago, he'd passed through town in the company of a young woman. It was the first confirmation Jesse had heard of him traveling with someone and it piqued his interest. The clerk could shed no light on her identity, but said she'd appeared to be with him of her own will. They'd spent the night at the hotel, then boarded a northbound train the next morning.

Jesse found himself dwelling on the story, unable to quell the concern that McGuire had repeated his crime. He worried that the girl might have met the same fate as the Jervais heiress.

And if McGuire struck twice, that meant he'd likely strike again.

Jesse had to find him before another child lost her life, and another family came apart at the seams.

Of course, he couldn't do a damn thing until he got Honesty safely settled in her brother's care. Why he felt so responsible for her, he couldn't say, except for that niggling worry that the Treat brothers had somehow sensed his attraction to her and made her pay the price as their revenge on him.

Then again, maybe their reason for taking her had nothing to do with him at all. She was a strikingly beautiful woman, he thought, looking at her profile, with those silky amber curls, mysterious eyes, and sensuous lips. A woman any man would want to possess. Even him. Especially him. He'd been lucky to get a wink of sleep last night, for thinking about it.

"Quit staring at me."

He tore his gaze away from Honesty and snapped open the newspaper he'd found on the seat. Obviously she still hadn't forgiven him for last night, but that was her own fault. She'd put herself in danger. "You look tired. We've got a long trip ahead of us. You might as well get some sleep."

"Gee, I don't think I can. Girls like me aren't used to keeping regular hours."

The remark drew the attention of several passengers sitting nearby. "Keep your voice down."

"Or what, you'll gag me as well?"

"Don't tempt me."

"Jesse, Jesse . . . I'd have thought a man as bright as you could come up with more creative ways to quiet a woman."

The little minx. He turned his attention to the open paper but couldn't make heads nor tails of the articles, and it was her fault. She consumed his every thought. It was more than her beauty, more than her sensuality—it was the damned mystery of her. A puzzle he couldn't solve by seduction or coercion.

Was she in trouble? Running from someone? No, she'd not have stayed so long in Last Hope if that were the case. Running *to* someone? That made more sense. Her brother? There was something off-kilter there. She had a map, a name. But maybe Mallory didn't exist. No, he'd heard the name before. Maybe Mallory wasn't a brother, but a lover . . .

Why couldn't she just trust him? If she would just tell him, he could help her. He had friends. Sources.

Damn, but he wished he could get his mind off the whole mess. It reminded him too much of the old days he wanted to leave behind: that zeal for answers, that unquenchable thirst for solving riddles. The game itself. The more he learned, the more he wanted to know.

And it was driving him insane.

With a frustrated sigh, Jesse folded the paper and let his head fall back against the seat. With luck he'd learn something when they got to New Mexico. He'd sent the report to McParland, along with an inquiry into George Mallory. Then he could get this cursed curiosity out of his system.

The clack of the tracks had a lulling effect, and soon Jesse's eyes drifted shut. The darkness behind his lids slowly became illuminated by the mellow glow of crystal chandeliers. A lovely woman with golden hair and changeling eyes materialized, pacing a room with marbled floors and statuettes. "Something's wrong, Jesse," his mother said. "He's never been away this long."

"No letter yet?"

"Not a one. No one has heard a whisper from him since he left. Jesse, where could he be?"

At seventeen, Jesse thought he had all the answers, but he didn't have an answer for this one. His father often disappeared for months on end on business, but this time even *he* had begun to worry. It just wasn't like Elliot Randolph to disappear for almost a year without a word. "Let me ask around, Mother. Someone must know something."

It had started with an innocent inquiry at the bank where Elliot Randolph kept an account. Jesse didn't want anyone knowing they hadn't heard from his father, for it left his mother vulnerable to scandal. So he'd pretended to withdraw a portion of funds at his father's request.

And discovered that money had been transferred from one account to another on a regular basis for the last six months. Fearing his father had met with foul play, Jesse embarked on a search that took him from their elegant Chicago home to war-torn Tennessee.

Four months later, he found himself standing at the gates of a magnificent plantation home outside Memphis. He could hardly believe the rumors that Elliot Randolph owned the slave-tilled fields and ten-columned antebellum house, for his father vigorously protested against slavery and all it stood for. Had, in fact, campaigned to free them.

That day, Jesse learned the true meaning of deception.

"I'm here to see Elliot Randolph," he told the butler who answered the door.

"Massah Randolph is away on business, suh."

"Who's at the doh-ah, Samuel?" came a sweet inquiry from inside.

"A gen'lman to see the massah, Missus Randolph," the butler answered, stepping aside to make way for a woman in her late thirties, with flame-red hair and vivid green eyes.

"May I help you, young man?"

The instant he looked at her face, he knew what his father had done, and the knowledge made him sick to his stomach.

Jesse swallowed the knot of dread in throat. "I need to speak to Elliot Randolph."

"As Samuel told you, he is away on business. Perhaps I can be of some assistance?"

He is away on business. It was the same line he'd been selling to his mother for almost twenty years.

It took only a moment for Jesse to recover enough from the shock to realize that he could not confront his father with his suspicions; he needed to arm himself with facts. "Yes, ma'am, I believe you can. I'm a reporter for the *Chronicle* and I'm doing an article on Mr. Randolph, and I'd like to ask you a few questions . . ."

He'd returned to Chicago after that "interview" to find Elliot Randolph sitting at the breakfast table as if the world hadn't just crumbled. Jesse remembered doubling up his fist and punching his father, then walking away, leaving the man he'd loved and respected more than anyone to explain to his Northern wife how he could have spent the last twenty years also married to her Southern sister.

"Jesse? Jesse, wake up."

He came awake with a start and found Honesty staring at him with concern. For a moment he struggled with an insane urge to throw himself against her, to lose himself in those soft brown eyes and comforting arms, to forget the memory of his father's betrayal and the launching of his sleuthing career.

"Are you all right?"

He straightened abruptly. "Of course I am." He glanced past her shoulder, out the soot-blackened window and realized the train no longer clacked down the rails. "Why are we stopped?"

"We're at the station."

"It's about damned time." He got to his feet and grabbed their bags from the compartment above their heads. "Let's see if we can find this brother of yours, shall we?"

He performed at a mission church?

Jesse studied the adobe buildings set on the dry plateau near the Apache Indian Reservation. Chickens pecked the ground near a stone well, a wagon with half its moorings shredded and a busted axle leaned precariously against an empty paddock, and two closed shutters on the steepled chapel were missing slats.

"The place looks deserted. Are you sure your brother was heading here?"

"I think so. I remember seeing it on the map."

"Let me see that thing again."

She reached into her pack and pulled the folded paper from the mason jar. Sure enough, there was a star pencilled in near the Texas border with the words "Sisters of Charity" Mission pencilled in below.

Still, this whole scenario had Jesse's nose itching something fierce.

"Maybe everyone is at Mass," Honesty suggested.

At ten o'clock on a weekday morning? "Maybe. Stay close." Jesse absently tucked the map into his vest pocket and gave Gemini a nudge with his heels. Honesty did as ordered, following behind on the roan gelding they'd picked up in Trinidad.

They reached the chapel and Jesse strained to hear voices that would tell him where everyone had gone to, but not a sound came from within. He drew his Colt and dismounted. "Wait here," he told Honesty, then sidestepped to the double doors, scattering a few hens. Obviously someone had been feeding them, for grain was strewn on the ground.

The chapel turned out empty, as did the commissary and the mess hall. But there was bread dough rising in the kitchen, so someone had been here recently. Figuring the occupants had probably gone to preach to the savages, Jesse returned to where he'd left Honesty, only to find her horse standing riderless near the dilapidated wagon and the door to the chapel ajar.

Sighing, Jesse entered the building. Hadn't anyone ever taught that girl caution? His temper started to climb when a search of the chapel didn't turn her up. Not in or under any of the hard wooden pews, not behind the black curtain of the confessional, or on the platform where the pulpit reined. A flash of her racing away from Last Hope with the Treat brothers in hot pursuit, then another of her stuck in the middle of a frigid creek, had his pulse picking up and the coppery taste of fear growing on his tongue.

Just as he turned to head out and begin a search of the grounds, he caught sight of a white granite statue near a side doorway, and the unmistakable curve of a calico clad bottom stuck high in the air. "Honesty?"

She jumped a foot in the air and smacked her head against the under edge of the statue. "Good Lord, Jesse, don't sneak up on me like that!"

"Let that be a lesson to you. What if I'd been one of the Treat brothers?"

"Point taken," she said, rubbing her head. "Did you find anyone?"

"No, but I expect they'll be back soon. What are you doing down there?"

"Down here?" She looked at the floor, then at the statue. "I was uhm . . . admiring the craftsmanship. The detail is amazing, don't you think? The stones seem to flow all the way down the base!"

Jesse's brows dipped into a scowl. He didn't see anything remarkable about the craftsmanship of a chipped-granite Jesus standing on a mountain with his hands raised to the heavens. In fact, the whole thing reeked of an amateur.

"I saw a tub in the pantry," he said. "If you want to take a bath, you might as well do it now, because you won't get another chance for a while."

"No, you go ahead," she said, picking herself up off the floor. "I think I'll go to the kitchen and see what I can scrounge up to eat."

"Again? We just ate a couple hours ago."

"Tell that to my stomach."

He watched her warily. Honesty did nothing without an ulterior motive; what was she up to now? Did he dare leave her alone?

As if sensing his suspicion, she rolled her eyes and declared, "Go take your bath, Jesse. I'm not going anywhere. I'll be right there when you get finished."

Yeah, right. But other than following her around like a puppy, he could think of no earthly reason why they had to spend every waking minute together. They weren't in any apparent danger, nor would anyone think to look for either of them here.

Besides, what kind of trouble could she possibly get into at a mission?

Chapter 13

He should have been more worried about himself.

Thirty minutes after their conversation, with a rolled cigarette clamped between his teeth, a bar of soap clasped in his hand, and his clothes piled neatly beside the well, Jesse climbed into the wooden barrel he'd set up in the middle of the grounds. He knew he was leaving himself vulnerable by bathing out in the open, but his revolver was nearby and at least no one could catch him unawares.

He recoiled at the first contact of cold water against his skin and gave himself a moment to adjust before allowing the shallow tub to swallow his frame. As he slid the soap up his arm, his thoughts turned back to another tub, another bath. For a moment he wished Honesty were here. He sure could use a bit of her "obliging" about now. Between the bone-jarring train ride and a few days of steady travel on horseback, his muscles were knotted so tight that he'd need a year to unwind.

But if Honesty remained true to nature, he had about ten minutes before he'd have to go searching for her again.

He shook his head with mild exasperation. What was he going to do with the contrary bit of baggage? Although he had to admit, she did add a certain spice to his humdrum days, a spark to dreary nights . . .

"You stay in there much longer, your skin will fall off."

He twisted his head and peered at the woman strolling toward him, holding what looked a like a chicken leg. "I see you found something to gnaw on."

"A whole basket of fried chicken in the ice box." She propped herself against the well, crossed her feet at the ankles, and pulled a piece of meat from the bone with her fingers.

Jesse closed his eyes, knowing he couldn't endure the sight of her putting the meat into her mouth without his imagination running rampant.

"How long will it take us to get to Texas from here?"

"In a hurry to get rid of me?"

Honesty wasn't sure how to answer that. Part of her was still so furious for the way he'd treated her in La Veta that she could spit; another part, relished the fact that he'd cared enough to keep her close—in his own barbaric way. That part also remembered his kinder moments of concern and tenderness, and the thought of continuing her search without him left a hollow, achy sensation in her heart. "I just assumed you would be eager to return to whatever it is you do."

He lifted his arm and the sight of water streaming from the bronzed skin made her pause with the food midway to her mouth. Again she was struck by the sheer perfection of him. Well, except for the scars: one near his shoulder blade, one on his chest, and if she remembered correctly, one high on his thigh—which was, regretfully, now hidden beneath the water. It relieved her that he was as flawed and vulnerable as the rest of the human race.

Leaning forward, she couldn't resist tracing the puckered pink scar on his chest. "How did you get this?"

At her touch, his skin tightened, his muscles bunched, and the nipple below her finger pebbled. "I told you—"

"I know. You got in a fight with a Winchester and lost." She searched his eyes, which had turned from light aqua to deep green. "But who was at the stock end of it?"

His Adam's apple slid down his throat and he seemed unnecessarily engrossed in scrubbing his arm. "A friend."

"Remind me to steer clear of your friends."

"He saved my life. I'd have died if he hadn't given the impression of killing me."

"How on earth did you get into a situation that called for you to take such a foolhardy risk?"

"If you must know, I trusted a woman with something very valuable and she betrayed me."

Honesty would have traded her last pair of bloomers to know who the woman was and what was so valuable that it had almost gotten Jesse killed, but she didn't dare ask. Jesse might start demanding answers of his own.

"Now it's your turn."

"My turn?"

"Truth for truth. Why are you so bent on getting to Galveston?"

She thought about the answer for a long while. She could continue with her story of a long-lost brother, but Jesse had made sacrifices for her and he deserved more than that. At the same time, experience was a harsh teacher; her very survival relied on secrecy.

"Because there's something missing in my life," she finally said, choosing her words carefully. "And I can't rest until I find it." Once the confession was out, she wished she could take it back. It made her sound weak and pitiful and dependent. She tossed the chicken into the dirt and brushed her hands on skirt. "I don't expect you to understand that, of course . . ."

"I understand it a whole lot more than you give me credit for."

The breath damned up in Honesty's chest as she looked into his changeling eyes and saw an unspoken history in the somber depths. And a bond formed between them, a tentative friendship, a fragile awareness that perhaps in another time, another place, under different circumstances, she and Jesse might have had a chance for something more. Something lasting and unique and indestructible.

Something she'd once longed for with every fiber of her being.

She almost laughed at her own foolishness. What kind of relationship based on lies and half-truths and vague admissions ever lasted? It would be wiser and so much safer to stay within the boundaries they'd set. Anything more was far too dangerous to contemplate.

"I'm tired, Jesse. I think I'll go lie down with the horses for a while."

"Just make sure you're still there when it's time to leave, Honesty. I won't waste my time looking for you."

Whatever peace they'd managed to attain in the last few minutes was spoiled by his harsh words. "Don't worry, Jesse. I wouldn't want you wasting anything on me, much less your time."

As she walked away, her spine so stiff it looked as if someone had shoved a steel rod down the back of her dress, Jesse cursed his careless tongue. Why did he say things like that to her?

The clatter of approaching wheels stopped him from examining the question and alerted him that he was about to have company. Jesse rinsed off the last of the soap, heaved himself out of the barrel, and reached for his pile of clothes.

His hand froze atop bare stone. "Aw, damn it! Honesty, what did you do with my clothes?"

With nothing but silence for an answer, a growl rose up in Jesse's throat. He wouldn't put it past her to have shoved them into the well.

"So help me, Honesty, if you don't bring back my clothes, I'll tan your fanny black and blue!"

A sudden screech behind Jesse spun him around. He froze, then clapped both hands over his privates to hide himself from the two nuns watching him from the wagon that had just arrived.

It got worse.

Behind the nuns loomed a face Jesse hadn't

seen in over ten years, and hadn't expected ever
to see again. J. B. Cooper had once been the top
tin in a tiny Kansas cattle town, and his purse
had always seemed to exceed a lawman's
salary. Suspicions within the town council had
resulted in Jesse appearing on the scene, posing
as a down-on-his luck drover to bust up what
turned out to be a profitable rustling ring.

"Did you hear him, Father?" the taller nun
gasped. "Did you hear how he threatened that
poor lamb?"

Poor lamb? "I hardly know her! I met her in a
saloon in Colorado—"

The sister gasped in horror. "Heaven have
mercy, he is defiling her, too."

"I'm not defiling anyone." The righteous
faces staring at him with disapproval told Jesse
that defending himself was pointless. "Look,
I'm taking her to her brother. That's it. Then I'm
heading back to Colorado."

"No doubt to corrupt the morals of another
young woman," the vocal one accused. "Father,
you must do something. We are but shepherds
for the Lord, entrusted to protect His innocent
lambs."

Innocent lambs? They couldn't be talking
about the same girl.

"Sisters, wait for me in the chapel while I
have a word with our brother."

Jesse almost thanked the man for dismissing

the women. Standing stark naked in the presence of two nuns wasn't his idea of a Sunday picnic. The sooner they left, the less awkward he'd feel.

With a final sniff, the taller of the nuns spun on her heel and started toward the chapel. When her companion did not immediately follow, she paused to hiss, "Sister Marguerite!"

"Oh! Yes, Sister Agnes. Right away."

Once they left, Cooper gave him an intense up-and-down study. Any hope that the man wouldn't remember the grief Jesse had given him all those years ago was dashed the instant he folded his hands before him and flashed that smirk Jesse remembered so well.

"Goodness. Look how far the mighty have fallen—or should I say, the mighty's clothing has fallen?"

"What are you doing in that get-up, Cooper?"

"It's Father Cooper. I am a man of the cloth now—which is more than you can say."

"You? A priest? Since when did hell freeze over?"

"I'll thank you not to use profanity, Brother Justiss," Cooper chided him imperiously. "And for your information, three years in prison gave me plenty of time to reflect on my sinful ways and turn my life around."

"Yeah, and I'm an angel come to give you your wings," Jesse scoffed. Cooper seemed to forget that he'd been caught with his pants down—so to speak—a heck of a lot more times than Jesse, and usually while in the company of another man's wife. "My guess is you stole the suit off a dead man and are passing yourself off as a priest for a free meal and bed."

That got the man's temper rising. "I can see that you haven't changed a bit, Justiss. You're still the same cocky upstart you've always been, showering your judgment upon the heads of others. So I'll tell you what I'm going to do for you—I'm going to return the favor you granted me."

"And what favor is that?"

The smile should have warned him. "I am going to place you under arrest—"

"What?"

"For public indecency and immoral conduct."

The gravity of the situation became unmistakable when Cooper clapped his hand on Jesse's shoulder and pushed him toward the outer edges of the mission grounds. "You can't arrest me—you're a priest, not a sheriff."

"Who now wears the badge of the Lord. Let's see if a month will be enough time for you to repent of your sinful ways."

"Oh, Sister Agnes, that was wonderful," Honesty praised the woman beside her after swallowing one last bite of cake. "You are truly a gifted cook."

"God blesses us all with talents to glorify His name." She clasped Honesty's hands with bony fingers. "I am so pleased that you came to us, child."

"I wish I could stay longer, but I had better get back to Jesse before he starts to wonder where I've gone to."

"Have no fear, child, you are safe from him."

"Him? As in Jesse?" Honesty almost laughed at the absurdity. For all his bluff and bluster, she'd never felt safer with anyone than him, with the exception of her heart. "Jesse would never hurt me."

"Such a brave child," Sister Agnes crooned in sympathy, then gave Honesty's hand a pat. "But you needn't be brave any longer. We often give sanctuary to women in danger of those heavy-handed individuals who seek to punish. You will come to no harm here. Father Cooper is seeing to it."

It took a moment for the words to register. When they did, Honesty felt her cheeks pale. "Oh, no, what have you done to Jesse?"

The penance chamber was exactly four paces wide, five strides long, and six and a half feet high, with nothing more than a bucket in the corner that Jesse couldn't bring himself to use, and a small square window cut high into a solid wooden door through which, if he stood on the tips of his toes, he could peer outside into the waning light of day.

He alternated between pacing the cell and squatting on the floor with his hands draped loosely atop his knees. The inactivity left him with ample time on his hands to do nothing but ponder his situation. He'd always known that the choices he'd made in his personal and professional life might have a later impact, and he'd thought he'd prepared for any occurrence.

But he sure hadn't prepared himself for this.

Cooper hadn't even given him the benefit of clothes, and the dampness of his surroundings clung to his skin.

He paced the beam of sunlight on the floor, eroding a path into the dirt with his heels. As the day wore on, the beam got shorter. The adobe walls shrank around him, pressing against his brain, closing around his lungs. Shapes shifted behind his eyes. A sense of desperation clawed its way up his throat. He had to get out.

No escape, no escape.

Hell and damnation, where was Honesty? If Cooper decided to use her against him, he'd be powerless to do anything to stop it. Or maybe Honesty had planned this, and somehow conned Cooper into getting him out of the way.

He couldn't imagine Honesty betraying him that way, but he hadn't dreamed Miranda would do so, either.

Put him in the Hastings shaft. Let him see what happens to people who try and cross me.

And Miranda's face, with that small smug smile, that spiteful glitter in her eyes. She'd played him all along. Plotted and planned from the moment he'd told her who he was, just to save her own skin.

Sliding his back down the wall, he fell hard onto the floor, sweat dripping down his brow. His heart slammed in his chest with bruising force. He drove his fingers through the hair at his temples and bowed his head. Of its own will, his body started rocking.

From somewhere above, the call of his name reached into the recesses of his mind.

"Jesse, are you in there?"

The voice seemed to beat at the fog around him, a distant beckoning that changed in tone and pitch, becoming hollow and distorted. *"Are you in there, darling?"*

"Jesse, answer me!"

"Answer me, darling."

He peered into the thick darkness but saw nothing. The stink of coal and mildew and bitter surrender filled his nostrils. "Was this your plan all along?" he asked hoarsely.

"Plan?" came a confused reply. "What are you talking about?"

"You know exactly what I'm talking about, Miranda. I might have fallen for that innocent ruse before, but not this time."

For several moments, silence ruled the night. Then she spoke again, slowly, distinctly. "Jesse, you're talking nonsense. I'm Honesty, and I've come to help you."

Honesty.

His mind latched onto the name, took it apart, tested each syllable. His heart rate dropped to a slow, emphatic thump. The stink of defeat receded.

"Did you hear me, Jesse? I've come to help."

Jesse blinked and came to full awareness. Honesty. Cooper. The penance chamber . . . "Go away, Honesty. I don't need your help."

"Really? Who else is going to get you out of here?"

"Let me rephrase it— I don't want your help."

"Come now, Jesse, you're being childish."

Jesse stared in her direction in astonishment. "*I'm* being childish? *I* am being childish? You stole my clothes! You have those mercenaries in black habits believing that I beat you!"

"I took your clothes to Sister Agnes for washing and was bringing you back a clean set. And they're not mercenaries, they're missionaries who are keeping my virtue at heart."

"Virtue? That's a joke. Do they know what you do for a living?"

After a moment's pause, she asked in a small, timid voice, "Are you telling them?"

A blade of guilt sliced through the tangle of helpless fury and humiliation that churned in Jesse's gut. "They wouldn't believe me if I did."

Honesty couldn't prevent the tears that welled up in her eyes. It was her fault he was in there. She'd thought that leaving him naked and defenseless would be a harmless and fitting retaliation. She'd had no idea her moment of satisfaction would see him punished, and in a manner that obviously took a deeper toll on him than she'd ever imagined. She wouldn't have blamed him if he shouted her sins to the world if it would save him. But even when she least deserved it, he maintained a sense of honor that moved her beyond words.

The need to touch him, to assure herself that he was all right, compelled her to reach through the window. Her hand met only the blackness that concealed him from view.

"I'm going to get you out of here, Jesse."

He snorted, and Honesty couldn't tell if that meant "don't bother" or "yeah, right." Either way, she'd get him released.

An hour later, she sat primly in a tiny room off the chapel across from the one man who could grant Jesse his freedom. Father J. T. Cooper was a tall, slender man with a beaked nose and narrow eyes, who looked more like an undertaker than a priest. The odds in Jesse's favor didn't look promising.

Still, she refused to give up. Jesse had saved her life more times than she wanted to remember; she owed it to him to do whatever it took to set him free. If it meant making a full confession to a man of God, then so be it.

"So you see, Father, this has all just been a misunderstanding. Jesse has not compromised me or defiled me or done anything to harm me. If anything, it's the other way around. I am the one who should be punished, not him."

Father Cooper leaned back in his chair and steepled his fingers under his prominent chin. "Let me see if I've got this straight," he mused aloud. "In the last three weeks, the two of you have been traveling alone, slept in houses of sin, engaged in premarital behavior, and deceived one another on more occasions than you can recall."

Having her many sins recapped made Honesty realize how compromising the situation sounded. She bowed her head in contrition. "Yes, Father."

Any moment, she expected him to toss her into the penance chamber alongside Jesse.

The last thing she expected to hear was a bark of laughter. "Oh, there is justice in the world, after all!"

She stared at the man in wonder. His grin stretched from ear to ear and his pale blue eyes sparkled with glee. "Tell me this, young lady. How has Jesse met the challenges posed upon the two of you?"

The question took her off-guard. She knew her answer would mean the difference between Jesse spending the next thirty days imprisoned, or riding out of here a free man. But she could not, under any circumstances, bring herself to lie to a priest. "With honor and courage, though I'm afraid he has not always maintained his sense of humor."

That seemed to please the priest immensely, for his smile nearly stretched off his face. "Then there is only one way to rectify this situation."

Chapter 14

"Married?" Jesse cried. "That's your idea of rescue?"

"Actually, it was Father Cooper's," came Honesty's muffled reply from the other side of the door.

"I'll just bet it was," he spat. Cooper was no doubt chortling with glee over his method of revenge. Jesse shoved one foot, then the other, through the leg of the trousers Honesty had stuffed through the window. "What exactly did you tell him?"

"I only told him the truth: that we met at the Scarlet Rose, and you're taking me as far as Texas. He seemed quite disturbed that I was traveling with you unchaperoned, especially when I . . . uhm, sort of mentioned that we'd been sleeping together."

"Damn it, Honesty, why did you have to tell him that?"

"He's a priest, Jesse. I couldn't lie to him."

It never stopped her before, Jesse thought, rolling up the sleeves of the shirt he'd just put on.

"When I explained the necessity of our journey, he said that he could not condone us traveling together unless we did so under the sanctity of marriage, and considering the circumstances, it's his spiritual duty to see that you make an honest woman out of me."

Her voice was so prim and righteous, so . . . *Cooper*-like, that Jesse wanted to choke her. Make an honest woman of Honesty? He was a man, not a damned miracle worker. And why was he the one stuck paying for the actions of every other man who'd taken his pleasure with her? "Well, you can just forget it, Honesty. I'd rather be trampled by a herd of longhorns than marry you."

"What's wrong with me? I'd make a fine wife!"

"For someone else! You are reckless and unpredictable and impulsive. You disobey me at every turn, you argue with everything I say—"

"All right!" she cut him off. "I get the picture.

You don't have anything against marriage, just marriage to me."

That wasn't exactly true but he didn't see any reason to discuss the issue.

"But if you ask me, you don't have much choice unless you'd prefer to spend the next thirty days locked up in here. It's not like this would be a real marriage, anyway: just the appearance of one, and only for as long as it takes to have a judge reverse it."

"Annul it," he absently corrected.

"What?"

"You can't reverse vows, you annul them."

"You sound as if you've done it before."

No, but he'd come so damn close it was frightening.

"Think of it this way, Jesse . . . you once let a man shoot you to save your life. Well, this is no different, except I'm the bullet."

A sudden image appeared in his mind, of Honesty as a bullet aiming straight for his heart. Except she wouldn't miss. His throat closed and his skin went clammy. Jesse swallowed heavily. "I won't marry you, Honesty."

His hoarse declaration hung in the air for several minutes before Honesty finally hissed, "Then stay here and repent of your sinful ways."

His eyes snapped open; his blood went cold.

Here? In this cracker box? Thirty days and nights with nothing but the suffocating darkness and ghosts of the past for company? She wouldn't . . . !

She would.

Jesse gritted his teeth and said, "Fetch the damn priest."

The ceremony binding Jesse "Jones" to Honesty "Mallory" was over in the blink of an eye, and before Honesty could even say farewell to their hosts, Jesse grabbed her by the hand and dragged her out of the chapel.

". . . Saddled with a damned wife," she heard him mutter as they collected their mounts. "Next thing you know, I'll be building picket fences and sowing crops for winter."

Honesty should have been used to such remarks by now. Jesse had been in a surly mood ever since she'd brought up marriage as a solution, and she'd been bearing the brunt of it for hours. But enough was enough. "You are not my ideal husband, either, you know. You're bossy, you're quarrelsome, and . . . and you snore!"

He stopped in mid-mount to stare at her. "I do not snore."

"Oh, I beg your pardon. That's just perpetual thunder that keeps me awake half the night."

He made a crude sound under his breath,

then climbed into the saddle, leaving Honesty to fend for herself. She glared at his backside, then turned to her own horse and grabbed the saddle horn. She should have left him in the chamber to rot. But no, she'd felt sorry for him. Indebted to him.

It took her several minutes of hopping and heaving before she finally managed to land in the saddle, but she did it, *and*, she thought with a smug smile, she'd done so *without* the scoundrel's help.

The darkness folded itself around them in an intimate embrace as they turned their horses toward the west. If necessity hadn't set a slow pace, she wouldn't have put it past Jesse to leave her eating his dust, but he had more concern for his horse than that. The night hid any number of dangers on the plains; all it would take was a careless step to ruin either of their animals.

Unfortunately, caution gave Honesty too much time to reflect on the mess she'd made of her life. Like most women, she'd dreamed of the perfect wedding since she'd been a little girl. And as she'd grown older, she'd sworn that if she never did find a man brave enough to take her to wife, it would be a moment that would live on in her memory until they were old and gray.

Well, this memory would live on, all right.

She expected it to give her nightmares for the next twenty years.

Once Jessie deemed they'd put enough distance between themselves and the mad missionaries, as he called them, they made camp on a flat patch of ground. Rocks hemmed them in on two sides. Jesse rarely chose spots out in the open; he'd told her that it left them too vulnerable to attack. From whom, Honesty didn't need to ask. Her brush with Robert and Roscoe lay constantly at the back of her mind, as did the knowledge that if Jesse hadn't come after her, she could very well be dead.

They'd developed a routine over the last couple of weeks; while Jesse unsaddled the horses, Honesty fed them their oats and helped groom them. Then Jesse would start the fire while Honesty prepared coffee and gathered makings for the meal. Tonight it was cold chicken she'd gotten from Sister Agnes, cheese, and fresh bread, all of which tasted like paste.

The silence between them stretched as vast and black as the sky above, and Honesty found that she missed the sizzling banter they'd once shared. She felt more alone now than she had since the night she'd fled Salida, her father's blood still on her hands, his final words echoing in her ears.

From across the fire, she watched her reluctant husband as he alternated between drinking his coffee, taking deep draws from a cigarette, and staring broodingly into the jumping flames. Firelight and moondust collided across his skin, turning it the color of polished mahogany, highlighting the angles of his jaw and the hollows beneath his cheekbones. His hair had grown another couple inches in the last few weeks and fell loose and flowing around his shoulders. She remembered the silky feel of it between her fingers all too clearly. In fact, she remembered every single look, every touch, every kiss she'd received from him since the day they'd met.

She sighed, and stirred the embers with a stick. She still found it hard to believe that she was actually married to this beautiful, remote man, even if the marriage was a sham. "Jesse?"

"Hmm?"

"Who is Miranda?" she asked, unable to contain her curiosity about the name he'd called her back at the mission.

After a long pause that had Honesty wondering if he would even answer her, he said, "Someone I knew a long time ago."

"Is she the one who betrayed you?"

Another long pause. "You ask too many questions."

"You once accused me of hiding something, but if you ask me, *you're* the one who's got something to hide."

"I didn't ask you." A flick of his cup sent the

dregs of his coffee flying into the fire. "You should get some sleep," he muttered. "We'll be starting out early."

"I'm not sleepy." It was her wedding night, for goodness sake! She should be slipping into something frothy and white and sipping wine by candlelight, preparing herself for a consummation that, by mutual agreement, would never happen between her and Jesse.

"Mind too busy concocting more ways to make my life miserable?"

"No busier than yours is trying to wreak misery on mine," she shot back.

He gave a mocking tip of his hat. "Just part of my job, ma'am."

"And what job is that, exactly?"

"Why, keeping your little fanny safe from the likes of the charming Treat brothers. Isn't that what got us into this mess?"

The anger she'd tried so hard to keep in check began to bubble. "You act as if this is the worst thing that has ever happened to you. Well, let me tell you something, Mister, it isn't. In fact, if you think about it, being married does have its advantages."

"Really," he drawled. "Like what?"

"Well, you always have someone to talk to."

"I'm a man, Honesty. Talking doesn't rank high on our list of priorities."

"Okay, then. You always have someone who

believes in you, who accepts you no matter what."

"That's what mothers are for."

Honesty wouldn't know, since she didn't have a mother.

She wracked her brain for another benefit of marriage, besides the obvious, of course. They both knew that sex could be had without vows. The only other thing she could come up with was the one closest to her heart. "You don't ever have to be alone."

"I like being alone."

Honesty sighed. Obviously this was not a conversation to be having with him now. Or possibly ever. Good cow feathers, even her experiences with men up to this point hadn't turned her off the idea of matrimony completely; it had simply taught her to be careful of her choices.

Of course, those choices had been slim to none over the last few years. What man wanted "a saloon trollop" for a bride?

Certainly not Jesse; he'd made that perfectly clear. It shouldn't matter what he thought about her, but it did. Maybe it wouldn't if she weren't so blasted attracted to him. Even now, as he spread his bedroll on the ground, the graceful play of muscles had her heart thumping so loud she swore he could hear it. If he'd given the slightest indication that he wanted her in that bedroll with him, Honesty wasn't sure she'd have the strength to deny him, despite the fact that he thought her a strumpet.

What would he do if he knew the truth? What if she admitted that the night they'd supposedly spent together hadn't really happened?

No, she could never tell him that, because then she'd have to admit that she'd drugged him, and she didn't think he'd take too kindly to hearing that. And then she'd have to tell him why, which would lead to more questions . . .

But would that be so bad? Having him know everything there was to know? What was the worst thing that could happen?

He'd never forgive her. Honesty knew it as surely as she knew her own name. Jesse could not tolerate betrayal of any kind; he'd shown her in all manner of ways—his hunt for her father, who had no doubt swindled him; his bitterness toward that Miranda woman; his constant demand for answers.

No, best just to leave things as they were. She had to think of her own safety, after all. They'd reach Texas soon, have their marriage annulled, find her another guide, and they'd never have to see each other again. It was the best thing for both of them.

So why did every mile toward the border give her such a hollow feeling inside?

* * *

They set out the next morning before the dew evaporated, following a stretch of the Santa Fe Trail.

Jesse kept his eyes on the horizon rather than on Honesty. Why he should feel guilty for keeping secrets from her, he couldn't explain. He shared only his name with her now, and even that was a temporary arrangement thanks to Cooper. He didn't owe her any explanations about Miranda.

They stopped in Clayton long enough to buy supplies, then headed out again, reaching the Texas border around midday. Jesse's spirits lifted the instant he stepped onto familiar ground. Some of his best and most rewarding work had been performed here. He'd exposed a ring of train bandits, sabotaged an assassination attempt on a government official, and most memorably, brought a crooked lawman to his knees and helped save the neck of a pretty little mustanger in the process.

Thoughts of Annie put a smile on his face. She and her husband were probably the only two people in the world that he could trust without question, and they often gave him sanctuary when he was running dry.

In some ways, Honesty reminded him of Annie. Both were survivors, both flouted adversity, and both were fiercely loyal to those they cared about.

The big difference was, he'd never wanted Annie.

But if Honesty had any idea how hard it had been keeping his hands off her last night, she'd probably chortle with glee.

Of all the nights he'd spent alone, relishing his solitude, last night was not one of them. Never had he been more aware of the woman lying nearby, close enough to touch; what made it worse was that last night was his wedding night. What was it about her that sent his senses spinning and put his emotions in turmoil?

Hell, maybe he should have bedded her and gotten her out of his system. Exercised his husbandly rights. Except, if he'd bedded Honesty last night, she might have gotten the idea that he wanted to make this a real marriage, and nothing could be further from the truth. As soon as he found a judge to undo the damage Cooper had done, he'd be a free man again.

And Honesty, he realized with a heavy heart, would be a free woman.

Chapter 15

~~❦~~

She was, without compare, the most stunningly beautiful woman Honesty had ever seen. She rode a pale brown horse inside a circular pen to the delight of two little girls standing on the fence. Her long blond hair had been caught into a ponytail high up at her crown, and the straight, silky hair brushed the curve of her bottom. Her skin was tanned golden by the sun, her eyes were as blue as the sky, and her face looked as if it had been sculpted by angels in heaven.

"Is she your sister?" Honesty asked. She and Jesse shared a slight resemblance, with their fair hair and slender builds, but the resemblance ended there.

"Something like that."

A stab of jealousy drove itself into her heart at the unconcealed adoration in his voice. It didn't make any sense. Of course Jesse would have known other people. Other women. She just hadn't expected to come face to face with one of them.

"Uncle Jesse!"

Honesty tore her attention from the woman on horseback as one of the flaxen-haired little girls threw herself at Jesse. He caught her up in his arms and smothered her chubby face with sloppy kisses.

The second one squealed with all the excitement of a three-year-old, and followed in her sister's wake. "Unca Jesse!" He caught her up in his other arm, and the sight of him holding the children unexpectedly swelled her heart.

"Mama, Uncle Jesse's here!"

"Jesse, you old scoundrel!"

Honesty glanced up just as the woman climbed over the fence. She had to turn her face away so she wouldn't have to watch the woman embracing Jesse. Or Jesse embracing her back.

"What brings you out this way?" the woman asked when he set her back on her feet.

"I'm hoping I can charm you into keeping Gem for a while and let me borrow a couple of fresh mounts."

"You could charm the skin off a snake."

"Everyone's got his talents."

Honesty couldn't decide what irked her more: the stupid grin on Jesse's face as he looked at Annie, or the obvious affection and respect between them. "Aren't you going to introduce me to your lady friend?"

He looked at her as if just then remembering her presence. "Of course. Honesty, Annie Corrigan. Annie, this is—"

"Jesse's wife," Honesty supplied.

Surprised blue eyes snapped to Jesse. "Wife?"

"I'll explain later."

Honesty ignored his warning glower, summoned a polite smile, and stuck out her hand. "A pleasure, I'm sure."

"I wouldn't be *too* sure," Annie countered. "Wait'll you get to know me, then be the judge."

"Uncle Jesse, did you bring us a present?"

"We got to ride Destiny today!"

"Girls, stop pestering him," Annie scolded the girls who clung to Jesse's legs.

"They're no bother, Annie." He caressed each cap of gold hair, then glanced around. His brows narrowed. "Where's Justine?"

"With Brett. She's been begging to go to the canyon with him and I finally couldn't resist letting her go."

Honesty's ears perked. "Canyon?"

"The Palo Duro. We had some land there

until we sold it to a friend of Brett's, but Charlie still lets my husband make a trip down there at least once a summer and look through the wild bands for breeding stock."

"I'd love to see it."

"Not this trip," Jesse answered, shaking his head. "It's too far out of the way."

"But wild horses, Jesse! I might not get this way again! And who knows? My brother may have gone that way."

"We will not discuss this now, Honesty."

She fumed from fury and humiliation when he left her to follow Annie to an outside pump by the stables. She and Jesse chatted while she washed her hands. And laughed. And touched. Innocent touches, yes—a hand to the shoulder, a playful slap to the arm—but touches all the same. A camaraderie and comfort with one another that made Honesty ache. Normally she didn't give in to bouts of self-pity, but it was hard to fight it when these two had something she desperately yearned for.

He returned to her side shortly and said tonelessly, "We've been invited to stay the night."

"I don't want to stay."

"You're being childish, Honesty, not to mention rude. Brett and Annie have been friends of mine for years. I'll not insult them by refusing their hospitality."

"And we wouldn't want to insult them, would we?"

"What's the matter with you?"

The genuine confusion in his eyes made her feel silly for letting her insecurities and petty jealousy reveal themselves. Of course it made sense to stay with his friends; they couldn't afford many more nights in hotels. "Nothing. Of course we'll stay."

While Jesse went to settle the animals in their temporary home and choose the mounts they would borrow, Honesty followed Annie onto the veranda that wrapped around the single-story ranch house. The girls played jump rope in the yard—actually, one played jump rope while the other perfected the art of lassoing a short-haired hound.

She took a seat in one of the whitewashed chairs, feeling awkward and unsure of herself. She didn't know what to say to this woman who seemed so important to Jesse. They shared a past, a present, a future . . .

"I've got to say, Honesty, you're quite a surprise," Annie said, handing her a bowl of freshly picked pea pods.

So are you, she almost said, but bit her tongue at the last moment. "I apologize if we are causing you any inconvenience."

"Not at all. Jesse knows he's welcome here

anytime, and so is any friend—or wife—of Jesse's. So where did you two meet?"

Honesty wasn't sure how to answer; she was almost ashamed to tell this woman, who'd probably never set foot in a bar in her life, that they'd met in a saloon. "In a little town in Colorado called Last Hope. He helped a friend of mine save her business."

"Sounds like something Jesse would do."

"You've known him a long time, then?"

" 'Bout ten years or so. He's been a good friend to Brett and me."

They fell into a companionable silence, splitting pods with their fingernails, breaking them open, and dumping the tiny round peas into another bowl. It was a mindless and mundane chore, and yet there was something about preparing a meal for her man that made Honesty feel womanly and content and . . . wifely.

Except she wasn't a real wife.

And Jesse wasn't her man.

"This canyon you were talking about earlier," she said, trying to keep up with Annie as she shelled peas with enviable speed. "How far away is it?"

"Two days' ride south as the crow flies."

"Are there by chance any stones that look as if they're flowing?"

"There's only one spot that I can think of that might be considered flowing. A sheet of sandstone that looks like a slide, with a pool of water beneath. It's on the north end, near a formation called the Spanish Skirts."

"It sounds beautiful."

"Maybe you can talk Jesse into taking you there."

"Maybe." But she doubted it. "He's different with you than he is with me," she confessed to Annie.

" 'Course he is. I'm not a threat to him."

She wished she could hate the woman. It wasn't as if she was easy to talk to; she wasn't. In fact, she was probably as wary of Honesty as Honesty was of her, and she made no secret of her place in Jesse's life.

But maybe that's what Honesty liked about her. She was a straight shooter who spoke her mind. "I would never hurt him, Mrs. Corrigan."

The soft declaration earned her a searching look from those striking blue eyes. "Is it that obvious?"

"That you care about him?" Honesty nodded.

Annie smiled. "Yes, I do. And I'm glad you wouldn't hurt him, but that isn't what I meant."

"What did you mean?"

"Jesse comes here when he's feeling lost. Off balance. Confused. He jokes around with me, plays with the girls, wrestles with Brett. Then he leaves. We're his friends, but he's not so involved with us that he can't live without us for weeks or months or even years. No threat."

Before Honesty could pursue the topic, the air filled with the sound of pounding hooves. Annie glanced toward the horizon. Her eyes glowed and a beaming grin split her face for a second before she checked the response. "There's my husband now."

Three horses bearing an older man, a younger man, and another young girl broke over the crest in the distance. Several head of horses trailed behind by lead ropes. Annie set aside the bowl of peas, brushed her hands down her trousers, then stepped to the edge of the veranda to wait.

The girls weren't that patient. They dropped their ropes and tore across the prairie as fast as their little legs could carry them. Annie's husband swooped one child in front of him, the other behind him, and carried both of them back to the house.

"Jesse! Jesse!" called his other daughter, trotting up on a black horse that looked far too big for her to handle.

"There's my girl!"

There was nothing tender about the way Annie and her husband looked at each other. It was pure sizzle.

He swung out of the saddle, set his girls on the ground, and swept Annie into his arms for a kiss that nearly singed the hairs off Honesty's arms.

Jesse stood near the corral with a little girl of ten or so; their gazes met over her head, then dashed away, but not before she saw her own longing reflected in his expression.

" 'Bout damn time you came home, gambler," Annie told her husband several moments later.

"I missed you, too," came his deep reply. When he could finally tear himself away from his wife, he turned to Jesse. "Hey, Jess. I thought that was your horse tied to my hitching rail. Who's your lady friend?"

"His wife," Annie announced with a cheeky grin.

Jesse sent her a glower that warned of later retribution.

"Ace, this is Honesty. Honesty, this is the biggest cheat in Texas."

Piercing green eyes looked Honesty up and down with such intensity that Honesty felt a flush creep up her cheeks.

"Have we met?" he asked.

Oh, Gosh, she hoped not. "I don't think so."

"You look really familiar."

Aware that Jesse was watching the byplay with avid interest, Honesty lowered her lashes. "I'm sure I would have remembered if we had met before."

"I'm escorting her to her brother."

"In the escort business now, are you?"

"Something like that." Jesse's smile never reached his eyes, though, and Honesty knew he'd not let go of Brett's statement until he learned why she was so familiar to him.

"Ah, never mind," Annie's husband finally said. "And please forgive me, Honesty. You probably just look like someone I know."

Supper at the Corrigan house had always been a lively affair that kept Jesse's mind off his troubles. But tonight, trouble was dining with them.

He could hardly keep his eyes off Honesty. She sat across from him, next to the Corrigan's son Dogie, wearing a dress he'd seen on her a dozen times before—the rose print one with the bits of lace at the sleeves and the heart-shaped neckline that left her skin bare, revealing the tantalizing curve of her breasts and the slender column of her throat. She'd brushed her amber locks until they shone, and caught them up at the sides of her head with combs in a simple but flattering style.

Honesty smiled at something five-year-old Emily said to her. It lit up her face and crinkled her eyes and made her look so damned desirable that his heart about stopped beating.

Funny, he couldn't remember seeing her smile all that much when she was around him.

Annie and Ace didn't make the situation any easier to bear with their heated glances and secretive smiles. Criminy, if not for Dogie's and the girls' presence, Jesse would have sworn they'd have gone at it right there on the supper table.

He regretted the thought the instant it hit. Images of doing just that with Honesty sliced through his mind with such clarity that he could only thank God Annie liked cloths on her tables. Long tablecloths.

"Justine is such a pretty name," Honesty told the oldest girl.

"Mama and Pa named me after Uncle Jesse, didn't you Pa?"

Jesse froze, and snapped a glance at Brett.

"How do you get Justine out of Jesse?" Honesty asked.

"Not from his first name," Justine giggled, "from his—"

"Girls, time for bed," Brett announced, rising from the head of the table.

"Oh, Papa, it's still early!" Justine wailed. Emily and three-year-old Amelia chimed in with their objections.

"It's eight o'clock." He set one hand each on the two older girls while Dogie plucked Amelia from her high chair. "Now, if you want to ride Destiny again tomorrow, I suggest you pop your little fannies in your rooms."

As they left the dining room, Jesse released a relieved breath. That had been close.

Seeming to take their leaving as her cue, Honesty set down her napkin and also got to her feet.

"Honesty, I put you and Jesse in the blue room," Annie said as she picked up plates. "It's the one Jesse always uses when he comes to visit. I think you'll find it to your liking."

She smiled at Annie. "I'm sure it will be fine." Then she looked at Jesse and softly asked, "Are you coming?"

The question swept him back to the first time she'd asked it, standing on the stairs of the Scarlet Rose in that heart-stopping red silk dress . . .

"I don't think it's a good idea if we sleep in the same room, Honesty."

He could have kicked himself for causing the hurt that flashed across her eyes. "Then I'll see if Justine minds sharing her room with me tonight."

"That's not necessary. You take the blue room. I'm gonna sleep in the barn." If he slept under the same roof as Honesty tonight, he wouldn't have the strength to keep away. At least in the stables he'd get a decent night's rest without images of her taunting him.

Or so he hoped.

* * *

Jesse awoke drenched in sweat and so hard it was a wonder he didn't bust a placket. Every time he closed his eyes, his mind filled with such explicit images of Honesty that he'd have sworn she'd been lying in the hay with him. Hell, the dreams he was having were a whole lot more memorable than the night he'd spent with her back in Last Hope.

Hoping the night air might cool him down, he went outside and took a seat in a chair outside the barn. A half moon looked down on him with pity.

He didn't know how long he stared the damn thing in the face before his thoughts turned to Brett's reaction to Honesty earlier. Brett had been quite the ladies' man before he'd married Annie, but never once since the day she'd agreed to be his wife had he so much as looked at another woman. And Honesty would only have been a girl during his player days, so he couldn't have known her that way.

The sound of footsteps on dried grass pulled him from his musings. He glanced around and found Annie strolling toward him, her arms wrapped around her waist. "What are you doing awake?" he asked. "It's three o'clock in the morning."

"I was thinking about you."

"Annie, we're married to other people," he jested.

Her smile was brief. And sad. "She doesn't know who you are, does she?"

He didn't have to ask who she meant. "Nope, and we're going to keep it that way."

"You can't judge all women by the actions of one," she softly scolded.

"If I did that, I wouldn't be here."

"You should tell her, Jesse."

"Why?"

"Because I don't want to see you make the same mistake I did."

"Ace always knew who you were, Annie."

"His knowing is one thing, my not telling him is another." She laid her arms over the top of the fence. "She has a right to know she could be in danger traveling with you."

"I won't let anything happen to her."

"You may not be able to help it."

Jesse thought about the close call in Last Hope, and his jaw clenched.

"Just what I thought—you've got feelings for her."

"Jeez, Annie, Ace is putting too many damn romantic notions in your head."

"I know a man in love when I see him."

"I'm *not* in love. I'm just helping the woman look for what family she's got left."

"Keep telling yourself that, Jesse." She

laughed and patted his shoulder. "But a word of advice from someone who knows: be careful what you look for. You just might find it."

After she disappeared inside the house, Jesse leaned back in the chair with the back of his head pressed against the rough log wall. Annie had gone out of her ever-lovin' mind. He wasn't in love with Honesty. In lust, yes. What man with breath in his body wouldn't be?

But in love?

With Honesty?

He'd never heard of anything so ridiculous in his life.

Still scoffing at the notion, Jesse dropped his hands to his knees and pushed himself out of the chair.

"You lied to me."

Startled by the voice behind him, Jesse swung around. Honesty stood at the corner of the wrap-around veranda, looking madder than a wet hen.

"What?"

"You *are* an outlaw."

"Hell, are we back to that again?"

"I heard Annie tell you that I could be in danger traveling with you."

Jeez, what else had she heard? "Eavesdropping, now, are we?"

"Is it true?"

Jesse raked his fingers through his hair.

Maybe Annie was right. Maybe he should tell her.

She walked toward him, her head tilted to the side. "Are you an outlaw?"

"No, I'm not an outlaw."

"Then who are you, Jesse Jones? Or is that even your name?"

"As much as yours is Honesty."

He'd cornered her there. Until Deuce's death, Honesty would have argued herself blue in the face, but now . . . now she didn't know anything. "Just tell me this, then. Am I safe with you?"

"As safe as you'd be with anyone."

She almost laughed. If he'd meant that to be assuring, he'd missed the mark by a mile. He cupped her jaw and turned her face toward his. "Honesty, I give you my word, you will come to no danger with me."

After searching his eyes for several seconds, she turned into his arms and laid her cheek on his shoulder. He tensed, but she ignored it. He was the closest thing to security that she had in this world right now, even though she couldn't trust him farther than she could throw him. She was so tired. So afraid. So alone. "Hold me for a minute, Jesse. That's all I'm asking."

Jesse stared at the head on his shoulder, protectiveness welling up inside him so strong and powerful that his chest ached. He shut his eyes

and as his arms closed around her, Jesse feared
that Annie might be closer to the mark than
he'd thought.

If he wasn't in love with Honesty now, he
was coming dangerously close.

Chapter 16

Honesty slid another sidelong glance at Jesse, who saddled his horse with swift, impatient movements. His lips were pressed in the same grim line they'd been in since she'd woken an hour ago. Not a word had passed between them.

He wouldn't look at her. He wouldn't touch her. He wouldn't speak to her. Was he so angry with her that he couldn't bear to be around her now?

Honesty blinked back a sudden sting of tears. She never should have gone down to the barn. Never should have overheard parts of his conversation with Annie. Never should have confronted him with it.

It was just that she'd gotten so used to him

sleeping nearby, that the room had been ...
well, so darn lonely.

Only dimly aware of what she was doing,
she buckled the bedroll onto the little gray mare
Jesse had picked out for her, then gathered their
filled canteens. Clutching them to her breast,
she carried them to Jesse.

"Where will you go?" Brett was asking him.

"Tascosa."

"Are you sure that's wise?"

"Probably not, but it's my best shot of finding
someone to take Honesty to find her brother,
and while I'm at it, I'll see what I can do about
getting this marriage annulled."

She caught Brett's eye over Jesse's shoulder,
and wished the earth would open up beneath
her feet and swallow her.

"You sure you want to do that?" he asked
Jesse, though his gaze never wavered from her.

Several heartbeats passed without Jesse's
reply, and Honesty didn't realize how badly she
wanted to hear him say, "Hell, no, she belongs
to me" until he said instead, "Yeah, I'm sure."

She shut her eyes and turned away. She
didn't know why it surprised her. He hadn't
said anything she didn't already know.

Well, this was it, she supposed, striding to
the little gray mare being lent her. They'd reach
Tascosa, he'd find her another escort, she'd pay
him the measly twenty-two dollars and thirteen

cents she had left, and they'd go their separate ways.

And she'd never know what it felt like to be loved by him. Or made love to by him.

She swallowed the thick knot of regret rising in her throat. As much as wished she could deny it, she'd been attracted to Jesse almost from the instant she'd seen him riding up that old dusty road back in Last Hope. And with each day she spent in his company, that attraction, that longing, had done nothing but grow until she could hardly bear it. To feel his hands on her, her hands on him, his breath whispering across her body . . .

"Sleep well?"

She gave Jesse a brief glance out of the corner of her eye and shrugged. "You?"

"Fits and snatches."

"Maybe you shouldn't have spent the night in the barn."

"If I'd have spent the night in that house, neither of us would have gotten *any* sleep."

Honesty's mouth fell open. He couldn't have meant what she thought he meant. The idea that he might actually have wanted her as badly as she'd wanted him sent a delightful warmth rushing through her blood, and lifted her spirits so high her feet barely touched ground as she attached her carpetbag.

They set out on a westerly path through the

eternal prairie blanketed with yellow amaryllis. Above her, the sky had never been more blue, and below her, the grass never so green. She didn't know what to say to Jesse, but she longed for the sound of his voice, so she said the first thing that popped into her mind. "Your Mrs. Corrigan is an unusual woman."

"That she is. But she not 'my' *anything*."

"Really? I thought there was something between the two of you."

"Me and Annie?"

"You clearly have feelings for her."

" 'Course I do. I respect her and admire her. The woman's got more courage in her little finger than most men I know. But that don't mean I love her. Besides, Ace would kill any man who looked twice at her."

"Would you?"

"Look twice at Annie?"

"Kill any man who looked at your woman."

"If she meant as much to me as Annie does to Brett, I'd tear him limb from limb."

Oh, gosh . . . "I envy her that love. To be the center of a man's devotion, his reason for coming home at the end of a long journey . . ."

"No reason you can't have that, Honesty."

"Someday, maybe, but not—"

"What?"

Not with you. Horrified at what she'd nearly divulged, Honesty quickly sought a safer topic.

"It's so beautiful out here. The way the wind makes the grass ripple and the sun turns everything to gold. Can you hear the music?"

"I don't hear anything."

"That's because you aren't listening. Close your eyes, Jesse. If you listen real close, you can hear the wind sing to you."

Jesse felt like an idiot when he closed his eyes, but she sounded so light and happy that he couldn't deny her.

At first, the only thing he heard was the eternal rush of wind. Then slowly, the steady beat of hooves provided the percussion. The birds up high resembled flutes and clarinets, and the wind through the reeds became a violin solo.

And for the first time in fifteen years, Jesse found himself humming aimlessly. The unknown notes came from a place so deep inside him that he'd forgotten it even existed. His spirit soared beyond his body, his mind filled with the sound of an orchestra, and his fingers. . . . he could almost feel the ivory beneath them.

Finally, with the last note of the composition drifting slowly back down, Jesse opened his eyes to the sight of Honesty staring at him, her mouth opened in speechless astonishment.

And Jesse wished he could just disappear.

He cleared his throat and gave his horse a nudge with his heels.

"I had no idea you could sing," she said, catching up to him.

"It's not something I do very often."

"Haven't you ever considered making a career of your music?"

"What for?"

She shrugged. "Fame. Fortune. Personal satisfaction. I'd be willing to wager that if you took to the road, people would stand in line to hear you play."

Jesse thought of all the years he'd performed for the scions of society, playing the piano and singing ballads, while his father stood off to the side, wearing that smirk that declared to one and all, "I created this."

"I don't want fame, have no use for fortune, and I find my personal satisfactions elsewhere." Most of the time, anyway, he thought with a twist of his lips. He hadn't had any personal satisfaction in months that he could remember.

"Then what will you do when our business is finished?"

The million-dollar question. Hadn't he been asking himself that same thing? And it hit him with sudden clarity: he wanted to be everything his father wasn't. The day he'd left Chicago, he'd given up his name, his fortune, even his music. He shrugged. "Might try my hand at ranching."

"You?"

"Why not me?"

"Good cow feathers, Jesse, you'd be as happy tending a bunch of steers as you'd be busting rock in a quarry."

"How do you know what would make me happy?"

"You're a man who thrives on challenge. There is no challenge or adventure in riding a fence that will pen you in as much as it does the dumb beasts meant for slaughter."

"Well, I won't know unless I give it a try."

"That's true," she conceded. "Most of life's greatest achievements are discovered because someone took a stab at it."

Jesse couldn't contain a laugh. "God, Honesty, you're beginning to sound like my mother."

"So where do you think you'll begin this little venture?"

"I'm not sure. Here in Texas, maybe. Or New Mexico. Might even try Montana. I've heard there's good grazing there. I'll know it when I find it."

"I suppose we're all looking for something."

"What are you looking for?"

"What everyone looks for I guess. A place to belong, someone to belong to."

"That's it?"

"To some people, that's everything."

* * *

Jesse had never given much thought to what turned innocent girls into soiled doves, but over the next couple of hours, he found himself dwelling on Honesty's comment. Sure, women went into the profession for all the reasons Rose had once told him: abandonment, desperation, greed.

But Honesty . . . He wondered if, in her quest to belong to someone, she would belong to everyone or anyone.

Including him.

And he found himself thinking about her family, what kind of upbringing she had. Dangerous thoughts for a man who wanted nothing more than to escort her safely into her brother's keeping so he could be rid of her.

She'd obviously been fond of her father; the ring she wore around her neck testified to that. And she obviously had a large measure of loyalty, or she wouldn't be risking neck and limb traveling across badlands to find a vagabond brother.

She had no fear of people, no qualms over taking off on her own and going afer something she wanted, and she was very good at hiding her thoughts. Hell, she'd make a damned good detective if she weren't so blasted annoying.

Would marriage to a woman of those qualities be all that much of a hardship?

But he could never have a relationship with a

woman he couldn't trust. If she would be truthful with him, he might understand. But he'd
given her plenty of chances to come clean, and
time after time, she'd come up with some
cockamamie story, or avoided the subject altogether. And he'd been burned too badly to be
truthful with her.

He should have left her at the Triple Ace; Ace
and Annie would have watched out for her. Except he'd given his word to find her another escort if they didn't find her brother by the time
they hit the Texas border and he'd do just that.

"This is Tascosa?" Honesty asked a couple
hours later as they approached the town where
Jesse had once posed as a deputy.

"What there is of it," he replied.

"I don't like this place, Jesse. It gives me a
bad feeling, like spiders crawling up the back of
my neck."

He studied her curiously, then scanned the
town. Nothing out of the ordinary: Mickey Mc-
Cormick's Livery, Jenkins' and Dunn's Saloon,
the Wright and Farnsworth General Store, and
the old courthouse, now Cal Farley's Boys'
Ranch. Most of the buildings were made of
brick, some of lumber, and a few even had
pretty shade trees in front of them. It was just a
town.

Yet, Honesty's face had gone pasty white.

"All right then, let's go." He pressed the

reins against the horse's neck to turn him around. "If we travel fast, we can be in Sage Flat by tomorrow."

"But I thought you wanted to find me another escort."

"And I thought you wanted to see wild horses?"

As his meaning dawned, her eyes lit up. "Really?"

"Really." He didn't dare examine why he'd suddenly turned against the idea of unloading his troublesome baggage. Except the thought of someone else spending their days and nights with Honesty set his teeth on edge. He found himself wanting to show her all the places he'd been, the things he'd seen and had taken for granted or just plain hadn't appreciated.

"Be careful, Jesse. I might start thinking there's a heart inside that glorious chest of yours." She kicked the little mare into a canter.

Jesse plucked his shirt away from his skin and peered down his shirt. She thought his chest gorgeous? He grinned. Damn minx.

He didn't know what in the Sam Hill had gotten into Honesty, but he liked it. Not once since leaving the mission had he been forced to track her down, bail her out of trouble, or rescue her from the clutches of any thugs. In fact, she'd been strangely cooperative and astonishingly obedient.

Maybe something he'd said had finally stuck.

* * *

They hit Sage Flat well after noon the next day, too early for the rowdy crowd, too late for the marketers. Jesse guided his gelding directly to the town's only hotel, which was directly across the street from the Two-Bit Saloon, but there wasn't much he could do to change that.

"Why are we stopping here?" Honesty asked as he helped her dismount. "I thought we were going to see the horses."

"We are." He wrapped his fingers around her elbow and ushered her into the lobby. "First thing in the morning."

She came to a skidding halt. "What?"

"I've got some business to tend to. We'll stay the night here, then head over to the canyon first thing in the morning."

"But I want to see the horses now!"

"I know, and so does everyone else in town now, too."

Suddenly aware that her outburst had drawn the attention of several guests, she lowered her voice. "What kind of business is so important that it can't wait one day?"

Jesse scribbled a false name into the register book, received the room key, then escorted Honesty up the stairs. "Well, seeing if your brother has been here, for starters. And I need to find out if the judge is in town; if he isn't, I want to know how long it will be before he passes through again." He also needed to send a wire to McParland, letting him know where he could be reached; he hoped there would be some news on George Mallory by now, too. "I shouldn't be longer than a couple of hours." He slipped the key in the door and turned the lock. "While I'm gone, I do not want you leaving this room. No more stunts like the one in La Veta, understand?"

She folded her arms over her breasts and pursed her lips.

Jesse sighed. He was beginning to understand that mutinous expression well enough to know that it didn't bode well. Two casual steps brought him close enough to feel the anger and the hurt emanating from her skin. "Honesty?"

She refused to look at him.

His lips quirked. He tipped his head to one side, then the other, trying to catch her eye.

She turned partly away from him.

"Now, darlin' . . ." He caught her chin with his finger and gently forced her to turn back in his direction. "You know I wouldn't be leaving you if it wasn't important, don't you?" he asked in his silkiest tone.

She peered at him from beneath her lashes. He could see her weakening. There really was something to be said for catching more flies with honey.

Pressing his advantage, Jesse moved in closer; his breaths mingled with hers, and his gaze fixed on her lips. In his mind's eyes, he saw himself leaning in, inch by inch. By inch. "I won't be long; I give you my word." He slid his finger along her jaw. "Will you wait for me?"

Those long, thick lashes of hers crept up. Her eyes locked with his. He saw his own reflection in her dilated pupils, and his breath damned up in his lungs at the desire in them.

An eternity seemed to pass before she finally nodded.

Jesse smiled inwardly. Women weren't the only ones who could use sensuality as a weapon of persuasion. It had just been so long since he'd used his own, he'd all but forgotten its power. "I promise, as soon as my business is finished, I'll come back and . . . keep you company." He gave her a slow wink and an even slower grin.

Her mouth fell open.

Then before he gave in to the temptation to test her responses further, he took a step backward. "In the meantime, try and relax, okay? I'll have a—"

"I know, you'll have a bath sent up." She sighed, and it sounded so defeated that he might have changed his mind if there wasn't so much at stake. He rocked his Stetson on his head, checked the load in his Colt, then headed for the door.

"Remember what I said, Honesty; do not leave this room. Believe me, this is one town you wouldn't want to be caught in alone."

The minute the door closed behind Jesse, Honesty's smile vanished. Scoundrel. If he thought he could seduce her into waiting meekly in the room while he jaunted about town, he was sadly mistaken. The man was up to no good, and the longer she stayed in his company, the greater the danger that he would discover her true identity. His errands would take him an hour, two at most, before he returned. If she hurried, she should have just enough time to slip over to the canyon, do a bit of exploring, then slip back.

Taking a page out of Annie's book, she borrowed a pair of Jesse's trousers. They were a bit too snug around the waist and hips, and she hated the way the coarse fabric felt against her skin, but at least it would afford her some protection. And there was a lot more freedom to split-legged garments than skirts, which had a tendency to get tangled in everything in her path.

Once she deemed the hall was clear, she closed and locked the door behind her, pocketed the key, then strode down the corridor to a door that, as she predicted, opened to an outside stairwell.

For just a moment she stood on the threshold, her hand around the knob, her heart stammering in her chest. Maybe this wasn't such a good idea. Maybe Jesse was right, and she should go back to her room and stay there and . . .

And what? Let him think that every time he snapped his fingers, she would blithely follow?

No. Something was wrong. She couldn't explain it, she couldn't define it, but she could feel it. There'd been a knot in the back of her throat the size of a melon for the last two days, the skin on the back of her neck burned, and she had a sinking sensation in the pit of her stomach that if she didn't find whatever it was her father wanted her to find soon, she'd wouldn't find it at all.

The canyon was easy to locate, but the slide-rock that Annie told her about wasn't so easy to find. Hands on her hips, she scanned the visible length of the Palo Duro. She didn't know what she'd expected, but an eleven-mile chasm of striated rock as wide as it was deep had not been it. There was no way she'd be able to explore the entire eleven-mile-long canyon in one hour.

She could, however, make a dent in it.

Lips pressed together, she fetched the rope

from the little mare's saddle and set about finding a place to descend where she wouldn't break her fool neck. Just as she spotted a decent decline and lowered one foot over the edge, a wailing sound from across the prairie stopped her in her tracks. Honesty swung around.

Her heart froze at the sight of the figure riding on horseback along the canyon's rim, toward her.

Roscoe Treat!

She'd have recognized him anywhere, even without the buffalo-hide coat.

She dropped to the ground and crawled backward. He was still too far away to see her. Or even if he could see her, surely he wouldn't recognize her. She'd just wait here until he passed.

How had he found her? And where was Robert?

She buried her face into the ground and slid backward a bit more, trying to make herself as small and flat as possible without slipping down the cliff as the wailing grew closer. Honesty realized he was singing, or trying to. The obnoxious volume and slurred notes left her with no doubt that he'd had quite a bit to drink. That could play to her advantage.

Or not.

The instant Jesse stepped from the telegraph office, a sense of foreboding prickled across his skin. Years of ingrained reaction kicked in, pushing him to the shadows. He reached for his Colt and snapped the safety strap free, even as he scanned the street for whatever had his senses going on instant alert.

He went to the room first. "Honesty? Honesty, we're in luck. I ran into an old friend who agreed to take—" The words fell on an empty room. Her bag was still on the bed, her money jar hidden inside, but no Honesty.

A red haze of fury clouded his eyes.

The little sneak had stolen off again.

Chapter 17

One hour passed.

Then two.

And still Roscoe roamed the prairie, singing himself hoarse. Honesty had managed to creep down to the floor of the canyon and climb back up a wall further north. She suffered one close call when he staggered to the rim, unbuttoned his pants, and peed barely two feet away from her. Nose curling, she inched sideways a couple of yards and tried to figure out how to get back to Sage Flat without him detecting her. Jesse would surely have returned by now and discovered her missing. He was probably tearing the town apart looking for her.

Or maybe he wasn't.

Maybe, like Roscoe, he was availing himself

of the local liquor stock and didn't even know she was gone.

She could hope, anyway.

If he found out that she'd disappeared on him again . . . She didn't want to contemplate what he would do, but she had no doubt he'd take more severe measures than tying her to his wrist.

It suddenly occurred to her that she hadn't heard Roscoe in a few minutes. Honesty peeked over the rim one more time. Hope flared when she saw him sitting less than ten yards away in the high grasses, his shoulders slumped. "Please be sleeping, please be sleeping . . ."

Keeping her eyes on him, she hoisted herself onto flat ground and crawled on her stomach behind him, using her elbows and knees for leverage. She briefly considered making a run for it, but if Roscoe caught sight of her, she was done for.

And so, calling on every ounce of patience she could summon, she chose the safer route of caution and crawled toward her horse. It seemed to take forever to pass him; he stirred several times, his head bobbing drunkenly, but he gave no sign of noticing her. At last, with nothing but open ground between herself and the mare, Honesty rose to a crouch and closed the distance. Then she climbed into the saddle and rode like the wind.

She arrived back in Sage Flat in a cloud of dust just as the moon edged its way above the horizon. Quickly she brushed down the mare, then sprinted up the outside staircase. The key made a loud click in the door and Honesty winced. Peering through the crack, she breathed a sigh of relief at finding the room empty.

She slipped inside, shut the door, and turned the key.

"Oh, my gosh," she whispered, noticing the clothes she wore. Jesse's trousers now had shredded holes in each knee, and dirt ground into the fibers, and one of the rolled leg cuffs had been torn half off. His gray cambric shirt was also beyond repair. She had to destroy the clothes before he saw them and guessed correctly that she'd once again been prowling about. She'd figure out something to tell him tomorrow when he discovered them missing.

After checking the livery stable and finding the little gray mare missing from her stall, Jesse then checked the Two-Bit Saloon, then the newly built theater, both restaurants, the bath house, the hotel lobby, and the four other gentlemen's entertainment parlors in various stages of class.

But Honesty was nowhere to be found.

After searching every nook and cranny in

town he realized there was only one other place Honesty would have gone—the Palo Duro. Why she would possibly want to go there today after he'd promised to take her tomorrow, he couldn't figure. There was nothing to see at night, and she sure as hell wasn't going to find her brother there.

Unfortunately, Honesty's behavior didn't always follow reason.

As concerned for her safety as he was furious at her reckless disobedience, Jesse returned to the hotel to fetch his saddlebags. There was no telling how long it would take him to locate her.

The instant he opened the door to their room, he came to a sudden stop at the sight of Honesty standing near the window.

Feeling equal parts fury and relief at finding her safe, Jesse found that it took all his restraint not to slam the door, storm across the room, and paddle her backside. She didn't even notice that she was no longer alone, which made Jesse's temper rise even higher. Anyone could have come into the room, and she wouldn't even know of the danger until it was too late.

But maybe that was a good thing—maybe the little sneak should be taught a lesson.

He slipped inside the room, shut and locked the door, then moved to the corner. There, he folded his arms across his chest and watched her fight her way out of her shirt. No, *his* shirt.

Not only had she stolen off, but she'd done so in *his clothes!*

By the time she finally freed herself from her cambric prison, she'd worked herself up into a mild frenzy. And Jesse's mouth had gone dry as a desert bone yard. The only light in the room came from a moonbeam shining through the window, and it caressed her bare breasts like a lover's hands, skimming the outside swells, lighting on the dark aureoles.

His tongue stuck to the roof of his mouth; his heartbeat echoed in his ears. God, she had beautiful breasts. Not too large, not too small. Just perfectly proportioned with her slender frame.

She tossed the shirt onto the bed, then turned her attention to the pants. For a moment Jesse wondered why she didn't light the bedside lamp, then decided he didn't care. There was something sinfully erotic about a woman undressing in the moonlight, especially when she didn't know she was being watched. She unfastened the three buttons in front, and worked the waist swiftly down her hips. With each inch of bare bottom she revealed, Jesse's mouth went drier and his pulse pounded with like a freight train charging down the line.

Haste made her clumsy, though, and Jesse almost gave away his presence by laughing when, hopping on one foot to untangle the pants leg from her foot, she fell backward with a squeal.

A dull thud, then a mild expletive, broke the hush, and for a moment Jesse wasn't sure if it came from her or him. She shot up quickly and scrambled to her feet. It didn't take him long to realize that she was trying to hide the evidence; with the clothes she'd been wearing balled in her hands, she swiveled from one side to the other, searching the room. She tried beneath the pillow first, then shoved them under the bed. A second later, she pulled them out again and stuffed them into a corner of the wardrobe. That didn't satisfy her, either, for she removed them just as quickly.

And Jesse couldn't resist. "Throw them out the window; he'll never know."

She shrieked and all but jumped out of her skin. Instantly she clutched the clothes to her front and searched the room. A shift in the blackness had Honesty honing in on a spot behind the door. "Jesse? Good God, you scared the life out of me!"

"I'll do more than scare the life out of you," came his low-timbred reply. The shadows slid away from his face as he stepped out into the open, filling the room with his presence.

Never had she seen such steely determination in a man's eyes. Jesse wore it the same way a gunslinger wore a pair of well-worn Colts, with a dangerous familiarity that at once fascinated and intimidated her.

Honesty backed up a step and lifted one hand as if it held enough power to ward him off. "This isn't what it looks like, Jesse."

"Really? You mean you *weren't* sneaking back into this room after I explicitly told you not to leave it?"

He continued walking toward her, and Honesty continued back-stepping until the rough wall at her back left no more room for retreat.

"What was it this time, Honesty? More gold? Another sandstone formation? Or maybe another performance?"

"Did you know that your eyes change color with your mood?"

He flattened his hands on the wall on either side of her head. Anger radiated from him in scorching waves.

"Do *not* try changing the subject. I want to know where you've been, and why you felt the need to sneak out the instant my back was turned. *Again.*"

"I . . . went outside to get a breath of fresh air."

He arched one brow. "Wearing my clothes?"

"You pointed out that this was not a place for a woman to be caught alone, so I borrowed your trousers, hoping it might make me less noticeable. Anyway, I went out for a breath of air, and that's when I saw him."

"Your brother again?"

"No, Roscoe Treat."

She waited for the name to sink in before pressing on. "He must have followed us, Jesse. And you know that wherever Roscoe is, Robert isn't far behind. I tried looking for you, but when I didn't see you, my only thought was to get away before he spotted me. So I hid until it was safe to come back here."

"Where you intended to destroy the evidence. Nice try, Honesty, but I'm not buying it."

What! Here she was, telling him as much of the truth as she dared, and he didn't even believe her! "What are you doing in here, anyway? How did you get in here?"

His smile held no humor. "It's one of the advantages of being married. We not only share a room, but a key as well."

"I think you had better leave."

"Why, so you can disappear again? I don't think so." They were now nose to nose. "I have done everything I can think of to keep you safe and still you defy me. So here's the deal: if you sneak off one more time, just *one more time*, there is no deal. All bets are off and you're on your own. I won't come after you again."

She stared at him a moment. "You're bluffing."

"Do I look like I'm bluffing?"

No, he looked calm and cool and dangerously collected. It frightened her. Worse, it excited her. "Maybe I like you coming after me," she whispered.

"What?"

Honesty swallowed. "I said, maybe I like you coming after me." No one had cared to before, except for Deuce. It made her feel important. Special. As if she really mattered to someone in this harsh, cruel world. "You're a beautiful man, Jesse. Any woman would be flattered to have your attention."

"Is that what all this is about? Getting my attention?"

He searched her eyes, looking for an ulterior motive. A payoff. Some benefit she might be expecting to gain beyond a moment's satisfaction. But finding none, he slid his hand under the fall of her hair, cupped the back of her neck, and dragged her mouth to his. He kissed her with savage possession, giving the desires he'd held in check for so long free rein.

She whimpered into his mouth, but the hunger with which she kissed him back told him the sound didn't come from pain, but from the same need that raged through him. Her hands reached under his arms to pull him closer; her nails bit into his shoulder blades. The press of her breasts against his front inflamed him.

He tightened his hold on her, pressed himself closer and slanted his mouth across hers, one way, then the other, tasting, pulling, demanding, sliding his tongue across hers, filling her with the taste of him.

Her nails scored a path down his back to his buttocks, and she clenched him in her hands. Of their own accord, his hips rocked against the mound of her womanhood, and pressure built in his loins. Stars danced behind his eyes. Oh, God . . . he had to have her . . . had to feel himself inside her . . .

With one hand at her nape, the other around her bare bottom, Jesse spun her around and guided her to the bed. The edge of the mattress hit the back of her knees and together they fell. He couldn't remember a time when he'd felt so out of control. So on the edge. So near detonation.

Breaking the fusion of their mouths, Jesse pressed his forehead to hers and clenched his eyes shut. His breaths came in raspy gasps; his nerves felt as if they'd been strung out across desert sands. Beneath him, her heart thudded against his chest. Good God Almighty, what was she doing to him? He was supposed to teach her a lesson on being caught unawares, not the other way around.

A bead of sweat tracked down his temple as he fought for control over his rampaging need. He slowly lowered his hand from Honesty's nape and forced himself to relax on his side, creating a bit of space between their bodies that allowed a chilly breeze to creep in from the window.

He knew what she was doing. The woman had a natural sensuality that scrambled a man's senses before he knew what hit him. Worse, he wasn't sure he had the power to fight it. And that made her more dangerous than he'd given her credit for. At any given moment, she could draw out that weapon, use it to torment, exact revenge, or simply bend a man to her will. Jesse knew the game; by God, he'd written the rules. "I won't let you do this to me, Honesty."

"Do what?"

"Make me lose control."

"Does it matter? We're never going to see each other again, Jesse, so why not make this night worth remembering? If you're worried about the annulment not being granted, I won't tell anyone we were together. Who's to know?"

She had a point. It wasn't as if they hadn't done this before—and she still owed him a memory.

Tired of fighting the need she roused in him,

Jesse once again covered her mouth with his own.

And Honesty came close to tears. She'd wanted this for so long—to belong to someone. To belong to *him*. She felt as if she'd been waiting her whole life for this moment, this man, and now that he was in her arms, she could scarcely contain her joy.

Needing to feel his skin beneath her hands, she fumbled with the buttons of his shirt.

Jesse ran his palm down her rib cage, then back up to cup her breast. He guided her nipple into his mouth. Honesty's entire body arched. She swung one leg over his hip and clutched his hair. Seeming to take her reaction as invitation, he stroked the back of her thigh. His fingertips teased the sensitive flesh near her womanhood, each time coming a little closer. Honesty's breaths came in tiny pants. Her mind began to swim. She didn't think the pleasure could get any greater.

Then his finger found the wet center of her and slipped inside. Honesty gasped.

"I can't . . ."

She didn't know what she wanted to say. She couldn't take the pressure? She couldn't bear the pleasure? *Both*, she thought, rocking against his hand in wanton abandonment. She felt herself grasping for something beyond reach, climbing higher and higher.

Suddenly Jesse's hand was gone. Honesty moaned and reached for him. "Don't leave me," she sobbed.

"Darlin', I'm just beginning." And then, *he* was sliding inside her. Thick. Strong. Slick. Stretching her to the point where she thought he'd surely tear her in half. Jesse moaned. Honesty bit her bottom lip and blinked back the tears forming in her eyes. Just when she didn't think she could take him any further, he withdrew.

Then he did it again. Pushing inside her, expanding her to that point of pleasure-pain, then withdrawing. Again. And again.

And Honesty no longer remembered the pain. She lifted her hips to receive him, and slowly, they fell into a glorious rhythm that opened up all her senses. She tasted the salt of his skin, smelled the wind in his hair, felt the strength of his body.

The pace picked up. His breathing grew ragged. His muscles clenched beneath her hands. And he drove into her with greedy precision that, each time, sent her to a higher plane of awareness. The skin drew tight around his cheekbones. His eyes went dark as a midnight forest.

"J . . . Jesse?" she cried softly as a dizzying pressure built inside her.

"Give it to me."

"Jesse, I. . . . oh, God!" She dug her nails into his shoulders and arched her back as her inner muscles convulsed around him and the sky exploded into a thousand shards of light.

Her limbs shaking, her bones like water, she went limp against the mattress while Jesse lowered his shuddering body onto hers.

She had no idea how long they lay there, arms sprawled across the sheets, legs tangled, hair an intimate blend of blond and amber, when the quivering finally abated and their breathing settled to a normal rhythm. But it must have been a while, for she was growing so sleepy.

"If we were half this good the first time, it's a wonder I'm not dead," Jesse mumbled against her breast.

"Then let's pretend this was the first time," she murmured back, barely able to summon the strength to talk. Jesse didn't seem to have that problem, for he pulled her gloriously sated body closer, tucking her hip between his thighs, stroking her skin.

"By the way," he murmured, "you owe me three dollars."

She socked him in the arm.

Jesse awoke in as fine a spirits as a man could be. He curled his arms around Honesty and snuggled closer to her. The instant reaction of his body surprised him, considering how many times they'd been intimate during the night.

Intimate, hell. They'd made love. Several times. And each time had been better than the one before it. He had no idea Honesty could be so . . . creative.

The memory made him smile.

Though Jesse would have liked nothing better than to spend the day in bed with her, they did have things to do. "Come on, lazy, we'd better get up."

"Do we have to?"

"We do if you want to see those horses."

Her eyes snapped open. "I'd forgotten all about them."

"Well, I didn't," he said, dragging himself to the edge of the bed. "I'm a man of my word." He reached for her hand and pulled her to her feet.

Then the morning exploded.

Jesse threw himself down over Honesty as the window shattered behind them, showering glass over his back and across the bed. Three more shots followed.

Shouts in the street alerted him that the shooting was over. For now.

He lifted his weight from Honesty and helped her sit up. "Are you all right?"

She clutched the blanket to her breast and nodded. "I think so." Brown eyes examined him with worry. "You?"

"Not a scratch," he assured her, touched by her concern. It had been too long since he'd had anyone worry over him.

"Were those shots meant for us?"

"I don't think so; the others came from further away." Nonetheless, it served a sharp reminder of the dangers that had been chasing him the last dozen years. "Come on. Let's get our stuff together and get out of here."

"Why don't you go saddle the horses? I'll get our stuff together."

"Are you sure?" He didn't like the thought of leaving her alone in the room.

"I'm sure. I'll meet you in the lobby."

It *would* be faster that way.

After throwing on his clothes, he left Honesty to rummage through the debris for their belongings. The instant the door shut behind him, Honesty's knees gave out. She stumbled to the corner of the bed. Her chest hurt, her eyes burned, and her lungs didn't seem capable of taking in air.

The last few minutes replayed themselves over and over again. The gunshot, the shatter of glass, Jesse's body covering hers . . .

Oh, God. Honesty brought her knees to her

chest and rocked back and forth. Jesse could have been killed, and it would have been her fault.

Maybe that bullet had been a stray shot, but what about the next one?

The bliss she'd felt barely an hour ago withered like an autumn leaf. She could not do this anymore. She had to tell Jesse the truth of her relationship to Deuce McGuire, of his death, and of the danger he might be in just by being in her company. She still didn't know what he wanted with her father, or what he would do when he learned who she was, but he had a right to know of the danger so he could be prepared. He'd be angry that she'd kept her identity from him all this time, and might never forgive her. But wasn't that better than seeing him dead?

With a sense of resignation Honesty wiped her eyes, pushed herself off the bed, and gathered her clothes.

No sooner had she gotten dressed than a knock sounded at the door. The porter from downstairs said, "A message for Mr. Jones."

She opened the door. "Thank you. I'll take it."

"I was instructed to give this only to the gentleman."

"I'm the gentleman's wife," she said. "I'll see that he gets it."

Plucking the folded paper from the porter's hand, Honesty then shut the door. Who would be sending Jesse a telegram? She turned the message over in her hand. No one knew they were coming to Sage Flat.

She split the seal with her fingernail and scanned the typewritten note. The letters blurred together in a senseless pattern, and Honesty almost folded the paper.

Then one word jumped out at her.

McGuire.

Voices outside penetrated the fog creeping through Honesty's mind. She whipped open the door, startling the elderly couple entering the room across the hall.

"Excuse me, sir, I wonder if you can do me a favor." With a smile that Deuce once told her could rival the stars, she handed the silver-haired gentleman the telegram. "I just received this message, but I'm afraid I've misplaced my glasses and can't read a word of it. Would you mind?"

"Certainly." The man cleared his throat and read.

Mallory possible alias for McGuire. Stop. Last known address Sweetwater. Stop. Report soon. Stop.

"Does it say who it's from?"

"I'm afraid not."

After thanking the man, Honesty returned to her room and drew the message through her fingers, sharpening the crease. It was a damning message, one that connected Honesty with two of the names her father had used. It wouldn't take Jesse long to put the rest together. She'd planned on telling him anyway, so that wasn't what disturbed her. But why would Jesse be getting a message like that? Who would have sent it? What business did he have with Deuce?

She and Deuce had spent some time in Sweetwater; that was one of the stars on her map. She couldn't have been more than eleven or twelve at the time, and they'd had to leave when those dreaded detectives had started snoop—

Honesty's hands stilled. Her blood turned to ice in her veins.

No . . .

She hastened to the bed and dumped out the contents of Jesse's saddlebags. She didn't know what she was looking for; something to tell her that her suspicions were unfounded. Some clue to his identity . . .

Her hand brushed the tinderbox and froze.

The catch sticks sometimes.

Her heart pounded erratically as she picked up the box and turned it over. Engraved at the bottom was the shape of an open eye, and in the center, the initials J J R.

A memory flickered at the back of her mind, a handbill pinned to the wall of a Denver store, with the picture of an open alert eye.

"It's their motto, lass," her father had once told her. " 'Pinkerton Detective Agency; we never sleep.' "

They never gave up, either. They pursued relentlessly and mercilessly, changing character and appearance as often as most people changed their clothes.

And she knew then why Jesse seemed so mysterious. He wasn't an innocent drifter-for-hire. He wasn't an unpredictable outlaw. He was so much worse. He was a detective. A *Pinkerton* detective, the best of the buch.

And heaven help her, she'd fallen in love with him.

Chapter 18

Jesse saddled the horses with swift efficiency, anxious to get the hell out of town. His mind kept clicking back to the night before, when Honesty claimed to have seen Roscoe Treat. He hadn't believed her then, but what if she had been telling the truth? What if the brothers had somehow discovered where he and Honesty were staying?

It had happened before. Marks he'd been trailing would catch wind that he'd looked at a woman with interest, and the next thing he knew, she'd be threatened, or her family would be threatened, her house ransacked or her pet killed mysteriously. A man in his line of work couldn't form attachments, because it put the innocent at risk.

It was one of the reasons he'd encouraged his mother to move to Montana, so she would be safe from the consequences of his profession.

But what was he going to with Honesty? Turning her away would now reduce her again to the kind of life she'd led before.

He'd married her, and made her his wife in every sense of the word. She was his responsibility now, and it was his duty to keep her safe. He couldn't leave her here, or anywhere else. The risk was too great; by not believing her, he could very well have put her in danger. So his only choice was to keep her.

And if he did that, he had to tell her who he was.

Did he risk it? Would she expose him, too?

Maybe it was time to have a little faith in her. As Annie had pointed out, she wasn't Miranda and he had to stop making that comparison. If he trusted her a little, maybe she would learn to trust him back.

He returned to the hotel. Honesty wasn't in the lobby. Figuring she was still trying to get their things together, he took the stairs two at a time and entered the room. "Honesty, the horses are—"

He came to a sudden halt inside the doorway.

No. She *wouldn't* have done this to him again. Not after the night they'd spent together.

Spying the contents of his saddlebags spread

across the bed, he felt a sense of doom creep through his chest. Jesse's hand met the butt of his revolver. "Honesty?" Weapon drawn, he searched the room. The window was shut, the wardrobe open, and glass still littered the floor and bed.

But no Honesty.

Had Treat seen her last night? Followed her here? Taken her again?

Fearing the worst, Jesse started shoving his clothes into his saddlebags and flipped it over his shoulder, only to be yanked back by the bed's blanket, trailing from one pouch. Cursing, he tugged at it and flipped the rumpled blanket onto the bed—and saw that spots of blood stained the white sheet. At first he wondered if Honesty had been cut by the glass, despite her denial. In the excitement, he hadn't examined her closely.

If she'd been cut, though, how had the blood gotten beneath the blanket? He took a closer look at the sheets. It wasn't fresh, which meant it must have gotten there last night. Had she been having her menses? No, he'd have known.

The only other way it could have gotten there . . .

No.

It was too absurd to consider. She couldn't have been a virgin. He'd seen her taking men upstairs. Hell, he'd been one of them.

Or had he?

That night *was* a blank in his memory. All he had was Honesty's word that they'd spent the night together.

Honesty's word.

Feeling as if the breath were being crushed from his lungs, Jesse examined every relevant moment from the night before.

She'd been so tight. She'd seemed unsure, even awkward at times. Then there had been that split second when he'd pushed against a resistance and her whole body had stiffened. He'd never been with a virgin before; there was no bigger trouble for a bachelor than an unsullied woman. But he'd heard stories from men who liked to boast . . .

Oh, God.

As senseless as it sounded, it all added up. The saloon strumpet he'd paid to bed, then been forced to marry, had been a virgin.

What the *hell* kind of game was she playing?

The winds blew a lonely wail across the plains as Honesty rode south toward the Palo Duro, the emptiness in her heart as vast as the plains surrounding her. Her eyes were dry and gritty from sand, and she wore a scarf over her nose and mouth to keep out the dust. Her heart felt cold and brittle.

Why hadn't she listened to her instincts the

very first time she'd seen Jesse? She'd known he was either evading someone or searching for someone, and that inkling had been clinched the night she'd overheard him talking with the Treat brothers. She was better off without him.

She would do this. She would survive. She would find whatever it was her father had left her, and she would build a future for herself. It was her legacy, and good or bad, it was all she had left to hold onto.

At the sound of hoofbeats, Honesty threw a glance over her shoulder and saw a cloud of dust bearing down on her at breakneck speed.

Jesse! How had he found her so quickly? Why couldn't he just leave her alone? She jabbed her heels into the mare's sides. The hoofbeats drew closer, and Honesty knew the little mustang would not outrun his faster mount. She pulled on the reins and brought her to a halt, intending on blasting Jesse with both barrels over his betrayal.

Instead, she found herself looking into the stormy eyes of Robert Treat.

Behind him, Roscoe chortled. "Told ye I saw her leaving the hotel."

"That you did, brother. You are one slippery little bird," he told Honesty, grabbing the mare's reins. "But you'll not fly the coop so easily this time."

"What do you want?"

"What we've wanted all along. Your father."

"My father is dead, Robert. You killed him three months ago."

"I'm certain you would like me to believe that, but we both know the truth."

"That *is* the truth. You shot him in the stomach down in Durango, and it killed him."

Something in her tone must have convinced him, for his face went a mottled red and he began to pace. She'd never seen Robert be anything but calm and composed, and his agitation worried her down to her toes.

"Why didn't you tell us this in the first place?"

"Would you have believed me?"

"What are we going to do?" Roscoe whispered. "If McGuire's dead, we're never going to get our money."

"We're going to have to kill her," Robert stated, as if her life meant nothing. "She knows us. She could turn us in."

"I ain't never killed a woman before."

"Just shoot her."

"That's awful noisy. What if someone hears the shot?"

"Then we'll hang her."

"There ain't no trees."

Robert gritted his teeth. "Smother her, then. I don't care how you do it, just get it done!"

Each method sent grisly pictures flashing in Honesty's mind. For just a moment, she wished Jesse were here, then chided herself for the thought. She'd spent most of her life depending on Deuce to be there for her when she needed him, and when he'd died, she'd been all but helpless.

Besides, he'd sworn not to come after her again. And when he gave his word, he meant it.

No, she'd have to get out of this herself.

"While you two are dickering over my murder, I hope you don't mind if I go collect the money my father hid."

Both swung around to face her with expressions of shock. "What did you say?" Roscoe asked.

"You know where he hid the money?" Robert cried.

"Of course. My father would never have kept a secret like that from me." It was as bold a lie as she had ever told, but desperation offered no other solution. Rose had once said that unless she had something to offer besides herself, her business would go under. Well, the same logic applied here. If she had nothing of value to offer these men, she knew she'd not live out the day.

Roscoe leaned forward. "Where is it, then?"

"Do you think I'm stupid? I'm not telling you anything."

"She don't know where the million is," he told his brother, who watched her with grave speculation.

"Are you willing to risk it?" Honesty challenged.

"What if she's trying to pull the wool over our eyes again, 'Bert? Last time she did this, that damn fool from the bar came after us. My nose still hurts."

"Honesty," Robert said smoothly, "it would really be in your best interests to tell us where that money is, or . . ."

"Or what, you'll rape me? Kill me? Torture me? Do what you will, I swear on my father's grave that you'll never see one red cent of that million."

He weighed her sincerity for several long moments before finally kicking his horse into motion. "If you are playing me for a fool, I promise that you will regret it."

She'd lied to him. The realization pounded through Jesse's brain as he went to collect his horse. Why it came as such a shock, he didn't know; Honesty had done nothing but lie to him since the day he'd clapped eyes on her. And he'd fallen for her anyway. What a fool he'd been to think one night with him could have changed her; to have trusted that she'd stay put and trust him to help her.

He'd not be anyone's fool ever again. He'd meant what he said, goddamn it. He'd not go after her. Let her face the harsh, cruel world on her own. He was sick and tired of putting off his own agenda to chase after her; it was time to focus his energies on picking up McGuire's trail.

"Jesse!"

He threw a glance over his shoulder, and recognition of the horse and rider galloping toward him had his brow creasing in bewilderment. "Ace?" What was he doing here?

Brett pulled his high-headed Arabian to a skidding stop. "I've been looking all over for you," he announced breathlessly.

"Nothing's happened to Annie or the girls—?"

"No, nothing like that. Jess, I finally remembered where I'd seen your wife before."

"Hell, man, you didn't have to send out the hounds to tell me that."

The humor he tried to inject fell flat at the grave expression his friend's face. "You said you were looking for a fellow named George Mallory."

"I was." He wasn't anymore; Mallory was Honesty's problem to deal with.

"Do you know what he looks like?"

"Not a clue."

"Then this might interest you." He reached into his shirt pocket and withdrew an old newspaper page. "I met him down in Sweetwater back in '76. The pair of them took me for a couple hundred dollars. She was quite a few years younger then, but it's her."

Jesse didn't understand how meeting Mallory ten years ago could have any bearing on this, until he took the clipping Brett handed over. He stared at the smiling picture of a young fair-haired girl in her early teens, standing beside a man whose face had been burned into his memory since he'd first seen the sketch three months earlier. His eyes blurred. His nostrils flared.

His one link of finding McGuire had been under his nose the whole time. And he'd just let her get away.

"Are you sure she's headed this way?" Brett asked him for the umpteenth time as they headed south out of Sage Flat. "I haven't seen a single sign of her."

"I'm sure," Jesse told his friend, as certain of Honesty's intentions as he was of his own name. "She has a map, and Sweetwater was on it. She'll go to Spring Creek next. Whether or not she's actually following a trail set by McGuire remains to be seen."

As he made the prediction, it occurred to him that it was something the old Jesse would say, and it caught him by surprise. When was the last time he'd let his instincts guide him? When was the last time he'd felt so confident? When was the last time it felt this good?

About a mile out of town, a flash of blue cloth in the amber grass caught his eye. Jesse dismounted, something about it reminding him of the bandana Honesty wore to keep from breathing the dust. He brought it to his nose and inhaled the faint fragrance of lilacs. "This is hers."

"Jesse, you need to take a look at this."

He glanced ahead to where Brett stared down at a section of crushed grass and hoof-churned earth. Three sets of tracks converged into one. The bottom fell out of his heart, and his mouth turned to cotton. "Hell, they got her again."

"They?"

"It's a long story," Jesse said. "Help me find her and I'll fill you in."

The trail led them to the edge of the Palo Duro Canyon. As it wound a crooked path down a steep and rocky decline, Jesse gave the lead over to his friend, who was more familiar with the area. He refused to let himself think of what Honesty might be going through. But as the hours passed with no sign of her, fearful anxiety joined the riot of emotions twisting inside him.

He didn't fool himself into thinking his drive

to find her stemmed from the fact that she was his only lead to McGuire. He blamed himself for the Treat brothers finding her. He never should have left her alone in the room. Never should have let her out of his sight. But after the night they'd spent together, he'd let her delude him into thinking she might want to stay with him. What was it that continuously tore her away from him? What was she was after?

A break finally came late that afternoon when they saw Honesty's mare galloping through the trees lining the river that cut through the canyon floor.

Jesse spurred his horse through a maze of hickory and huckleberry with Brett close behind. At the edge of the wood, he slowed, prickles of unease dancing up the back of his neck. He dismounted, leaving the reins trailing on the ground. Signaling for Brett to cut to the left, Jesse circled right and crept forward.

He spotted Honesty the instant he reached the edge of the tree line, sitting on a rock near the river bank, watching Robert stumble around the inert form of his bulky brother, who lay on the ground. Jesse reached for his Colt, prepared to barge in and rescue Honesty, when Robert's cold, slurred voice stopped him at half charge.

"You bitch!" he hissed, swaying in place. "What did you put in our whisk . . . ?" Then the flask in his hand fell to the ground, and the man tumbled face down into the dirt.

Honesty leaned forward to poke his shoulder. "Robert?"

No response.

Jeez, what had she done to them?

The answer hit him when a smug smile slid across Honesty's face. "Sweet dreams, Mr. Treat. Thanks for an unforgettable afternoon."

Jesse's chest swelled with admiration over her resourcefulness. Then his mind spun back to that foggy-brained sensation he'd felt upon waking that morning in Last Hope. So that's how she . . .

She'd drugged him! The conniving little wench had put something in his whiskey!

A rush of cold anger brought Jesse to his feet and he approached Honesty as she rifled through each man's pockets.

He folded his arms across his chest. "Well, well, well, if it isn't my sweet little wife."

She spun around. Her eyes widened at the sight of him. For a moment relief filled the deep brown depths, and she started toward him, arms lifted in welcome.

Then she caught herself. Alarm replaced the relief.

And she bolted.

Jesse cursed. Forgetting the Treat brothers, he tore off after his fleeing wife. They leaped over logs, splashed through brooks, and climbed over rocks before he finally tackled her.

She fought him tooth and nail. "Get off me, you filthy snake!"

Jesse finally grabbed both of her wrists and pinned them above her head. "Now, is that any way to talk to your *husband?*" he gritted out, breathing heavily with exertion. "The game's over, Honesty. We can do this the easy way or we can do this the hard way—but either way, you're coming with me."

"I'm not going anywhere with you, you Judas!"

"Judas?"

Her lips curled in a sneer. "I know who you are."

Jesse masked his surprise beneath a mask of indifference. "Is that so? And just who do you think I am?"

"You're one of those filthy Pinkerton Agents. Don't try and deny it."

"Actually, I'm a damn good Pinkerton Agent. And is it a coincidence," he drawled, then adopted a cold smile, "I know who you are, too."

Chapter 19

❝**G**eorge Mallory, Deuce McGuire—
they're the same man." His voice was
silky steel. "So now that you know who I am
and I know who you are, let's call an end to this
little charade."

Dread uncoiled in Honesty's stomach as she
stared into Jesses's turbulent eyes. She'd known
he would figure it out eventually, she just didn't
know when he'd done it or how, since she had
the telegram on her. "I don't know what you're
talking about."

"Damn it, Honesty!" The dull light of fury
turned to hot rage. "I've given you every opportunity to tell me what you've been after,
why you needed my protection so badly, and

now, even when I confront you, you still can't trust me enough to be honest with me."

"Trust a Pinkerton Agent? That's a joke! You people are nothing more than glorified bounty hunters. Why should I trust you?"

"Because right now, I'm probably the only one you can trust."

Oh, how she wished she could believe that. She hated keeping all these secrets from him; they ate at her insides like an incurable disease. But give him control over her destiny, the power to destroy her dreams? He asked more than she could give.

Jesse sighed. "I can see we're going to have to do this the hard way." His left hand disappeared behind his back and reappeared with a pair of metal cuffs.

"What are you doing?"

"Taking you to Denver. Maybe ten years in prison will loosen that stubborn tongue of yours."

Honesty writhed beneath his weight, frantic to get away from him. But the strength and power that had once been so attractive were now a prison she couldn't free herself from. Tears of helpless frustration stung the back of her eyes as he caught one wrist in the manacle, then the other.

"What do you want from me?" she cried, hating that he could see her weakness.

"The truth. Who is McGuire to you, and why are you willing to foolishly risk life and limb to find him?"

"He was my father! And you want to know where he is? Fine, I'll tell you: buried in a little grave outside Salida."

Jesse searched her eyes, and her heart warred with apprehension and relief that she'd finally confessed her secret.

Then his eyes once again hardened, and his lips turned up with a cynical smile. "Nice try, but I'm not buying it." He rolled off of her, then hauled her to her feet. "The tears are a nice touch, by the way."

"It's the truth! He was shot down by Robert Treat four months ago in Durango. We jumped a train, and he died from a gunshot wound to the stomach just outside Salida. Ask the old hermit who lives on the mountain, if you don't believe me. He helped me bury him."

"That's a good idea—let's go."

She wrenched out of his grasp, yanked his revolver from his holster, and aimed. "I said, I'm not going anywhere with you."

He eyed the weapon she held on him, then looked at her. "You're out of your depths with me, Honesty. Now, look at this reasonably; I can either help you, or I can hurt you. If you don't put the Colt down, I'm going to have to hurt you." He held up his hand and took a step toward her.

Honesty retreated just out of his reach and pulled back the hammer. "One step closer and I'll shoot. My aim isn't very good, but from this distance I can do some damage."

"You aren't going to shoot me."

She didn't waver. "I don't want to, but I will."

"If this is the way you want it, so be it. But know this, my sweet Honesty: you will not get away from me. I will track you down to the ends of the earth if need be, but I will see McGuire brought to justice."

"Why?" she cried. "What did he ever do to deserve being hunted down like an animal?"

"He stole two little girls sixteen years ago for ransom. After the money was paid, he killed them, then fled."

Honesty paled, and the gun went limp in her fettered hands as the news hit her like a blow to her stomach, stealing her breath. "No." She shook her head in denial. "He would never have done that."

"He would and he did, and there's a ransom note to prove it."

"There must be some mistake! My father might have done a lot of lawless things, but he would never hurt anyone, much less little children!"

"Then maybe you don't know him as well as you think you do."

Jesse closed the distance between them, pulled the gun from her hand, and looked her over with contempt. "He's a crook, Honesty. A man who's left a trail of fraud and theft across half the country—and he made you a part of it."

Honesty wished with all her heart that she could deny that, but it would be futile. Deuce *had* swindled people, and he *had* made less-than-scrupulous choices. But if Jesse expected her to believe that the laughter-loving, gentle man who had raised her could have done something so heinous as to steal two children from their family . . .

A sudden, crushing memory surfaced. *No matter what happens, sweet lass, remember that I've loved ye with all me heart.*

Her mind spun back to a lifetime of evasive answers and outright avoidance, to her earliest memory—of a sky so blue it hurt the eyes and grass so green one could sink into its depths. Of salty winds and the rugged chisel of rocks and the mournful whisper of her name across a diamond-tipped sea.

Ye'll know soon enough.

The truth is hidden in the flowing stones.

"Oh my gosh . . ." She closed her eyes against the wash of pain that overtook her. If it was the truth, and she was one of the children he had taken, then that meant that the greatest con man in the west had played the greatest con of all.

On her. She lifted her lashes and fixed anguished eyes on the imposing man before her. "Jesse, I think I'm one of those little girls he took."

Jesse stared at her with incredulity. Honesty? One of the long lost heiresses to the most profitable shipping company in the United States?

"You really are something. Rose was right about one thing—you do belong on the stage."

"Listen to me, Jesse. When Robert caught us in the alley, my father told me that if we should become separated, to run as far away as I could, that I would know all there was to know soon enough. And later, the day he died, he told me to go back to where we began, that the truth is hidden in the flowing stones. I've been looking for it ever since. Don't you understand? This is what I've been searching for, what he wanted me to find! He *wanted* me to know!"

"Did you just see this as an opportunity, and take it? Or did you and McGuire concoct this from this beginning?"

"Look, I know it sounds crazy, but think about it. My fath—Deuce—never talked about my mother. He was always on the run, never stayed in any one place for long. And what about the people who have been after him all these years?"

He folded his arms across his chest. "You've

got this all worked out in that scheming little brain of yours, don't you?"

"You can't ignore the facts, Jesse."

"Except for one small detail; those little girls are dead."

"You're certain of that? Isn't it possible that people only *believe* they're dead? Don't you owe it to their family to consider the possibility?"

"Fine; we'll let them decide."

"No, Jesse, not yet. The girls have been gone for sixteen years. If I'm wrong, all it would do is reopen old wounds. But if I'm right, it would be best to have proof. And I think that as soon as I find the flowing stones, I'll have it."

Jesse stared at her long and hard. She looked so damn convincing. And she made so much sense it was frightening.

Hell, after all the lies she'd told, he wouldn't put it past her to grasp at any straw that might save her skin. No doubt McGuire was still alive somewhere and she was trying to lead him on a wild-goose chase to throw him off the scent.

The easiest way to verify her story about McGuire being dead was to make quick tracks to Salida and find the old hermit.

But if there was a single chance that she was telling the truth, the only way he'd ever know was to find this "proof" she sought.

"Help me, Jesse," she implored, seeming to sense his weakening. "Help me find whatever my father wanted me to find. If he did this terrible deed, then I must know. If he didn't, then neither of us have lost anything except time."

Despite every rebelling instinct the prospect of the search had his blood humming in a way it hadn't in years. "All right, we'll go to the flowing stones. But if you pull one more stunt, if you flee from me one more time, if I find out you've been trying to pull one more con on me, you will regret the day you ever double-crossed me."

The days passed in a blur of windswept prairie and stony silence. After taking a small detour back to Sage Flat to turn the unconscious Roscoe and Robert Treat over to the marshal, and for Jesse to send a wire to his superintendent updating him on the current development, they headed southeast.

They stopped at every point on Honesty's map, questioning every person they ran into, searching every rock formation and creek bed they came across. Jesse spoke to her rarely, and then his words were terse and forbidding. On the occasion when she did try to carry on a conversation with Jesse, he cut off her attempts to bridge the chasm between them with a stare so sharp she felt its sting. It seemed impossible to believe that the man who rode beside her was the same man who had brought her to the highest bliss only days before. Honesty couldn't even think about those moments in his arms without regret piercing her heart.

Maybe she'd gotten what she deserved, going weak in the knees and dim in the head over a handsome face. How could she have been such a fool as to trust him?

From the moment she'd seen him riding up the empty street of a forgotten town, she'd known he posed a greater danger to her well-being than the most ruthless thief. Yet she'd let herself believe that he might be different. That he might be the one person in the world whom she could depend on and trust. Whom she could belong to, body and soul.

Look where her silly notions had gotten her.

On the third morning of the second week of their search it began to rain, but even the soggy weather didn't deter Jesse. He seemed driven by some invisible demon, and she almost felt sorry for those he'd pursued in the past.

The mud and rain finally forced them to make camp late that afternoon, and as they huddled beneath a crudely constructed lean-to, listening to the wind and the rain and the thunder, Honesty could bear his silence no longer.

"How long do you intend on punishing me?" she asked, watching him nurse a cup of coffee.

"Now, why would I want to punish you?"

"For telling you about my father. You've been

hounding me for weeks to tell you the truth, yet when I do, you act as if I've committed a mortal sin."

"Because it isn't the truth. Every word, every gesture from you, has been a lie from the start."

She thought about the way she'd responded to his touch, the way he made her heart sing and her soul soar. "Not everything." Even now, she ached for Jesse to take her in his arms and hold her. Except this was not the gentle or passionate man she'd given herself to. This was a man who could destroy her.

"No, only every word you've uttered from the moment I set eyes on you back at the Scarlet Rose," he scoffed.

"What?" Honesty went still, the shift in direction throwing her off-balance.

"I saw the proof of what happened that night in Last Hope. You remember: the night you made me believe you obliged men for a living and rooked me out of three dollars?"

"You want your money back?" she snapped.

"No, I want to know why the hell you never told me you were a virgin."

There was a note of pain beneath his anger, and Honesty felt shame stir in her belly. She averted her face and fixed her sight on a patch of weeds near her feet. "You wouldn't understand."

"Try me."

"I needed traveling money."

"So you drugged me and made me believe I'd bedded you."

Honesty hesitated, then nodded. "Most men would be pleased to find their wives untouched."

"Most men don't expect their *wife* to already be deflowered."

"Are you saying you'd rather I had been a sporting girl?"

He set his jaw, but didn't answer.

"You are such a hypocrite. What makes your lies any different than mine?"

"I never lied to you."

"No, but you didn't tell me the truth, either, and that's just as bad. You could have told me at any point that you were a detective, yet you didn't."

"Because it had nothing to do with you before."

"So you portrayed yourself as a drifter with no past, no future."

"I've only been doing my job."

"And I've only been protecting my life! That may not mean much to you, but it's all I've got!"

As she flopped onto her bedroll and curled into a ball beneath the saddle blanket, Jesse found himself gripping his cup in a white-knuckled fist. He stared at the curve of her back and thought how alone she looked lying there. How could she think her life meant nothing to him? Did she think he'd put the most important case of his career on hold for the joy of it? Or that he'd chased after her time and time again because he had nothing better to do? Or that he'd put up with more nonsense from her than from any other woman for his health?

If she had any idea just how deeply she'd burrowed under his skin—

Muttering a profanity under his breath, Jesse emptied his cup into the struggling fire and watched it sizzle. He could have walked away a long time ago if he hadn't cared what happened to her. But he admired her tenacity as much as he cursed it; he respected her loyalty as much as he loathed it. And despite his own judgment to the contrary, he'd spend his last breath keeping her safe.

He jerked to his feet and strode out of the shelter of the oilskin to the fringe of the campsite. Drizzling rain sprayed against his face but didn't dampen the turmoil inside him. He'd spent more lonely nights on the prairie than he could count, but never had he felt so alone. They needed to find the stones pretty damn soon, or he might just start forgetting that Honesty embodied everything he'd come to detest in his life.

His father had shattered his illusions. Miranda had bruised his ego. But Honesty . . . if he let down his guard for an instant, she could do the most damage of all. She could break his heart.

She had the dream again, stronger this time, and more vivid than at any other time. Blues and greens and golds and rusts. The colors blended together, colliding, separating.

Ho-ne-sty . . .

She tossed her head from side to side.

Come out, come out, wherever you are . . .

The girlish voice beckoned, yet something held her back.

Ho-ne-sty . . .

"Honesty, wake up!"

Her eyes snapped open, and a man's face came into focus. Whiskered jaw, piercing blue-green eyes, golden hair flowing past his shoulders. "Jesse?"

"Expecting someone else?"

Ignoring the cynical slant to a phrase she'd come to find comforting, she sat up and pressed her fingers to her brow. "I dreamt someone was calling my name."

"I'm not surprised; I've been trying to get you up for ten minutes." He rose from where he knelt on one knee by her side and strode toward the horses. The packs on their backs and the odor of charred oak told her that Jesse had been up for some time. "We've got a lot of miles to cover today, so don't dawdle."

Despite his impatience, Honesty couldn't bring herself to hurry. A heaviness invaded her limbs and her heart, and it was hard to find the energy to face another day that would no doubt end in disappointment.

As Honesty rolled off her woolen pallet, she had to face the fact that she might never find Deuce's hiding place. They were running out of stars on the map. What would happen if she didn't find the stones?

Fighting discouragement, she donned her ankle-high shoes and rolled up her bedding, then joined Jesse by the horses. "Jesse, tell me about them," she said, strapping her bedroll behind the saddle.

"Who?"

"The people who hired you." The question had been haunting her since she'd first learned of the little girls' abduction. What her parents must have gone through, the grief they must have suffered . . . "What are they like?"

"I wouldn't know; I never met them. My orders were to find McGuire."

"But you must know something." She stepped into his cupped hands and let him boost her into the saddle. "Their names, where they're from, if they have other children."

"Hoping I'll feed your story?"

"If it's my family, I deserve to know something about them."

"*If* it's your family, I'll tell you what I know."

Well, there was her answer. If she couldn't prove her identity, she could look forward to spending the next ten years behind bars. Jesse would see to that.

The rain had left shimmering rainbows in the grass as she and Jesse set out across the rolling land. She blanked her mind of everything save the motion of her mare, unable to find the strength to deal with Jesse's bitter anger or the discouragement of trying to find a legacy that might or might not have been left by a man who might or might not have been her father. That numb, mindless state got her through the morning and part of the afternoon.

Then a strange tingling crept up the base of her neck, drawing Honesty's head up to the undulating land before her.

Ho-ne-sty . . .

Was it the echo of a dream?

Or the shadow of a memory?

Honesty's heartbeat slowly quickened as, in her mind, she saw herself as a very young girl, traveling across the grasslands with a much younger Deuce. "It's here," she whispered, reining in her horse. "Jesse, this is it—the place of the flowing stones; I know it is."

"Here? There's nothing but trees."

"This is it. Don't ask me how I know, I just do."

Kicked into action by the knowledge that filled her, Honesty swung herself out of the saddle and gazed at the terrain. Mile upon mile of grassland spread before her, with patches of live-oak woods here and there, and litters of rock. Her mind flashed back to an image of herself running across the grass, laughing so hard as her father chased her that she stumbled and landed in a pile of petticoats. But when she picked herself up and looked over her shoulder, Deuce was nowhere to be seen. There was just an echo of her name, coming from the ground.

Her heart picked up a faster rate; her skin tingled from her toes to her fingertips. "He fell. I remember thinking the ground ate him."

Jesse scanned the ground. "Honesty, we could spend days searching this area."

"Then we'll spend days searching the area. Jesse, I'm telling you, this is the place. There's a hole in the ground—I think it's near some rocks, but I can't be sure . . ."

"A hole like this?"

She spun around. Jesse was hunkered near a weather-eroded ravine banked by craggy red stone. Honesty hastened to his side and braced her hand against his shoulder. A spark shot up her arm at the contact and Jesse stilled, as if he'd felt it, too. "What's down there?" she asked, her breath catching.

"It's too dark. I can't see a damn thing." He rose quickly, refusing to meet her eyes. "Fetch me one of your petticoats and I'll fetch the tinderbox."

Elation rushed through her bloodstream as she hurried to her packs, whether from Jesse's discovery of the hole or her own discovery that he wasn't as immune to her as he wanted to believe, she didn't know. Perhaps a combination of both.

They met at the opening. Jesse soon fashioned a torch using one of her petticoats torn into strips and a green oak limb he'd broken off a tree. "It looks like some sort of underground cavern," he said, poking the lighted torch into the hole.

Honesty bent over his shoulder, trying to see past him.

The salty maleness of his skin assailed her senses, and for a moment she forgot why she stood so close. She shook her head to clear it. "How far down do you think it goes?"

Jesse stared at her in awe. "If you think I'm letting you go in there, you're out of your mind. There's no telling what's down there."

"My future is down there, and if you think you can stop me, you're out of *your* mind."

She'd spent the last four months searching for this place, and nothing or no one, not even Jesse, would stop her.

Her respect for him soared when after several moments, he grudgingly conceded with a short nod. "Then I'll go first. It doesn't look like too much of a drop, but appearances can be deceiving."

She granted him that favor. Still, the minutes dragged by after he fetched a rope from his horse, then lowered himself feet first through the opening, then disappeared. She heard a thud, then a curse.

Finally, his voice echoed up from below. "Hand me the torch, then come straight down. It's a bit of a drop, but I'll catch you."

After tossing the torch down to him, Honesty gathered her skirts in one hand and backstepped into the hole. Her courage almost deserted her when she found herself dangling from the mouth of the hole by her fingertips.

"Just drop, Honesty. I'm right here to catch you."

And she understood, as she released her grip, just what it meant to take a leap of faith.

She landed hard against his chest, and for the second time in as many minutes, the contact with him had her light-headed and giddy.

Then he set her on her feet and stepped

away, his expression almost guilty as he picked up the torch.

Honesty glanced away, wanting to ask him if her touch was so abhorrent, but the sight that met her eyes stole conscious thought from her mind. It looked as if a thousand giant fingers speckled with diamonds dripped from the ceiling. The torchlight caught every single one and turned them into sprays of glittering jewels. "Oh, my gosh," she breathed. "Oh, my gosh! Have you ever seen anything so beautiful in your life?"

Not until the moment he looked at Honesty's face. The majesty of the underground caverns faded in comparison to the splendor of her expression—one of such bliss that he wished he could capture it on canvas. The closest he'd come to ever seeing her so alive, so uninhibited, was in the throes of lovemaking. Knowing the danger of that line of thought, Jesse pressed his mouth into a tight line and scanned the cave with the torch. Several chambers branched off the main area where they stood. Before he could decide which tunnel to start exploring, Honesty lifted the hems of her soiled skirts in her hand and moved toward the one farthest to the left.

"Do you hear water?" she asked.

"Don't go wandering off, Honesty. We have no idea where those tunnels lead."

He could have been talking to one of the sta-
lagmites, for all the attention she paid him. She
was like a child as she wandered in and out of
chambers, exploring every formation, gasping
in wonder and clapping in delight, and it was
all Jesse could do to keep up with her and still
mark their passage with a chunk of slate. The
deeper they got into the caverns, though, the
tighter the band grew around his chest. Forbidden memories began to crowd into his mind,
turning his hands clammy and creating beads
of sweat above his lip. "We'd best get out of
here," he told her when she started venturing
down another narrow corridor.

"You go on. I'm going to keep looking."

"We'll come back later when there's more
light. It's going to take us weeks, maybe months
to search this place."

"I don't care how long it takes. It's here, and
I'm not leaving until I find it."

Jesse fought the sense of panic creeping into
his bloodstream. His lungs felt as if they were
shrinking, and spots were starting to blur his vision. He couldn't stay in here any longer; it was
a wonder he'd been able to hold the memories
at bay this long.

Then the torch, having lost its source of fuel
over the last few hours, sputtered and died.

The darkness closed in on him like a clamp

around his heart. Darkness had long since fallen outside, leaving them with no illumination save the torch. Jesse stumbled toward Honesty, hands outstretched, calling her name, trying to find her.

"I'm here, Jesse."

Forever seemed to pass before his fingers made contact with soft, warm skin. He grabbed her to him and held on, fearing that she, too, might disappear as quickly as the flame that had guided them.

"Jesse, you're shaking."

"It's colder than a well-digger's ass in here."

With the eyes and instincts of a cat, she guided them to a wall where they slid down to sit. Jesse propped his hands on his knees and searched the darkness, feeling caged and anxious. "Can't we light a fire?"

"There's nothing in here to burn," she said. "You don't care much for the dark, do you?"

"I don't mind the dark. I just don't like being *underground* in the dark. Reminds me too much of being in tomb."

"You don't have to stay in here with me, Jesse. I'll be fine on my own."

"I'm not leaving you alone down here. There might be bats or something." He didn't realize he'd been clenching his fists until Honesty's hand covered his own. Then one arm crept around his neck. She smelled so damn good, sweet and womanly, so different from the rank, musty odor that permeated the walls of the cavern. "What are you doing?" he asked over the knot in his throat.

"Holding you."

"That's obvious, but why?"

"You don't like being held?"

"I didn't say that." In fact, he liked it too much.

"You held me when I was afraid. It's my turn to now."

She just had to remind him of that day at the Triple Ace, didn't she? "What makes you think I'm afraid of anything?"

"You're ready to come out of your skin, Jesse," she pointed out.

He decided not to tell her that her nearness had as much an effect on him as the damn cave. With her head on his shoulder, her breasts pressed against his arm, and the scent of her hair teasing his senses, it was all too easy to forget the lies that lay between them and remember the nights he'd spent in the pleasure of her arms.

They sat in silence for quite a while listening to the hollow drip of water somewhere in the distance. He could almost hear Honesty trying to figure out a way to appease him. It was one of the things he liked about her—the way she had of sensing his moods, his fears, his thoughts, and making him feel as if no matter what he did or how he behaved, she would adjust to it. Sometimes it meant getting back in his face, at times she'd used her womanly wiles, and at still other times, like now, she'd just sit beside him with her head on his chest and listen to the dew drop.

And then, she began to hum.

Low at first, it took him a moment to recognize the tune as his own song, the last one he'd written before the music died inside him. "Tell Me No Lies," inspired by his father.

And his throat tightened as her voice carried him back to the past.

She stopped, looked up at him, and touched two fingers to his cheek.

"Thank you for helping me search for the stones, Jesse."

"You could have saved us a lot of time and a whole lot of misery, if you'd been truthful with me from the start."

"I know, and I'm sorry. I wanted to tell you about Deuce a long time ago, but I was afraid."

"Of me?"

"Of what you wanted with my fath—with Deuce." She lifted her head and rested her hand on his chest. He felt her looking at him in the dark. "Try and understand, Jesse, there are people who would have stopped at nothing to get to him."

Like the Treat brothers. "Why didn't you go to the law after he was shot?"

"What could the law do? The man who killed him was dead—or so I thought."

"They could have protected you. Helped you find out where you belonged."

"I considered it, but I was raised to run *from* the law, not *to* it. Anyone with a badge was someone who could tear me and my father apart, someone to fear. I was afraid if they knew who I was, they'd put me in jail for all the years I helped him swindle people." She brushed her cheek against him and tightened her arms around his waist. "You're the only one I've ever felt truly safe with since he died."

Jesse shut his eyes against the pleasure-pain of having her so close. Of smelling her hair and hearing her sweet, smoky voice. She sounded so damn sincere . . .

"How did you become an operative?" she asked.

Maybe it was the intimacy of the moment, or the fact that his identity was no longer an issue, but Jesse sighed and leaned back against the cold, damp wall. "A stroke of fate. My father was gone a lot on business. As I grew older, his visits home got scarcer and scarcer. When I was fifteen or sixteen, they stopped altogether and my mother was worried out of her mind. So I went searching for him." As if aware that the outcome was not one of pleasure, she let her hand clasp his. Strangely enough, though, as Jesse told her the story, the bitter anger that he usually felt didn't materialize. "It took me about a year, but I finally tracked him down to a plantation in Tennessee where he was living with his other wife."

"He had another *wife*?"

"Not just any wife—my mother's sister. He'd amassed a fortune through cotton and wanted a son to carry on the Randolph name. She came from a good family and was pleasing to the eye, so he courted her and they fell in love, so he said. The problem was, my aunt couldn't bear children."

"Why didn't he just adopt a child? The war left thousands of orphans."

"You don't know my father. He wants what he wants, no matter who it hurts. He wanted a son from his own loins to inherit both the fortune he'd amassed and the old money that came from my mother's family."

"But without a child, he couldn't get the old money."

"Exactly. So he married my mother and used her to breed himself a legal heir."

"And she went along with this?"

"She had no idea. She and her sister had a falling out over the War between the States and hadn't seen each other in years. My aunt was a staunch Southern supporter, my mother a Yankee to the bone."

"She must have been devastated when she found out what he'd done."

Jesse had to smile at that. "Spittin' mad was more like it. She sold the house in Chicago and we moved west. Neither of us wanted anything to do with him again, so she gave him back everything he'd given her: his name, his money, his music . . . everything except me."

"And your aunt?"

"She died two years later."

"And you joined the Pinkertons."

"In a manner of speaking." Jesse's arm was starting to go numb, trapped beneath Honesty, so he shifted it to around her back. "I happened to tell an acquaintance of mine how I tracked down my father; he relayed the story to a friend of his, who just happened to be the supervisor for the Pinkerton Detective Agency. Next thing I knew, I was being recruited. I had nothing better to do at the time, so I took the job. I've been with them ever since."

"I think it's amazing that you were able to forgive your father for what he did."

"Forgiving him means I'd have to care. And I don't. He lied. He cheated. He used people for his own advantage. He broke my mother's heart and shredded her good name. To me, he doesn't exist."

"He must, or you wouldn't have spent half your life going after those who preyed on the innocent, the way your father preyed on you and your mother."

His chest shook with laughter at her naiveté. "Oh, Honesty, you couldn't be more wrong. Joining the agency wasn't some sort of noble effort to right the wrongs of my father, it was a way to get back at him. To be everything he detested: wild, reckless, uncivilized. I didn't realize until it was almost too late that that kind of anger can get you killed."

"How so?"

"Years ago, I was assigned to a case involving a gang of criminals who'd taken over a mining operation. These were dangerous men, men who killed and raped and stole for the thrill of it. My job was to be accepted as one of them, cozy up to the leaders, and expose them. I thought I was smarter than they were, and I got involved with a woman who promised to help me bring them down since they'd killed her husband.

"Soon after that they suspected I was an informer, and I got a coffin notice. But they didn't kill me. Instead, they kept me in the deepest bowels of the mines for months. That way I couldn't possibly know what was going on, or get a message to the outside." His voice dropped an octave with raw emotion. "But something big was going down; I could smell it. I bribed a guard into giving Miranda a message for my superintendent, who was also working undercover, but he never got it. She took it to the body master instead and put the whole operation in jeopardy. McParland was forced to shoot me to prove he wasn't part of the operation, or hundreds of lives would have been lost."

"So that's what you meant when you said he had to kill you to save your life."

Jesse nodded. "Once I recovered, I went back to Denver and turned in my resignation. But McParland wouldn't take it. Instead, he offered me the moon. All I had to do was solve a sixteen-year-old case."

"My father." She sighed. "I supposed when this is all over, you'll go back to Denver."

"Well, Honesty, that's going to depend on you."

"What do you mean?"

"You know things about me that no one else knows."

"You think I would betray you?"

"If it meant saving your own skin, I'd expect you to do it in a heartbeat."

"I'm not Miranda, Jesse. What she did to you left a mark that cannot be erased, but I'm not her. I know what it feels like to be betrayed, to feel as if there is no one in the world you can trust. But if you never believe anything, believe this: I love you. I've loved you since the day you sat down in the Scarlet Rose and made Rose's piano sing, and I've fallen more in love with you every day. I would never betray you; I would never leave you in the dark."

There was a pause.

"Time will tell, won't it?"

Honesty got little sleep that night. The things Jesse told her about his father and Miranda played in her mind over and over, and she understood how hard it must have been for him to tell her. He was not a man who gave his trust lightly. She couldn't help but feel as if he were testing her, somehow.

He'd given her the truth; she owed him the same.

When the first fingers of dawn began to seep through cracks in the ceiling, she pushed herself off his chest, careful not to wake him. Jesse admired courage? Well, she had that. And if he wanted the truth, she would find it.

Avoiding the tunnels he'd marked the afternoon before, Honesty set out exploring. The stones were in here somewhere, and when she found them, she'd also find out if she was indeed the child Deuce had allegedly stolen sixteen years ago.

She lost track of time and got off course twice before finally venturing into an unfamiliar area where she came to a sudden stop, unable to believe her eyes. Soft yellow light streamed into a room where an underground brook cut a path into the floor, and melted rock poured forth in a massive display of flowing stone.

She stared at the glorious spectacle in disbelief and apprehension for several long moments before her feet began to move. As if guided by an unseen hand, she found herself stepping onto the formation and moving to the back, where the rocks gave the appearance of growing out of the wall.

Within minutes, her searching hands came into contact with a grainy surface she instantly recognized as wood, and she pulled out a long box that had been stuffed behind the stones.

Honesty's heart thundered as she set the two-foot-long box on the ground. Part of her wanted to run, for she knew that the instant she opened the lid, her life would never be the same; another part of her knew that unless she opened the box, she'd never learn if Jesse's accusations had any merit.

Summoning up her courage, she wiped her moist palms against her skirts, pressed her thumbs and index fingers at each corner, and popped the lid.

She fell back on her heels with a gasp.

"Holy mother of God . . ."

Honesty twisted around and stared at Jesse, who stood frozen at the entrance of the room. The shock on his face mirrored that in her soul. Her mouth moved, but no words came out.

Drawn by the contents, he moved forward and fell to his knees at her side.

"Jesse," she finally managed to whisper. "It does exist. I didn't believe Roscoe when he told me my father claimed to have hidden a fortune, but it's real. This is what they were after."

In slow motion, Jesse pushed his hands beneath the mounds of bank notes, lifted them up, and let them fall from his hands. "There's got to be thousands of dollars here."

"This is why the Treat brothers were after my father! They wanted this." She shook a fistful of money at him.

Spurred into action, he rifled through the notes in a frantic search for something she could only guess at—until he pulled up a packet wrapped in aged brown paper.

Honesty's stomach sank with dread.

Jesse licked his lips and pulled the string.

Within lay a pile of papers, topped by a folded, yellowed one with her name printed there in bold letters.

"Open it," she urged Jesse.

Setting the rest of the packet on his lap, he carefully opened the paper.

My Sweet Honesty,

If you are reading this, then the worst has happened and I am no longer with you. So it is here that I must confess my sins, and pray that you will one day forgive the unforgivable. My dearest lass, I am not your father.

Jesse's voice faded away, and as he scanned the rest of the letter his face paled even more.

"What does it say?"

He stared at her in horror. "My God, you *are* the Jervais heiress!"

"The Jervais heiress?" she echoed.

"One of the little girls McGuire took sixteen years ago."

It was a good thing she was sitting down, or she'd have fallen flat on her face.

Her? An heiress? Hysterical laughter bubbled up in her at the absurdity. She couldn't read much, she couldn't write. She wouldn't know social graces if they crawled on top of her and said "howdy."

"There's got to be some mistake."

"There's no mistake. This is his confession." Jesse lowered the letter and sifted through the rest of the contents. "These are newspaper clippings from the *San Francisco Chronicle*. TWIN HEIRESSES ABDUCTED. MANHUNT FOR MCGUIRE BEGINS."

"But I've never been to San Francisco. We came to Galveston from Scotland."

"That's what he told you, Honesty. Or should I say Aniste?"

"Aniste?"

"That's your real name. Aniste Jervais."

She tested the name out, but it just didn't fit.

"He must have hidden this here within months of taking you," Jesse said.

"How could he have done such a terrible thing? How could he have made me believe, all these years . . ." Through shimmering vision, she sought the answers from Jesse. "Why would he do this?"

"For money, Honesty. He says that he met a man who promised him wealth beyond his dreams if he stole an object of great value and held it for a time. That object was you."

"That doesn't make any sense. If he wanted the money, then why leave it in the box?"

Jesse turned back to the letter. "He says when he learned that the man who hired him never intended to return you, he took you and the money and fled. He says he tried taking you back but feared for your life, just as he knew if his part in the kidnaping was ever discovered, he'd spend the rest of his life in prison and leave you in danger."

"Is that all?"

"He finishes with, 'My only regret is that you are not the daughter of my blood, but you will always be the daughter of my heart, and as such, I shall protect you till my last breath.'"

Tears sprang to Honesty's eyes, and the items spread before her blurred. "He died trying to protect me." No sooner did that realization dawn than Honesty's mind captured another point. "Wait, did one of those clippings say 'Twin Heiresses'? I have a twin?"

"You had a sister. It doesn't mention any names."

Ho-ne-sty! Come out, come out, wherever you are . . . "Faith," she said with unwavering conviction. "Her name is Faith. And if I survived, then maybe she did, too."

"Maybe." But he didn't sound too hopeful.

"There's only one way to find out." Honesty lifted pleading eyes to Jesse. "Will you take me home?"

Chapter 20

❦

Slack-mouthed, Honesty stared through the ivy-leafed iron gates at the four-columned mansion atop Knob Hill. It had taken over three weeks of travel by coach and train to reach San Francisco. "*This* is the Jervais house? It looks more like a fortress. How are we ever going to get inside?"

"Through the front door." He wrapped his hand around her arm and started to pull her through the gate.

Honesty dug in her heels. "Wait—Jesse, I can't do this. Let's go back to Colorado."

He pressed a finger to her lips. "Honesty, you can't turn your back on this. This is your family. This is where you belong."

"I feel like an imposter." Twin or not, nobody

in his right mind would believe that streetwise
Honesty McGuire was Aniste Jervais, heiress to
the biggest shipping company in the country.
What did she know of living the life of a society
damsel? She, who knew dance halls and mining
camps and wayside inns . . . she couldn't read a
lick and was lucky to know how to spell her
name, for Betsy's sake! "What if they don't like
me?"

"Just be yourself. If they don't like you for
that, then they don't deserve you."

She looked up into the face of the man who'd
made her his wife, and stored his features in her
memory. He'd insisted on stopping at a shop in
the city so they could clean up and purchase
clothing befitting her station. She wore a red
lace-lined gown with flared sleeves and a bus-
tle, and Jesse had bought a fine suit. His long
blond hair was slicked back in a tidy ponytail
and tied with black silk. A starched collar
banded his neck. In the coattails and cravat, he
fully looked the scion of a wealthy planter, who
could easily fit into this world.

As they approached the door, she thought of
how strangely quiet he'd been since they'd discovered Deuce's hidden trove. She didn't know
what to make of it. No doubt he was glad to be
getting rid of her; she'd caused him so much
trouble.

Tears pricked her eyes. She wanted to stand

here and stare at him for the rest of her life, for once they proved beyond a shadow of a doubt that she was indeed Aniste Jervais, he would leave.

And he'd take her heart with him.

Impulsively, she cupped his jaw in her cheek and placed a tender kiss on his lips.

"What was that for?"

"Courage," she replied.

He cleared his throat. "Are you ready?"

Nerves set up a riot in her stomach once more, but she nodded with determination. Jesse was right. If they didn't like her, didn't want her, she'd find someplace else. She'd done it before; she could do it again.

Jesse rapped on the door, and it opened a moment later.

"We're here to see Anton Jervais," Jesse announced with authority.

The butler stared at Honesty, then stepped back to allow them inside. Jesse's hand burned into the small of her back as they followed the man through a marble-floored foyer into a library.

It was a monstrosity of a room, with shelves from floor to ceiling along three of its four walls, and a ladder that rolled on tracks around the perimeter to reach the higher volumes. The fourth wall seemed entirely made up of windows and allowed a vast view of the bay. Honesty couldn't resist approaching the desk, which looked out over the sea. Diamond-tipped waves crashed against the rocks below. The blues and greens and golds of her dreams crashed back to her memory.

"Honesty, come look at this."

She turned toward Jesse, who stood in front of a floor-to-ceiling fireplace. Above the bare mantel hung a large portrait of a man, a woman, and two young children. Unlike most portrait subjects, these were smiling. The man had thick black hair parted down the center and combed back from a wide brow, a narrow nose between deep brown eyes, and muttonchop whiskers. The woman had light brown hair and the bluest eyes Honesty had ever seen, a wide brow, a slightly large nose, and a wide mouth. She wasn't the prettiest woman Honesty had ever encountered, but there was a refined grace about her that made her compellingly attractive.

Yet it was the children who captured Honesty's attention. Two girls, two or three years old; both with the woman's fairer coloring.

"That's my ring! Jesse, she's wearing my ring!"

A tall broad-shouldered man near Jesse's age entered the room.

"May I help you?"

Honesty swung away from the portrait toward the tall, dark-haired man in the doorway.

"We're here to see Anton Jervais," Jesse announced.

Eyes of pewter gray narrowed immediately. "Mr. Jervais is upstairs resting and is not to be disturbed."

"Please tell him that his daughter Aniste is here to see him."

The sun-tinged hue of the man's face turned ashen. "That's not possible. My cousin is dead."

"I'll bet you'd like that to be true, wouldn't you?" Jesse said cynically.

"Jesse—"

"No, Honesty, look at him. If you don't come back, he gets all this."

"How dare you! This house has been in mourning for sixteen years. If I could bring Aniste back, I would do so in a heartbeat. You have no idea how many times I've wished I had been the one fished out of the bay, if only to spare the man up there his pain." He collected the emotions getting the better of him. "I don't know what sort of game you are playing, but I want you out of this house."

"He stays with me," Honesty asserted, clasping Jesse's hand in her own, drawing strength from it.

"I see. Then you leave me no recourse." He rang a bell that sat on a polished round table near the doorway and immediately a servant appeared. "Summon the police immediately."

"Good idea. Summon your lawyer, too. You're going to need one."

"Just who do you think you are?"

"I'm an agent for the Pinkerton Detective Agency, hired to find Deuce McGuire."

"A detective?"

"But maybe you knew that. Maybe you also knew that Honesty wasn't dead. Are you the one who hired me to find her, then set goons after her? Did you want to make sure she didn't return?"

"We hired detectives to find McGuire, but that was years ago."

"Then if you didn't hire Jesse, who did?" Honesty asked.

A new voice said, "I did."

Three faces turned as one to the stately man standing in the doorway. He wore a brown silk robe over pressed trousers and a snowy white shirt open at the throat.

Alex strode to his side and helped him to a nearby Queen Anne chair. "Uncle, what are you doing up?"

"I've come down to welcome my sweet Aniste home." He smiled through his tears.

"Uncle, Aniste is not here, much to my regret."

"She stands before us, Alexander. Do you not recognize her mother's glorious curls?"

"You . . . are my father?" Honesty asked.

"Uncle, she is but an imposter, come to capitalize on our tragedy for whatever gain. Extortion . . ."

Jesse took a threatening step forward. "One more word out of you against her, and they *will* be fishing you out of the bay."

"Alexander means no ill-will," the distinguished gentleman said. "He means only to protect me. This would not be the first time someone has appeared on our doorstep, claiming to be one of my daughters. But if my nephew will only look closely, he will see that this is indeed our beloved Aniste." He lifted a frail hand in her direction. "Look into her eyes, Alexander, and tell me who you see."

With obvious reluctance, Alex approached Honesty, and as his uncle bade, stared deeply into her eyes. Slowly he turned to look at the portrait, then back at her, his mouth going slack.

"My God, it *is* you!"

"That's what I've been trying to tell you."

He sank to an ottoman. "But . . . how? I was there the day they took you. I'd turned my back for only an instant . . . and I was there the day your dress . . ." His voice cracked. "A beautiful blue dimity with black sash and tiny collar . . . washed up on the shore . . . All these years I have carried the burden of my guilt."

Honesty's throat clamped shut. She closed the distance between herself and the broken man, and knelt at his feet. "Alex?" she softly called. And a memory surged to the surface of her mind. "Lex, it's all right. I'm here now."

He lifted eyes filled with despair and cupped his big hand around her cheek. "I turned my back only for an instant. I was charged with watching you that day, and I failed in my duty. Even worse, I gave up hope. Can you ever forgive me?"

"There is nothing to forgive."

"Child, come let me look at you."

With a guilty start, Honesty realized she'd forgotten all about her father, the man who'd sired her. She'd thought she would feel an instant bolt of recognition, but the man who sat before her was as complete a stranger as Jesse had been when she'd first seen him. Shyly, awkwardly, she approached her father.

"You have grown into a beautiful young woman, just as I always knew you would."

She shot a glance at Jesse and blushed. She hoped her father couldn't see just how much a woman she'd become . . .

"Your mother said that one day you girls would be returned to me."

"Is she here?" Honesty asked with barely restrained eagerness. "May I see her?"

His face fell. "I'm afraid that is not possible. You see, your mother died the day you were stolen from us."

* * *

The history of her abduction unfolded as they sat around a dining table set with gold-rimmed plates. Honesty had never seen such expensive china, much less eaten off it.

Anton Jervais sat at the head of the table, his manservant hovering close behind him, while Alex occupied the seat directly across from her. Jesse had opted to sit at the far end of the table. Honesty wished for his closeness.

She heard the story of how her mother had died of a wasting disease, and how the very day of her funeral, Honesty and Faith had disappeared. The next day, the family received a demand of one million dollars in ransom. Frantic to have the girls returned, the family produced the money through the quick sale of two of his finest ships, then dropped the money at the designated spot on a nearby wharf.

But they never saw either girl again—until a few short hours ago.

"We know that he wasn't the one who manufactured the whole plot, though."

Alex flushed.

"It was my brother, Alex's father, who conceived of the idea to steal my children."

All the while, Jesse sat in stony silence at the end of the table, his face expressionless, arms crossed over his chest.

Honesty absorbed the story as if she were

not the one they spoke of. She told them of her life and her search after Deuce's death, leaving out many of the details. What she had shared with Jesse was too private to share with anyone, especially two men who were little more than strangers.

"He was a good man. I know it's hard to believe that considering what he did, but he was." She showed them the letter. "And I have something else for you, too." She dragged her carpetbag close to her, opened it, and pulled out a stack of bills. Their eyes widened. "You can count it. Every penny of it is here—well, except for the train fare to get Jesse and me here."

Anton Jervais cleared his throat, then addressed Jesse. "We owe you a debt we can never repay. Please, take the money."

Jesse glared at the men, then, to their collective astonishment, pushed back his chair and stormed out of the room.

Jesse watched the waves crash against the jagged rocks that lined the beach below the Jervais home, feeling as if each one were battering away at his heart. He'd thought he could do this: bring Honesty home, reunite her with her family, then walk away without a backward glance.

He owed her that, for the way he'd doubted her story.

But the instant Jervais tried pushing off the ransom money on him as reward for finding his daughter, it all became too clear: he'd have paid twice as much to keep Honesty with him.

"Jesse?"

He felt her approach, but couldn't bring himself to look at her. What for? To remind him what he'd be missing for the rest of his life?

"You're leaving, aren't you?"

He gave a single stiff nod, and wondered if she'd come to say goodbye before taking up her duties as heiress to Jervais Shipping.

"My father wants you to find my sister."

"If he's looking for a detective, he'll have to look elsewhere. I'm not for hire."

"You mean you're not going back to Denver?"

"I don't know what I'm going to do, Honesty. I loved working for the agency, but . . ." Hell. What *was* he going to do with himself now? She was right; he'd never be happy tending a bunch of cows. He wanted passion in his life. Unpredictability. Adventure. He wanted all the things Honesty had brought back into his world—the challenges, the excitement. He wanted the rush of the chase, the thrill of the escape, the risk of the unknown.

And he wanted her at his side.

The thought of spending another single, solitary night under the stars without her made his chest hurt. An intense sadness came over Jesse as he realized what he should have known months ago. "I just don't think I'm cut out for this line of work anymore."

"But why? You're a wonderful agent!"

"Once, maybe, but that was before I lost the edge." It was the first time Jesse had admitted the truth aloud, even to himself.

"Oh, Jesse." She slipped up behind him and wrapped her arms around his waist.

Jesse closed his eyes in agony.

"You didn't lose your edge," she said. "It just got dulled a bit."

"I lost it. If I doubted that before, you became a sharp reminder."

"Why, because you didn't know of my connection to Deuce? Jesse, give me some credit; I didn't spend a lifetime with the greatest con man in the West without learning a few tricks."

He knew she was trying to lessen his sense of failure, but the attempt fell flat. "I should have known who you were."

"How could you have known, when I didn't even know myself? Deuce was very good at what he did, or he wouldn't have gotten away with it for sixteen years. And you are very good at what you do, or I would have picked up on your identity a long time ago."

"Maybe. Maybe not. But it doesn't change anything. A man gets tired of always watching his back."

"I'll watch your back."

Jesse didn't know if he was more surprised or touched by the offer. Honesty might be impulsive to a fault, but she didn't make commitments lightly. He turned in her arms and studied her face. "What are you saying?"

She laid her palms on his chest and stared at the tiny pearl button at his throat. "I'm saying that I don't know how you expect me to carry on as if we never met. As if I never fell in love with you."

Tenderly, he brushed her cheek, savoring the softness of her skin. "Honesty . . . do you even know who I am?"

"You're my strength. My music. My safe harbor. Everything's off-balance when I'm not with you."

He crushed her to him, and felt her soul clinging to his with greedy, grasping fingers.

"Without each other, who are we?"

There was a wealth of meaning behind the simple question. Like him, Honesty seemed to be looking for an identity. And a certainty filled him then that they had found it.

"We're the same people we were yesterday, and the day before, and the day before that. Our names might be different, but our hearts haven't changed."

"Do you really believe that?" she asked, her eyes alive with hope.

"It's the only thing in life I believe without question."

"Then why can't you believe that I feel the same for you now as I did the day I met you?"

"Because if I believed it, I'd never be able to walk away from you."

"Then don't. Stay here with me."

"I can't stay here. I left this kind of life years ago."

"Then take me with you."

He spun around and gazed at her in shock. "This is where you belong, Honesty."

"No, this is where Aniste Jervais belongs. I'm not an heiress, Jesse, I'm the daughter of the greatest confidence man in the West. Imagine the damage I could do to a shipping company."

A sad smile touched his lips at her attempt to make light of her own talents.

She stroked the lapels of his jacket and in that velvety voice that had captivated him from the first, said, "I don't blame you if you aren't willing to take a chance on me after I've been so dishonest with you, but I've spent too many years wandering the land to spend the rest of my days trapped in a glass cage. I'd much rather spend them sleuthing with my husband—if he'll have me."

Astounded and humbled that she would give up a future most women only dreamed of for him, Jesse realized that it wasn't the truth he prized above all things, but Honesty. "Promise me one thing: that you will never lie to me or keep secrets from me. You're the one person I need to trust."

"Does this mean you'll take me with you?"

His heart soared, and his arms tightened around her. "Someone's got to put those skills of yours to good use." She threw her arms around him with an elated shriek, and Jesse couldn't resist taunting, "You've got a few other skills that need putting to good use, too."

The wicked smile she gave him was easily worth a million dollars.

Dear Reader,

Now that you've come to the end of your book I'm sure you're like me—eager to discover something new to read and longing for a fresh, exciting, sensuous romance to entertain you.

Remember, each month there are four delicious Avon romances to choose from, so even if you've just finished one, there are three more awaiting you where romances are sold. And *next* month you'll be able to choose from these four unforgettable titles.

A Notorious Love by **Sabrina Jeffries:** She's a proper young lady, compelled to join forces with a dashing rogue to rescue her runaway sister. He's a man no proper young lady should be seen with—but he's devastatingly attractive . . . and oh, so irresistible. Sabrina Jeffries is a rising star, whose work sparkles with wit and sizzles with passion—this book is truly unmissable!

Next Stop, Paradise by **Sue Civil-Brown:** If you love contemporary romance that is high-spirited, delightful, and truly unique, then don't miss this one! When a small town lady cop matches wits with a handsome, smooth-talking TV journalist, well, you know something special is going to happen! With a touch of magic and a whole lot of charm *Next Stop, Paradise* should be on your book-buying list.

Secret Vows by **Mary Reed McCall:** It's always exciting to bring you a book by a brand-new author . . . one who has a spectacular career ahead of her. In *Secret Vows* you'll find a soul-stirring love story between Catherine of Somerset and Baron Grayson de Camville. And though severe punishment faces Catherine if she fails in her mission, she can't help but fall in love with this man she's been forced to marry—and ordered to destroy.

An Innocent Mistress by **Rebecca Wade:** He's a rugged bachelor sworn to avenge his imprisoned brother; she's the fiery woman known as the mistress of a fabled bounty hunter—but is she concealing a secret identity? Passion flares . . . and no one is quite who they seem to be in this surefire blockbuster of romance.

There you have it—four brand-new romances from the premiere publisher of romance . . . Avon Books.

Enjoy,

Lucia Macro

Lucia Macro
Executive Editor